"Seven years," he heard her whisper. "Haven't we had our share of bad luck without breaking a mirror? What'll happen to us now?"

Danny didn't know. But a growing sense of having lost what little control he might have had—of being able to manipulate his world to get what he wanted—crept over him like the lengthening shadows stealing in through the bedroom windows.

Beneath his bed, scuttling claws made strange noises.

He wanted to run to his mother and beg her forgiveness, throw his thin arms around her hips and cry his eyes out into her warm apron. He wanted to tell her he didn't mean it when he yelled "I hate you! I hate you!"

Instead, he stayed rooted to the bed—unable to move a muscle.

And then, he knew, it was too late.

Backing out of the doorway, she closed his door behind her and latched it securely from the outside, trapping Danny in the dungeon-like tomb of his own room, imprisoning him here where the monsters were.

Panic gripped him with icy fingers as the boy's horrified eyes saw the long shadows cast by the closet door actually move!

And, when the last ray of sunshine faded with the coming of the night, Danny doubted that he'd even survive his curse of bad luck till tomorrow morning—much less seven whole years.

DADDY'S HOME

BOOK 2 OF THE INSTRUMENTS OF DEATH

BY PAUL DALE ANDERSON

For Wayne
Great to see you again

[signature]

9-29-2017

DEDICATION

This book is affectionately dedicated to Gretta McCombs Anderson— my wife, lover and best friend.

To Jordan Elise Anderson, aka my daughter Tammy Jeanne Anderson, on the occasion of her 21st birthday.

To Elizabeth Flygare, who urged me to kill again.

And to everyone who believes, as I do, that it's never too late to have a happy childhood.

PROLOGUE

It was a stupid thing to do.

She should have gone the long way around. Risking her life for the few minutes a shortcut saved was pure stupidity.

But how could she have known when she entered the park that a maniac would be waiting for her with a knife?

Sure, her mother had warned her, as a child growing up, never to cut through the park at night.

But she was a big girl now—nineteen, almost twenty—and she'd long ago learned that her mother worried needlessly about almost everything: "Don't go out without a scarf or you'll catch your death of cold; don't let a boy touch your breasts or you'll get pregnant; don't talk to men or accept candy from strangers; don't wear short skirts or gaudy lipstick; don't stay out after midnight or drink liquor. Terrible things are bound to happen if you do.

"And never ever walk through the park alone at night."

Glenda had done all those "don'ts" tonight, beginning with the short skirt and gaudy lipstick and ending with leaving David's— she didn't even know his last name—party long after midnight. Giddy from too much alcohol and a more-than-satisfying romp on David's king-size water bed, with a man she'd never met before and probably would never see again, she thought she'd save time by taking the shortcut through the park.

And now her own stupidity was about to get her killed.

"Please," she begged. "Don't...."

But it was already too late. The knife arched menacingly in the moonlight before beginning its downward plunge to her heart.

In that instant before her death, she looked into the glazed eyes of the madman and wondered why he wanted to do something so hideously cruel to a perfect stranger. *Why me*? she wondered. *What have I done to you to deserve this*?

As the cold steel sunk deep into her flesh, and as she heard her blouse rip and felt warm blood bubble out of her chest, staining the lacy fabric of her bra, Glenda Rose Williams screamed.

CHAPTER ONE

Michael blew out the match and quickly lit another.

"Superstitious?" Wayne Gillespe asked the new vice president of sales.

"Why take chances when you don't have to?" Michael laughed, lighting his own cigar with the second match. "Isn't it usually better to be safe than sorry?"

"I've never known you to play safe," Bill Blake remarked around the fat cigar in his smiling mouth. "Giving up a seventy-thou-a-year salary to sell for us on commission was a hell of a risk."

"One that's paid off handsomely," Michael added. "I wasn't worried."

"You make it sound like a sure bet."

"With a superb product line like Blake Blades that practically sells itself? Of course it was a sure bet."

"What'd I tell you?" Gillespe smiled at the chairman of the board. "This man can sell ice cubes to Eskimos!"

"He's good all right," Blake admitted.

Michael Thompson puffed silently on the celebration cigar Blake had handed him after announcing the new vice presidency. Being good had nothing at all to do with it was what Michael wanted to tell the pompous ass that owned sixty percent of Blake Blades corporate stock. It was all merely a matter of the right kind of luck.

But he didn't dare tell Blake and Gillespe that. Let them think what they wanted.

When Michael had been a child, he'd stumbled across the truth quite by chance. While playing with friends at the age of eight, he literally put two and two together and came up with four. And, miraculously, he had irrevocably changed his life forever.

Now, at age twenty-four, Michael Thompson had become the youngest vice president of sales that Blake Blades—the leading manufacturer of precision cutting tools and surgical instruments— ever had. In another year, barring any unforeseen accidents, Michael was sure he could replace Wayne Gillespe as president of the company.

But, Michael knew, it would take a lot more than hard work and a golden tongue to unseat Bill Blake as chairman and CEO of the business he'd founded and still owned.

It would take a special kind of luck.

Michael listened—amused—as Gillespe continued to praise Michael's virtues to the old man. Poor Wayne was still trying to justify the unprecedented decision to fire Jud Dobson, one of Blake Blades' original employees and the previous vice president of sales, and give the job to this twenty-four-year-old newcomer. Though Michael had single-handedly doubled the company's sales figures in the six months since he'd come aboard as a rep, older employees seemed to resent the upstart's meteoric rise to power. Some—Jud Dobson among them—had threatened to quit when, less than a month ago, Gillespe appointed Michael district manager over men with more seniority. Yesterday Dobson had cut his own throat by confronting the old man with an ultimatum: "Either Thompson goes or I walk. I can't—won't—work with a man as ruthless and unethical as Michael Thompson."

"Sorry you feel that way, Jud," Blake was rumored to have told Dobson. "Don't let the door hit you in the ass on your way out."

"You're siding with *him* over *me*? Are you crazy?"

"I'm siding with Blake Blades, Jud. You've seen the latest sales figures. Michael Thompson is evidently worth more to this company's bottom line than are you, my friend. I'm sorry, but that's just the way it is in this business. Money talks and bullshit walks."

Michael harbored no illusions. Blake had made it abundantly clear that he'd cut anybody's throat to make a buck, and Michael wasn't about to stick his neck out to prove he could be an exception.

Not yet, anyway.

"… fourteen new accounts," Gillespe was saying. "One-and-a-half million in new orders. We'll need to start a third shift at the warehouse just to keep up…"

Blake's eyes caught Michael's and locked on. *How'd you do it?* the old man wanted to ask. *You're nothing but a two bit punk.*

But a valuable two-bit punk, Michael responded, by blowing concentric smoke rings at the chairman of the board. *Someone you intend to use as long as he produces positive results for your goddamn precious bottom line. I know you, asshole; I know what makes you tick. And I intend to use you, too—in ways you never dreamed possible.*

Danny Norman was scared.

He'd been scared a lot lately. First he'd been scared of the fights Mom and Pop used to have. It seemed Danny was always caught in the middle, and he was somehow sure that he was the cause of Mom and Pop breaking up and getting a divorce.

Then, as scared as he was that his father would hit him as a justifiable punishment for causing the breakup, Danny became ever more scared when Pop moved away and Mom had to go back to work, which meant Danny had to go to a dreadful place called "Day-Care." As an only child, he didn't take kindly to sharing toys with other children. And he absolutely hated sharing the teacher's attention with thirty other three- or four-year-olds, each screaming bloody murder for his or her own slice of the pie.

Things only got worse when Danny grew up and had to go to kindergarten in the mornings and day-care in the afternoons. Now there were sixty kids competing against him daily, and the world seemed extremely hostile and very scary. He didn't know how to deal with it anymore.

He cried a lot, but it didn't do any good.

The others kids called him "cry-baby" and "scaredy-cat," and taunted him mercilessly. He tried to avoid fights, but found it increasingly impossible. Danny Norman was an easy victim that five-year-old boys knew they could pick on with impunity, and there was nothing he could say or do to stop them.

So he withdrew more and more into his own safe world of imaginary friends where he wasn't looked upon as a forty-eight-pound weakling ripe for bashing. In his own mind he was a hero, a rescuer of the weak and downtrodden. A Superman. A Batman. A Transformer.

But in real life Danny Norman was just a cry-baby, a scaredy-cat, a wimp, a nothing, a nobody. A loser.

When Mom picked him up after school, however, Danny became a somebody and the center of attention again. Mom hugged and kissed him, catered to his every whim, and suddenly life seemed worth living. She listened to all his tall tales, even told him stories of her own, and gave him ice cream and cookies whenever he asked—provided they wouldn't spoil his supper. Danny really and truly loved his mother.

And he knew his mother loved him, too. But lately a new worry had intruded into his consciousness. It had snuck up on him like Johnny Radcliff—the school bully—liked to sneak up behind Danny's back and yell "Boo!"

He was afraid something bad would happen to Mom, and she would leave him all alone to face the world by himself.

"I'll never leave you, Danny," his mom had said reassuringly when he finally told her of his worst fear.

"Never ever?"

"Never ever."

"Promise?"

"I promise."

He wanted to believe her, but something inside him refused to accept a promise as fact. "Not even when I grow up?" he asked.

"When you grow up, Danny, you'll want to start a family of your own. I'm afraid you'll forget all about me the first time a pretty girl captures your interest. Maybe I won't leave you, but sooner or later you'll leave me."

"No, I won't."

"Wait and see."

"I won't ever leave you, Mommy. Never ever!"

"Maybe you say that now, but someday you'll change your mind. It's only natural, Danny."

"Is that why Dad left? 'Cause a pretty girl captured his int'rest?"

Danny could tell he'd reached a raw nerve. Mom's smile left her face and tears crept into her eyes. For almost a full minute Danny thought his mother was going to hit him with her fist.

Then her fists unclenched, her smile returned, and she blinked back the tears.

"Mommy and Daddy wanted different things out of life," she

explained. "Your father left us because he didn't want to be trapped by the responsibilities of marriage."

"Isn't he ever coming back?"

"No, dear."

"Why can't I have a daddy like other kids?"

"You just… can't." The tears were in her eyes again. "Go to sleep now, like a good boy. It's past your bedtime and tomorrow's another school day."

Danny's protests didn't do any good. His mother quickly turned out the light, tucked the covers around his shoulders, and kissed him goodnight. Then she left him alone in the dark to face, all by himself, the terrible monsters that dwelt in his closet and under his bed.

And in the dark, as he listened for the scraping sounds of giant claws coming for him across the hardwood floor, he heard instead his mother brushing her teeth, flushing the toilet, and crawling beneath the fresh sheets in the bedroom next door.

Her soft sobs continued to haunt him long after he fell asleep.

"Why?" sobbed Ellen Norman. "Why did I marry Bob? Why couldn't I have picked someone else?"

Because you were a romantic teenager and Bob Norman was the handsomest man you'd ever seen, her mind answered. *You were too flattered the first time he asked you out to think of refusing him, thrilled to pieces when he seduced you in the back seat of his car on your second date, and head over heels in love when he finally asked you to marry him. You fell for every line he ever fed you. You're a fool, Ellen Lester, thinking a man like Robert Daniel Norman could love you. Beautiful Bob doesn't love anyone but himself.*

"He remarried."

So? Don't tell me you feel sorry for his new wife. She deserves what she got!

"He told me he loves her."

He lied. He lied about loving you, didn't he?

"Not at first. I think he really loved me until…"

Until Danny came along?

"Yes."

And you think Bob was so self-centered that he resented his own son?

"Uh-huh. He was jealous. He couldn't stand it when I paid more attention to Danny than him."

And that's why he left you?

"Yes."

You don't really believe that, do you?

"Danny was awfully sick. He had a fever of a hundred and four and needed me all the time. Poor Bob felt left out."

He just used Danny as a convenient excuse, Ellen. While you were home taking care of a sick baby, Bob was free to chase around with other women. He would have done it anyway, you know. But Danny's illness was perfect for his plans.

"What plans?"

To make you feel guilty. He made it look like the divorce was all your fault, not his; and his scheme worked. You didn't ask for a penny of alimony, did you?

"He's paying child support."

But what little he pays isn't enough for you and Danny to live on, is it? He got off cheap, and you're the one who feels guilty about the break-up!

Ellen fought to control her tears, but it was a losing battle. Danny's questions had opened old wounds, and Ellen Norman—née Lester—was bleeding to death. From a broken heart.

It had been three years since the divorce, and Ellen's wounds weren't healing. Though she could mask the pain, she couldn't stop still-festering sores from turning ugly. Like a cancer, they grew inside her mind and spread through her heart and corrupted her soul.

And sometimes, when she least expected it, the sores erupted like vile pustules that splattered corruption everywhere, contaminating anyone near—even Danny.

Ellen had been especially careful with her son, aware how fragile and delicate he'd been since a viral infection had ravaged his body and nearly burned out his brain. For the entire first year of his young life, Danny Norman had hovered on the brink of oblivion. Only his mother's devoted ministrations had kept him alive after his doctors abandoned all hope and sent the boy home to die. Now Danny had recovered completely and, as far as anyone could tell, suffered no ill side effects except the aftermath of divorce.

Bob had claimed that Ellen's slavish devotion to their son ruined his marriage, driving him elsewhere to look for love. Ellen didn't deny that she'd ignored her husband for more than a year, that she hadn't slept with him for almost two years. Bob got the divorce he wanted—no alimony, minimal child support, and absolution of any responsibility to care for a sick child. In exchange, Ellen got what she wanted: complete custody of her infant son.

"Why can't I have a daddy like other kids?" Danny had asked, and Ellen had wanted to tell him the truth—almost letting the words slip before she caught herself.

"Because, Danny Norman, you're not like other kids," she'd wanted to say.

But that wasn't completely true, either, she now knew. Danny was a growing boy—normal in almost every way—and he needed a father. Ellen wasn't being fair to Danny or fair to herself.

After Bob's betrayal, Ellen hadn't wanted—or needed—a man in her life. Her job as a receptionist at Evans Surgical Supply Company, besides providing an excellent income and valuable insurance benefits, gave her ample opportunity to meet people. More than once, good-looking men had asked her out to dinner or the theatre, but she'd politely refused their invitations in order to spend the time with Danny. Her son needed her, she knew, and a man would only unnecessarily complicate their lives. Besides, Ellen couldn't bear the thought of being hurt again.

But now, if Danny were to be normal, he needed a father, someone to teach him to play baseball and take him to football games and do all the things mothers didn't do. Since Bob had no interest in the boy at all, it was up to Ellen to find someone else to take his place.

Yes, she thought, running her hands over her body—down her stomach to her open thighs, caressing her breasts, pinching her nipples. *There were some things men could do that women couldn't.*

Her sobs became moans as fingers found the forbidden place, rubbing, kneading… her back arched off the bed as her breathing increased… and suddenly she was THERE… touching… entering… gushing… screaming—

Screaming?

Someone was screaming, but it wasn't her. Even at the height of her ecstasy, Ellen had been aware that her son might hear in the next room, might awaken from a sound sleep and hear her climax.

So she'd stuck her tongue between her teeth and clamped down hard, literally biting her tongue to keep from crying out.

But the screams continued—hysterical high-pitched shrieks that shattered any sense of well-being she might have felt.

They were coming from Danny's room.

Ellen threw the covers aside, leapt out of bed, and ran next door as fast as her legs could carry her.

"Danny!" she shouted as she flipped on the light switch in her son's room. "Danny!"

As soon as the light came on, the shrieks ceased. "Oh! My God! Danny!"

The boy cowered against the headboard of his bed. His eyes were wide with fright and his whole body shook with fear.

"Danny! What's wrong?"

Ellen ran to the boy, gathering his frail form in her arms, cradling him against her bosom. "Danny!" she cried as she held him close. "Oh, Danny!"

"The monster, Mommy," the boy sobbed, his tiny voice trembling. "The monster..."

"It was only a nightmare, darling. Only a nightmare."

"I saw it, Mommy. I saw it."

"You saw a monster in your nightmare, dear, but it wasn't real. Now that you're awake, the monster's gone and you're safe."

"Wasn't a nightmare..."

"Of course it was."

"No, Mommy," he insisted. "I saw it."

Ellen released the boy and reached for a box of Kleenex. She dried his eyes and nose with tissue.

"What did it look like?" she asked gently, deciding to humor the boy. "Was it like the Cookie Monster on Sesame Street?"

Danny shook his head.

"Can you describe it, then?"

"It was big."

"How big, Danny? As big as me?"

"Lots bigger'n you, Mommy."

Ellen hid a smile. At five-two and ninety-seven pounds, Ellen wasn't surprised. Almost everything seemed bigger than her.

"Bigger than the doorway?"

"Yes."

"If it was bigger than the doorway," Ellen asked, "how did it get into your room?"

"The monster was outside."

"Outside the door? I didn't see a monster outside the door when I came in a minute ago," she teased. "How come you saw a monster out there, and I didn't?"

"I don't know, Mommy."

"And what was the monster doing outside your door?"

"He was trying to get in but you wouldn't let him."

Ellen smiled. The boy's overactive imagination had conjured up a monster, and now Danny was trying to embellish his tall tale by reconciling imaginary details with reality. He wasn't ready yet to admit it was just a nightmare.

"See?" she told her son, hugging him close. "Mommy protects you, darling. Even in your nightmares I keep the monsters out of your room. So you don't need to worry about monsters any more, do you?"

"Yes, I do!" Danny said, crying again.

"But why?" Ellen asked, surprised by her son's reaction. "Why, when I kept the monster out of your room?"

Danny let out a wail that rattled the window panes and made Ellen's ear drums ache. His body, racked with sobs, shook the way it had when he'd been sick with the fever.

"Why?" Ellen asked again, needing an answer. "Why are you still afraid?"

"Because," the small voice said between sobs, "I saw... the monster... cut you up... and he killed you... and then he came into the room... and wanted to cut... to kill... me!"

CHAPTER TWO

"This," Michael demonstrated by cutting a raw T-bone steak in half with a single flick of his wrist, "is what a Blake Blades scalpel can do. Please note the accuracy of the incision and depth of penetration. No other surgical instrument is quite as precise."

"Or as expensive," Lane Evans sneered.

"Cost is never a factor when a surgeon needs to control his cut."

"Cost is always a factor," Evans contradicted. "Quantity not quality is how wholesalers like me make our meager profit. I'd rather sell a quick thousand at ten bucks apiece than try to move forty or fifty at a hundred bucks each. Get my drift?"

Michael had rehearsed dozens of rebuttals for Evans' arguments about price, but the man had obviously already decided against Blake Blades and any argument now would only fall on deaf ears. Maybe it'd be better simply to cut his losses by moving on to the next potential buyer on today's list of cold calls. Why waste valuable time trying to beat a dead horse to death, especially when he knew of easier ways to get what he wanted.

"Here's my card," Michael smiled graciously, handing Evans his business card. "When you're ready to offer your customers what they want and deserve, just give me a call."

"Sure," Evans said, his terse tone of voice meaning Michael shouldn't hold his breath waiting for the phone to ring.

Lane Evans was a tough nut to crack, a real challenge. Michael made up his mind to add the account by hook or by crook. Everyone had an exploitable weakness, and Lane Evans was no exception. Sooner or later he'd break the bastard down and make him beg— literally beg on his knees—to carry Blake Blades.

Still smiling, Michael exited the office and walked past a bevy of young women inputting invoices into CRTs. Looking for a way to get his foot in the door to the closet where Evans hid his skeletons, Michael analyzed each clerk-typist in turn and rejected them all. Not one was even close to what he wanted.

Somewhere in this building, Michael knew from previous experience, was a woman with access to the information he needed. Someone Evans trusted with secrets.

A personal secretary, maybe, or an accountant—someone who'd been with the business for at least two years, who knew Evans' idiosyncrasies, his schedule, his appointments, his private indiscretions—someone older than these bimbos just out of high school.

It would most likely be a single woman, Michael guessed, perhaps a divorcee. Someone discreet who depended on her job for financial and emotional support, someone Evans could take into his confidence because she couldn't afford to quit or chance being fired. Someone who knew everything that went on inside this building and who controlled access to the big boss by screening his phone calls, scheduling his appointments, and opening his mail.

Now who, Michael wondered as he reached the lobby without uncovering a single candidate, *have I overlooked?*

"Any luck?"

Michael stopped in his tracks and turned around. "Did Mr. Evans buy anything?" the voice asked again.

Michael stared at the mousy-looking woman sitting at the reception desk. "No," he said, deliberately allowing his disappointment to show.

"Maybe next time," she offered optimistically. "Mr. Evans seldom decides to try a product until he's had time to think about it."

"Thanks for the tip," Michael said, turning on his smile. "Let me repay your advice by giving you a gift."

Michael opened his sales case and extracted a Blake Cutlery catalog. "Pick out any set of steak knives that we manufacture, and I'll give them to you tomorrow when I come back to see Mr. Evans."

Her eyes lit up magically when she saw the Blake name on the front page of the catalog. "Blake Cutlery? Their knives are so expensive! I couldn't possibly accept..."

"Of course you can," Michael said. "You did me a favor, now I want to do you one. Go ahead. Pick out whatever you want."

"No," she said, reluctantly handing the catalog back. "I didn't do anything…"

"Sure you did. You made me feel better," Michael beamed. "I felt horribly rejected when Evans didn't give me an order, but you cheered me up and gave me hope. That's worth a lot more than the price of anything listed in a silly catalog, isn't it? Besides, I get free samples and—since I'm not married—there's no one I can give them to. I've got more knives than I know what to do with, and you'd actually be doing me a big favor by taking a set or two off my hands."

He had her now. Maybe it was mentioning he wasn't married or maybe the implied offer of more than one set of knives, but her eyes lit up like a Christmas tree again.

"Go ahead," he suggested, lowering his voice to make it sound husky, sensual. "Anything you want. Anything at all…"

Did she dare?

Ellen flipped through the pages, longing to own a set of the high-priced carving knives bearing the Blake Blades' "double B" trademark of quality. Bob had promised her a set for their second anniversary, but that promise—like others he'd made—never materialized. And Ellen knew she'd never be able to save enough from her salary to afford to buy Blake Cutlery on her own.

Should she take a chance? Employees weren't allowed to accept gifts from salesmen even at Christmas time, and Lane had threatened to fire anyone who did. Would it be worth losing her job just to own a set of super-expensive Blake Cutlery?

"I'm sorry," she reluctantly told the salesman. "I really can't accept."

"I'm sorry, too," he said. "But I'm still in your debt, Ms.…" he glanced at the nameplate on her desk "… or is it Mrs. Lester?"

"It's Ms. Lester."

His smile broadened, exposing near-perfect teeth. "If you won't take a gift, how about dinner?"

"I beg your pardon?" Ellen wasn't sure she'd heard him correctly. "Are you asking me out to dinner?"

"Everyone has to eat, don't they? Why not eat together?"

Ellen didn't believe this was happening. Wasn't it just last night that she'd made up her mind to accept the next invitation to dinner from the first eligible man who asked? But this seemed much too soon, and she wasn't really sure she was ready. Or was she? Besides, she didn't even know the man.

She glanced up at his face—the sensitive ice-blue eyes, the pug nose, the blond hair with every strand razor-cut perfectly in place, the sensuous lips stretched in a broad smile over two rows of evenly-spaced, pearly-white teeth, the square jaw dotted in the middle with a dimple—and felt her heart skip a beat.

Delicious thrills raced up and down her spine.

She decided he wasn't such a total stranger, after all. She knew his name from his business card, knew he was the vice president of sales for Blake Blades—surely a reputable firm like Blake wouldn't make a less-than-virtuous man a vice president of their company, would they? Of course not!

He was impeccably dressed in a dark-blue suit, powder-blue button-down shirt, and red-white-and-blue striped tie. She couldn't even detect a single speck of dandruff flaking his tailored lapel, and that spoke well for his personal hygiene, didn't it? Only one thing about him bothered her.

"How old are you?" she asked, blurting out the words before she caught herself.

"Twenty-four," he answered truthfully. "But I've always been mature for my age. How old are you, if you don't mind my asking?"

"I'm twenty-six," she admitted. "Isn't that too old for you?"

He laughed. "I like older women," he said. "Besides, I really am mature for my age and two years doesn't make much difference when understanding adults like each other. Does it?"

Ellen was speechless.

"Look," he said. "I like you. Talking with you has brightened up my day and I'd love to stay here and talk for hours, but I've a sales meeting this afternoon I can't afford to miss—and I'm late already. Tell me you'll have dinner with me tonight and well talk to our hearts' content. Can I pick you up at seven?"

"Yes," she said on impulse. "Seven."

"Here," he handed her his card and a pen. "Write your name, address, and phone number on the back, and I'll be there at seven sharp."

"How should I dress?" she asked, scribbling frantically. "Where will we go?"

"Dress up," he said, grinning from ear to ear like a Cheshire cat. "I like to take my women out in style."

Exactly how many women, Ellen wondered with a pang of jealousy, *did Michael Thompson take out?*

And what kind of pain, she worried, *am I letting myself in for?*

"I don't wanna!" Danny wailed.

"Sure you do," his mother said. "You like to visit Aunt Suzi. You said so yourself just last week when we were there."

"That was diff-rent."

"Why was it different?"

"Cause you were there, too."

Danny felt tears well up in his eyes, and he knew he was going to cry. Maybe if he cried a lot, his mother wouldn't make him go to Aunt Suzi's house while she went somewhere else without him.

Didn't Mom realize how much he needed her? Why was she still dressing when her son was crying like Niagara Falls? Didn't she care about him anymore?

Obviously, his tears wouldn't work on her tonight. Mom was sitting on the edge of her bed rolling panty hose up her legs while Danny was dying inside from momentary neglect.

Did he need to smash something valuable just to get her attention?

The possibility of punishment crossed his mind, but he rejected the thought immediately. Wasn't Mom punishing him already by making him stay at Aunt Suzi's without her? What could be worse?

Stifling a sniffle, Danny walked to his mother's vanity and picked up the bottle of French perfume she'd inadvertently left sitting out where he could reach it. The bottle felt heavy in his hand—it was made of cut crystal and still half-full of "smells-good." He lifted the bottle above his head...

"Danny, no!" his mother yelled from across the room.

... and flung the fragile crystal...

"No!"

... right at the full-length mirror...

"Danny, don't!"

... less than three feet away.

The mirror shattered into a thousand tiny shards and glass flew everywhere. A sharp fragment of broken mirror grazed Danny's forehead and another gouged his cheek. It never occurred to him that his open eyes were vulnerable, too, until a piece of glass struck an eyelid and made him blink.

Terrible pain filled his head. Blood gushed from torn capillaries and obscured his vision. Suddenly he was scared out of his wits.

And then his mother was at his side, picking him up and laying him gently down on the bed, wiping away the blood and granules of glass from his face with a corner of the top bedsheet, holding his injured eye open with her fingers and looking for splinters—all done with the kind of cool efficiency Danny had come to expect from this woman who'd cared for him all his life and who could fix almost anything with her tender loving touch.

He felt safe and secure under her ministrations. The stark panic and incredible pain he'd endured only moments ago was already dissipating, and he knew his mother would soon make everything all right again. His mother would never let anything bad happen to her son. If it did when she wasn't paying attention, she'd quickly set things right as soon as she noticed something was wrong.

His foolhardy tantrum had worked even better than Danny expected in making Mom realize how much he needed her, depended on her. He could tell that by the way she was crying tears of joy at the discovery that his wounds were only superficial, that he would recover without scarring, without loss of vision. He knew they must be tears of joy because she was smiling and laughing at the same time she was crying.

Mom needed to be needed, and it made Danny happy when he found ways like this to provide for her needs, as she always provided for his needs.

"Oh, Danny," she cried. "You had me so worried!"

Mom told Danny to stay still while she went into the bathroom for bandages, a washcloth, and boric acid solution. In a matter of minutes she had him fixed up as good as new.

And then she laid into him with a fury he'd never seen before as her simmering fears and frustrations boiled over into anger. Instead of hitting him with her fist or paddling his bottom with the palm of her hand—punishments he'd anticipated and wanted and probably deserved—she lashed out with her tongue and cut him in two with pointed phrases that hurt far worse than he thought possible.

Withering under words like "hateful little boy who spoils everything" and "I wish you'd never been born," Danny's whole world collapsed in ruins. His mind tried to withdraw in self-defense, but her verbal tirade penetrated through to his subconscious and, no matter how hard he tried, he couldn't shut the words out completely.

For what seemed like forever, the vicious remarks continued unabated. Some words he'd never heard before and didn't recognize, but others he knew and took to heart. The tone of her voice was deadly serious and did far more damage than the words did themselves.

Somehow Danny had stepped over the bounds into unknown territory, and now there was no turning back. Subtle changes had taken place, of which he was consciously unaware, and nothing could ever be the same between this mother and son ever again. A vague feeling of loss overcame him, and he wept for what was and, he knew, could be no more.

"I hate you!" he screamed at his mother when at last she paused to catch her breath. "I hate you! I hate you!"

"Go to your room," she demanded. "Go to your room and stay there until you've had time to think about what you've done."

Not daring to disobey, Danny ran to his bedroom and continued to cry until all his tears were used up. Finally, mercifully, exhaustion claimed him and be fell asleep. He was awakened, an hour later, by the doorbell. Aunt Suzi's cheery, "Hi, Sis," resounded up the stairs from the foyer below.

"Thank God, you're here."

"Thank the cab driver. He ran a few lights and almost got us killed, but we made it here in record time. The way you sounded on the phone, I thought I'd better tell the cabbie this was an emergency of incredible magnitude. What's wrong, Sis? What's that awful smell?"

Danny listened as his mother explained, saying things like "ruined my best dress with blood" and "he did it deliberately"; broke the "antique mirror over the vanity" and "going to have seven years of bad luck"; the perfume was "the only thing that bastard Bob gave me worth keeping" and "that's why the whole place smells like a

French whorehouse."

"What about Danny?" Aunt Suzi asked. "How bad is he hurt?"

"I suppose his pride was hurt more than anything else. I lost my temper and shouted at him, but he'll more than likely be over it by morning. Nothing I say to that kid sinks in enough to teach him the lesson he needs, so I sent him to bed without supper. Suppose he'll listen to reason when his stomach complains loudly?"

"That never worked on us," Aunt Suzi laughed. "Or maybe you don't remember all the trouble we managed as kids?"

"I remember," Mom said. "That's why I want Danny to learn a lesson before he does something he'll regret for the rest of his life."

"Ease up, Sis. Go get dressed before your boyfriend arrives. Let me worry about Danny tonight."

"Oh, the time! He'll be here any minute!"

"Go! If he gets here before you're ready, I'll fix him a drink. Where do you keep the booze?"

"There isn't any."

"Okay. I'll give him a Pepsi. Hurry up, will you?"

Danny heard his mother's footsteps on the stairs. A minute later, when she peeked into his room, he pretended to be asleep.

"Seven years," he heard her whisper. "Haven't we had our share of bad luck without breaking a mirror? What'll happen to us now?"

Danny didn't know. But a growing sense of having lost what little control he might have had—of being able to manipulate his world to get what he wanted—crept over him like the lengthening shadows stealing in through the bedroom windows.

Beneath his bed, scuttling claws made strange noises.

He wanted to run to his mother and beg her forgiveness, throw his thin arms around her hips and cry his eyes out into her warm apron. He wanted to tell her he didn't mean it when he yelled "I hate you! I hate you!"

Instead, he stayed rooted to the bed—unable to move a muscle.

And then, he knew, it was too late.

Backing out of the doorway, she closed his door behind her and latched it securely from the outside, trapping Danny in the dungeon-like tomb of his own room, imprisoning him here where the monsters were.

Panic gripped him with icy fingers as the boy's horrified eyes saw the long shadows cast by the closet door *actually move*!

And, when the last ray of sunshine faded with the coming of the night, Danny doubted that he'd even survive his curse of bad luck till tomorrow morning—much less seven whole years.

CHAPTER THREE

A *Willow Woods homicide lieutenant shouldn't vomit on the corpse at the scene of the crime,* Tom Wesley chastised himself as warm bile clogged his throat and his stomach muscles convulsed uncontrollably. *Hold it down, boy, or you'll contaminate valuable evidence with your own barf.*

"Ripe, ain't she?"

"Tell me something I don't already know," Tom croaked, swallowing back most of the bile.

"Well, it wasn't rape," the deputy coroner said. "Wasn't robbery, either."

"Not unless the perpetrator got interrupted before he finished," a young patrolman eagerly suggested. "Maybe he didn't have time to take her clothes off or grab her purse."

"He had time to drag the body into the bushes, though," the coroner mused. "Seems to me that was time enough to take her purse—if he'd wanted the money, that is."

"How long, Doc?" Wesley asked, glad to have an excuse to look away. "How long has she been here like that?"

"Four or five days, Lieutenant."

"Who found her?"

"I did," said the uniformed patrolman, a kid in his early twenties.

"Johnson, is it?" Wesley noted from the name badge and scribbled the name in his notebook.

"Yes, sir."

"Tell me, Johnson, what made you look in these particular bushes? The body isn't visible from the road, is it? What tipped you off?"

"The smell, of course."

"You had the windows rolled down in the patrol car and could smell her all the way out on the street? You've got a better nose than me, mister."

"I..." the kid flustered.

Wesley decided to jump on the boy with both feet: "Don't lie to a homicide lieutenant, mister. Not unless you feel like doing time for obstructing justice in a murder investigation. What really happened?"

"I... I stopped to take a leak," the boy admitted, blushing.

"In the bushes?"

"Yeah."

"Couldn't hold it until your break?"

"I didn't have another break coming," the kid—Wesley thought of anyone who'd been on the force less than five years as still a kid—said sheepishly.

"And you didn't want to radio in an unscheduled pit stop, did you?"

"No."

"Did you take your leak?"

"Yes."

"Where?"

The patrolman pointed to a spot in the bushes some fifteen feet from the body.

"And that's when you smelled it? Something ripe? While peeing in those bushes?"

"I ..."

"Answer me, dammit!"

"Y... yes."

"Then what did you do? After you zipped up, I mean."

"I went back to the car for my flashlight."

"And radioed in?"

"I reported the smell and told the dispatcher I was investigating."

"Then what?"

"I followed my nose to the body."

"Did you touch her? Did you touch any part of the body?"

The boy blushed again. "No, of course not! I didn't need to feel for a pulse to tell she was dead."

"Then what did you do?"

"I radioed in for assistance."

"What about her purse? Did you open the purse and look inside?"

"I checked for identification."

"Did you move the purse? Or did you leave it where it was?"

"I..."

"You moved it, didn't you?"

"I put it back," the boy said proudly. "Exactly where I found it."

Wesley sadly shook his head. Kids these days didn't know the first thing about rules of preserving evidence, and they had to be taught the hard way what they should have learned day one at the academy. Maybe the next time Johnson smelled a dead body he'd think before pissing on possible clues, leaving his own footprints and fingerprints on almost everything at the crime scene, or moving material evidence before it could be mapped out, examined and photographed by Forensics. It'd sure make Wesley's job one whole hell of a lot easier if rookies knew what they were doing, or had one ounce of common sense in their brains.

"Get out of here," Wesley growled. "Go sit in the squad car while Doc and I determine how bad you've messed up."

Crestfallen, the patrolman did what he was told.

"Aren't you being a little hard on that boy?" the coroner asked when Johnson was finally out of earshot.

"He's got to learn," Wesley replied, irritated.

"Same way you did?"

"What's that supposed to mean?"

"Seems to me," the doctor said, "there used to be a young rookie who'd puke his guts over the remains every time he came across a ripe stiff. How is that queasy stomach of yours behavin' these days, Tom? Any better?"

"Not good, Doc. Wouldn't be bad if I had time to digest my food, but stiffs always seem to turn up when I'm halfway into a big meal."

"Ever thought of another line of work? One with regular hours and uninterrupted feedings?"

"Sure. Haven't you?"

"All the time. But I'm getting too old to start over again in private practice. You're—what—thirty? Thirty-two? That's young enough to get off the public payroll and look for something better. Isn't it?"

"Did I say I disliked being a cop?"

"No, you didn't."

"The only thing I can't stand about bein' a cop is looking at ripe bodies. Especially the carved-up bodies of young women."

"Kind of makes you mad, doesn't it?"

"Makes me real mad."

"Think you'll find him, Tom?"

"Who?"

"The killer."

Wesley glanced around the park, his trained eyes taking in the frantic activity of forensics specialists combing the sealed off area for bits of minute evidence. Yellow plastic streamers marked "Police Line—Do Not Cross" bobbed up and down in the autumn wind, and a string of floodlights that turned night into day illumined the entire crime scene. "With all this modern technology to help," the lieutenant said, "it should be a piece of cake."

"If you really believe that," the doctor said, smiling, "I've got a bridge you can buy."

"In Brooklyn?"

"Yeah."

Wesley grinned. "You're too late, Doc."

"Too late?"

Wesley slapped the old man's shoulder with a conspiratory cuff.

"I already own the Brooklyn Bridge," he said, and walked away.

"Danny?"

Aunt Suzi was at the door.

"Want some supper?"

Danny didn't answer.

"If you don't tell Mom, I'll let you out."

Huddled in a ball under the covers, Danny desperately sucked at one of his thumbs.

"Danny?"

It sounded like Aunt Suzi, all right, but Danny didn't dare trust his ears. Maybe it was a horrible monster just pretending to be Aunt Suzi. Monsters liked to pretend, Danny knew. They could pretend to be anybody. The worst monsters were the ones who pretended to be someone you loved. Like the wolf in Little Red Riding Hood pretended to be Red's grandmother.

"Go 'way," Danny whispered.

"I'm baking cookies, Danny. Chocolate chips. Can you smell them?"

Danny tried to test the air with his nose. All he could smell was stinky perfume. Like in a French "Ore-house."

"Go 'way," he said again, this time a little louder.

"Are you all right?" she asked, her voice sounding concerned.

"Go 'way!" he shouted.

At the sound of the latch snicking open, Danny cringed. He burrowed under the covers, completely covering his whole body—even the top of his head—as he heard the doorknob start to turn. He peed his pajama pants, warm liquid soaking the sheets and mattress beneath his butt, when painted hinges shrieked loud like a banshee. Though he didn't want to lay there in a big pool of his own piss, he knew he had to. The monster was coming in to get him, and there was no place else he could hide.

The light switch clicked on.

"I seeeee youuuuuu," Aunt Suzi sang as if she were playing a familiar game of hide and seek.

Danny waited—his breath caught in his throat and his heart beating a mile a minute—for the monster to grab him.

And then she did.

And his heart stopped.

"Drive," Wesley ordered.

"Where to?"

"Anywhere."

"Don't you have your own car?"

"No," Wesley said.

"How did you get to the crime scene?"

"I took a taxi," said Wesley.

Johnson put the squad in gear. Still smarting from the lieutenant's harsh words, it was obvious he expected another ass chewing. Wesley decided to let him stew.

"Go ahead," the kid said when he couldn't take the silence any longer. "I guess I deserve whatever you're going to say."

"Oh? And what do you think I'm going to say?"

"I fucked up royally."

"Did you?"

"Yeah."

"How?"

Johnson glanced incredulously at his passenger. "How? For starters, I left my vehicle without calling in. Right?"

"Right so far."

"Then I contaminated or destroyed valuable evidence by urinating in the bushes."

"Keep going."

"By checking her purse for identification, I may have smudged any prints the killer could have left. And by moving the purse, I disturbed the exact lay."

"Not bad," Wesley said, actually impressed. "Anything else?"

"Not that I can think of."

"What about footprints?"

"What about them?"

"You left size eleven boot tracks everywhere I looked," Wesley said. "Next time try and stay in one place until Forensics has a chance to go over the lawn with their proverbial fine-toothed combs."

"Next time?" The kid couldn't believe his ears. "What next time?"

"You figure it out."

Johnson pulled over to the curb and looked the lieutenant in the eye. "Let me get this straight," he said, hoping he'd heard right. "You're not going to report me?"

"Why should I?" Wesley asked, returning the kid's stare. "Everyone fucks up when he's a rookie. The important thing is to learn from your mistakes and not do the same dumb things the next time. Right? The way I figure it, you got all the real dumb things out of your system the first time out. Next time you'll be a fucking Einstein and do everything smarter, won't you?"

"Yes, sir. Thank you, sir."

The kid's gratitude was nauseating. Wesley was afraid for a moment that Johnson was going to kiss him or want to shake his hand or offer to buy him a cup of coffee or something stupid like that.

But before the kid could open mouth and insert foot, the patrol car radio blared an emergency call for anyone in the vicinity of Fourth and Elm, and that was less than a block away from where they now sat chewing the fat.

The kid reacted automatically, even before Wesley could think to respond himself. He radioed in their location, got an exact address and nature of the emergency, and they were off and running...

CHAPTER FOUR

"You look *gorgeous!*" Michael Thompson had told her as she walked into the living room where Michael and Suzi were sipping Pepsi Colas on ice.

Now, after Michael had again complimented her appearance at least a dozen times more, Ellen finally began to believe him.

Despite Danny's unsettling antics, Ellen had allowed nothing else to spoil the remainder of the evening. After locking her son safely in his room where he was sure to stay out of trouble, she'd miraculously managed to complete her dressing ritual in record time. The results, Michael claimed, were quite spectacular, and Ellen had to agree with him.

She tried to remember when she'd last felt so alive, so complete, so like a real woman. It had been her wedding day, she realized with a start; but that night Bob viciously brutalized her for the first time, making her feel worthless and degraded. Before their marriage, he'd always thought to treat Ellen like a lady, like a fragile doll to be treasured rather than toyed with. But after the ceremony was over, after family and friends had congratulated them both and Bob had celebrated with glass after glass of expensive champagne, he'd taken her to a sleazy motel room and treated her like she'd suddenly become his personal slave.

The next morning, of course, he'd apologized.

But the real Bob Norman wasn't the same man she'd imagined she'd married. The kind, gentle, caring *man* she'd fallen in love with.

Bob Norman was a *beast.*

One drink was all it took to change him into an inhuman monster that sought to dominate life by brute force, tearing at her clothes, ripping her flesh, subjugating her will to his whims. Any move she made to escape was met with debilitating blows to her body that left her, both inside and out, bruised and bleeding.

And broken.

And then, before she could find some way to finally leave her husband without being killed, she became pregnant.

Bob did his best to abort the baby, but Ellen found amazing strength in knowing she wasn't alone anymore. Feeling responsible for the fetus developing inside her body, she decided she had to protect herself. The next time Bob began to beat her, she pulled an eleven-inch butcher knife, and threatened to cut off his balls if he even tried to touch her.

Taking her threat seriously, Bob kept a respectable distance until Danny was born. Once she came home from the hospital, still weak and vulnerable from a difficult delivery, the beatings began again, worse than before.

And then Danny got sick.

The doctors said it had something to do with unusual stress depressing Ellen's immune system, and somehow she'd picked up and passed on a deadly virus to her son. His own immune system, at such a tender age, lacked the ability to form antibodies potent enough to overcome such an illness, and his raging fever was merely a symptom—not the cause—of a more serious malady no one knew exactly how to treat.

They tried to reduce his fever, but nothing seemed to work. Ellen stayed at the hospital night and day for months, hoping and praying, while Danny was fed, intravenously, every drug imaginable.

Eventually, the doctors exhausted all options for a cure—at about the same time as they exhausted all available insurance benefits— and they sent Danny home to die.

Bob, afraid the fever might be contagious, quickly moved out of the house—and into an apartment with one of his many girlfriends— and immediately filed for divorce.

It had taken her years to recover—longer than Danny took to recover from his fever—but now, at last, she was sure recovery waited just around the corner.

Or maybe, she thought, *it's seated across the table from me at this very moment.*

"I still can't believe the change," Michael was saying. "When I saw you this afternoon, I thought you were pretty. But tonight you're *gorgeous!*"

Not knowing what to say, Ellen simply smiled.

"Talk to me," he urged. "Tell me everything about you. Please."

"I'm divorced," she began, watching his eyes for adverse reactions. "And I have a son named Danny who's almost six..."

"I like kids," Michael said, showing no hint of rejection.

Encouraged, Ellen continued to talk. She told him about her sister Susan, whom he'd already met, her mother who'd died when Ellen was a senior in high school and Susan a freshman, her father who'd remarried and moved to Arizona. She told him about Danny's illness and eventual recovery, and she found herself, once again, claiming her son's illness was the cause for her divorce, even when she knew it wasn't true.

But Michael seemed to accept what she said with an eagerness that surprised her. It was almost as if he knew she were lying to herself—and him—and was perfectly willing to overlook the lie, something Bob would never have done.

No, she chastised herself. *You can't compare apples and oranges. Bob and Michael are different people.*

And Bob, thank goodness, was out of her life completely.

While Michael was here right now—right there across the table, close enough to touch.

"How long have you worked for Lane Evans?" he asked, redirecting her train of thought.

"Almost three years."

"Do you like your job? Seems to me it'd be boring to sit at a desk all day."

"Oh, no. I meet all kinds of interesting people sitting behind that desk." She smiled at him. "After all, that's how *we* met, wasn't it?"

"Touché," he said.

"Besides, I never have time to be bored. Mr. Evans makes sure I keep busy with other things."

"Other things?"

"Answering phones, opening mail, making travel arrangements. You know. Busy work."

"A little of everything?"

"Um hm."

Their waiter interrupted to ask if they wanted dessert. Neither did.

"I'm stuffed," Ellen said. "The food here is excellent."

"Then we'll have to come here again," Michael suggested. "Or would you prefer to try one of the other restaurants in town?"

Ellen felt her heart flutter. Had he asked her out *again*? Oh, Lord! What should she say?

Yes Yes Yes Yes Yes, any place, wherever you want! Whenever you want, yes!

She said instead: "I'll fix you a home-cooked meal, if you'd like. I'm not a bad cook. Really, I'm not."

He smiled appreciatively. "I'd love it," he said. "When?"

"Tomorrow night?"

"You're on." He reached across the table and took her hand. "But tonight is still young. I know this club with a fantastic band you've just got to hear. Grab your purse and let's go!"

I can't, she knew she should have said. *I have to go home because my five-and-a-half-year-old son needs me.*

But she also knew Suzi was there with Danny. And Ellen was here with Michael.

And Danny needed to learn a lesson and what could it hurt if she stayed out a little longer and she really loved to dance but never got a chance anymore and...

She grabbed her purse.

Michael paid the bill.

And, holding hands like a couple of teenagers, they left the restaurant and went out into the still-young night that Ellen hoped would never grow old.

Johnson took the stairs three at a time. He was out of breath when he reached the bedroom, but he wasn't about to stop even for a moment, not till this child was out of danger.

He pried open the child's mouth with practiced fingers, pulled the swollen tongue out of the esophagus, and pushed on the boy's abdomen hoping to dislodge any foreign matter blocking the airways.

"C'mon," he urged. "Breathe, dammit!"

But the boy didn't.

Couldn't.

"He's dead!" Johnson heard the young woman who'd opened the downstairs door scream again and again. "Omigawd! He's dead! He's dead!"

"Take it easy, lady," Lieutenant Wesley told her. "Sit down and take it easy. Hysteria won't help."

Johnson felt his own hysteria break to the surface and quickly shoved it aside. Wesley was right. Hysteria wouldn't help.

Using a combination of CPR and mouth-to-mouth, Johnson continued to work on the boy. Finally, in sheer desperation, he grabbed the child's ankles, lifted the body upside-down from the bed, and shook the limp form until...

Did he hear a gasp for breath? A cough? A cry? A wail?

Had it come from the still-hysterical woman? From Lieutenant Wesley?

Or had Johnson's own hysteria finally become audible? Had he made those sounds himself without realizing it?

Sudden warmth spread to the flesh he held in his hands, and Johnson thought the boy's circulatory system was indeed starting to pump fresh blood to the child's extremities. That meant the tiny heart was beating regularly, the small lungs breathing in and out, and vital blood was once again reaching the boy's oxygen-starved brain.

Or had he merely imagined it?

No. The flesh was warm.

Two toes moved, then wriggled, and then the whole body seemed to come alive.

Squirming like a bag of snakes, the boy struggled to right himself. Johnson lost his hold on one ankle and the loose foot kicked him in the face, bloodying his nose and chipping a tooth.

"Ungh!" he gasped, caught completely by surprise.

"Aieeeeeeeee!" keened the boy, kicking free with the other foot. The small body dropped back to the bed, bounced once or twice into the air, and rolled off the side of the mattress and onto the floor, screaming all the way.

Wesley and the woman came running, their footfalls like a herd of elephants trampling up the stairs. "Danny!" the woman shrieked as she entered the room. "Danny!"

Pandemonium ruled. While Wesley tried to calm both the boy

and the woman (whether she was the mother or only a babysitter, did it matter?), Johnson sank exhaustedly to his knees, and, at last, took the time to catch a much-needed breath of his own.

He'd gone away completely, but he came back.

He remembered holding his breath as the monster that pretended to be Aunt Suzi entered his room, remembered willing himself invisible in the bed, remembered the monster reaching for him anyway—grabbing both the covers and his cloak of invisibility and pulling them off—grabbing for his body with hideous claws that threatened to cut him in two like a pair of giant scissors slicing a sheet of paper. Everything after that was blank.

Just as the claws reached him, though, he remembered he'd tried to will himself away to Never Never Land like Peter Pan told children to do in the famous fairy tale—like Danny did when Johnny Radcliff beat up on him at school—only this time it really worked!

Now he was back in his own room, just as Wendy and her brother had returned to their bedroom after visiting Never-Never Land.

"Th-th-the m-monster didn't g-get me?" he asked incredulously, his throat sore from screaming.

"Oh, Danny," his aunt wept, holding him tight. "You didn't die. You didn't die. I thought you were dead, but you didn't die."

With the lights on in his room, he could see he was safe from the monsters. His real Aunt Suzi, not a monster pretending to be her, was protecting him now.

And, if Aunt Suzi needed help to keep the monsters at bay, she could ask the uniformed policeman sitting right there on Danny's bed to shoot the monsters with his gun.

"Son," a man's voice said. Danny turned his head and saw a tall man in an ordinary-looking brown suit standing off to the side behind Aunt Suzi. The man held a notebook in one hand and a ballpoint pen in the other. "Son, can you tell me your name?"

"Danny."

"Do you know your last name?"

Of course Danny knew his last name. He even knew how to spell it. "N-o-r-m-a-n," he said.

"Do you know where you are, Danny?"

"Home," the boy said. "In my room."

"And what's the address here? Do you know the address where you live, Danny?"

Danny tried to remember. "One-four-six-three Elm Street," he said, not sure if he had the numbers right. He always had trouble with numbers.

"Close enough," the man said. "It's four-one-six-three, Danny."

"Yeah," Danny agreed. "Four-one-six-three."

"I think he'll be fine, Mrs. Norman," the man said to Aunt Suzi. "We can drive him to the hospital, if you'd like, or you can wait until morning and take him to your own doctor. It's up to you."

"I'm not Mrs. Norman," Aunt Suzi said. "I'm Susan Lester, her sister."

"Oh? Where's Mrs. Norman?"

"She went out to dinner with a friend. I expect her back in about an hour."

"I see."

"Are you sure Danny's all right?"

"I'm not a doctor, Ms. Lester. But the boy's memory seems intact and his skin color's near normal. I don't think there's been any brain damage." The man looked at Danny again. "How do you feel, son? Do you feel okay now?"

"I'm hungry," Danny said.

"Sounds normal to me," said the policeman on Danny's bed.

Aunt Suzi smiled at the policeman. "How can I ever thank you?" she asked. "You performed a miracle. We'll never be able to repay you for saving Danny's life."

The policeman smiled back. "All in a day's work," he told her, suddenly blushing the way Danny sometimes did when he got embarrassed. "But I'm glad we got here in time to help."

"You okay?" the man in the suit asked the policeman. "You don't look so good."

"I just need some air. The smell in here's making me lightheaded."

The other man wrinkled his nose. "What is that smell?" he asked. "It smells like—"

"Like a French Ore-house," Danny finished for him, making everyone laugh so hard it looked like they were going to cry.

CHAPTER FIVE

"You got a first name?" Wesley asked when they reached the car.

"Leonard."

"You did okay back there, Leonard."

"Thanks. At first I thought we'd lost him. I really thought he was dead."

"He was," Wesley said. "I've seen enough stiffs to recognize dead. Believe me, the kid was dead."

"How could he be dead one minute and alive the next?"

"Dunno," Wesley shrugged. "Just happens sometimes."

Johnson buckled his seat belt and started the car. "Where to?" he asked.

"Station house. We've had enough excitement for one night, haven't we?"

Johnson radioed in, slammed the car into gear, and pulled away from the curb. Though he tried to keep his mind on the road, it was to no avail. Susan Lester's lithe body and beautiful face intruded on his thoughts, and he couldn't get her face and figure out of his mind.

Forget it, he told himself. *You'll probably never see her again, so why don't you just forget about her and concentrate on your driving?*

At twenty-two, Leonard Johnson considered himself a dedicated bachelor. There were two or three women he went out with when he wanted to have a good time, but he hadn't had anyone special in his life since he and Kathy broke up at the beginning of his sophomore year in college.

It just wasn't worthwhile to get involved again, was it? No, of course not. A police officer worked crazy hours and made a poor candidate for marriage. If he wanted to be a cop, he needed to be footloose and fancy-free. Marriage would only complicate things, and his life was complicated enough without a family to worry about, wasn't it?

So who's talking about marriage? You just met the girl, for chrissakes. You aren't thinking about getting serious. All you're thinking about is...

Seeing her again.

Being with her.

Hearing her voice.

Holding her.

Kissing her.

Yeah, sure. You know what that leads to.

He pictured his hands sliding under Susan's yellow sweater, caressing the smooth skin of her stomach, moving upward to touch the fabric of her bra, reaching around her back to find the fasteners.

It wouldn't hurt to call her, he decided. Maybe just to see how the boy's doing—make sure his recovery was more than temporary.

"Kids," Wesley said, shaking his head.

"What about 'em?" Johnson asked.

"Always getting into trouble. I feel sorry for Danny's mother. Don't you?"

"Yeah. Kids like Danny make me glad I'm still single."

"Wait a few years," Wesley said. "You'll change your mind."

"You married?"

"Not anymore."

Why not? Johnson wanted to ask, but thought better of it.

"What bothers me," Wesley said, "is how Danny died so quick. According to his aunt, she saw his body moving under the blankets when she entered the bedroom. But when she pulled the blankets off, he wasn't even breathing. It doesn't make sense."

"Doesn't SIDS—Sudden Infant Death Syndrome—work like that?"

"Yeah. But Danny's too old for SIDS."

"Maybe he smothered under the blankets?"

"I doubt it."

Johnson gritted his teeth. "You don't suspect foul play, do you?" he asked, fearing Wesley's reply. "Not the aunt, surely."

"Never can tell," the lieutenant said, studying Johnson's face. "You want to do me a big favor? Help put my mind at ease?"

"Sure. What?"

"Give the girl a call and check her out. You know, make a date with her. See if she had a reason for killing the kid. You're about the same age. Maybe she'll open up and tell you what really happened."

"I can't do *that*," Johnson said.

"Why not? You're a cop, aren't you?"

"I'm a rookie patrolman," Johnson said, "not a homicide detective."

Wesley's mouth twisted up at the corners. "I guess I didn't tell you, did I?"

"Tell me what?" Johnson wondered.

"As of fifteen-hundred hours tomorrow you'll be transferred to the homicide division."

"*What!*"

"Starting tomorrow night," Wesley said, his mouth twisting the rest of the way into a full-blown grin, "you're going to be my new partner."

"The night's still young," Michael said, sipping his third scotch. "You don't want to leave yet, do you?"

"No," Ellen admitted. "But I've got to go to work in…" she glanced at Michael's wristwatch. "Oh, my God! It's almost one AM!"

"Time flies when you're having fun."

"And it's been fun, Michael, but I do have to work tomorrow. Please. Either take me home or call me a cab."

"Okay," Michael slurred. "You're a cab."

Ellen stood up and reached for her purse, but Michael stopped her before she could leave. "Hey," he said. "I was only joking. C'mon, I'll drive you home."

"Sure you can drive?" she asked sarcastically.

"I'm still sober," he said, downing the last of his drink. "I only had three of these things, and the way the bartender waters booze it's like I only had one. Don't worry. I'll get you home."

"I'm not worried," Ellen lied.

For three-and-a-half hours she'd forgotten about everything except the music and Michael. She'd had a fabulous evening filled with fun, and Ellen wished it could continue forever.

But, like Cinderella, she knew she had to leave before the magic disappeared, and Michael turned into a pumpkin.

His first drink seemingly had no effect on him, and Ellen didn't argue when he'd ordered another. While the band was playing, they stayed on the dance floor and worked off the alcohol with their wild gyrations.

But each time the band took a break, Michael went straight to the bar and came back to the table with another round of fresh drinks.

Ellen had started with white wine and stayed with the same drink all night. Michael, also, had started with white wine, but an hour or so ago he'd switched to scotch on the rocks.

And, with each sip of hard liquor, he had gradually become more and more aggressive.

Ellen hadn't minded when his hands first moved below her waist on the dance floor. The light pressure on her buttocks had been stimulating and a welcome hint of growing intimacy. Nor had she minded when his fingers "accidentally" brushed the bodice of her dress. She'd deliberately gone without a bra so he'd want to discover whether or not she wore one.

Even the hand—creeping up her inner thigh under the table— hadn't bothered her until he tried to force her legs apart and reach inside her panties.

"No, Michael," she'd whispered. "Not here."

But he'd insisted.

And, finally, she'd let him.

Other couples—some in similarly compromising positions— paid no attention when Michael forced her hand to his lap and asked her to unzip him.

"No one will know," he urged.

But after she did and he demanded more, she flatly refused. As if in retaliation, he removed his fingers from her wetness and pulled down her skirt. Then he zipped himself up and headed for the bar to order another round.

"Haven't we had enough?" she'd inquired as he started on the third scotch. "What time is it anyway?"

A parking attendant brought Michael's Audi to the door and left the motor running. Michael tipped the man and climbed behind the wheel. Ellen got in on the passenger side, and, before she'd even closed her door completely, Michael slammed the car into gear, stepped on the gas, and peeled an eighth of an inch of rubber off each of the tires as the bright-red Audi squealed out of the parking lot and disappeared into the night.

Danny didn't want to watch television, nor did he want another chocolate chip cookie. What he wanted was his mother, but she wasn't home. Maybe she wasn't coming home, either.

Ever.

That thought had occurred to him more and more as time wore on.

He was much too tired to sleep, and Aunt Suzi had given up trying to make him.

Though he knew how to tell time by the positions of the big and little hands on a clock, he didn't know what time it was, only that it was real late and he'd never been allowed up this late in his entire life. After the policemen left, Aunt Suzi had catered to Danny's every whim. She'd let him eat as many cookies as he wanted, let him watch TV though he didn't understand the adult programs and couldn't find cartoons on any of the channels, and even let him make a mess of the kitchen tablecloth with his coloring crayons. Yet never once had she yelled at him or told him to quit his whining.

"I don't know," she'd nervously admitted each time he'd pressed her for an answer. "I don't know where she is, and I don't know when she's coming home."

Now Aunt Suzi was worried, too. Danny could tell by the way she'd talked on the telephone to the policemen at the police station.

And the people at the hospitals.

No, the policemen had said, Mom wasn't at the station. Aunt Suzi had given them a 'scription and they promised to call if Mom turned up dead. And no, she wasn't at any of the hospitals either. They had no record of anyone matching her 'scription being hurt in an accident. They, too, would call if she turned up dead.

Danny was afraid the phone would ring any minute now, and he didn't want Aunt Suzi to answer it.

So, while Aunt Suzi watched someone named "Letterman" on TV, Danny crawled on his hands and knees to the telephone jack, played with the wire until it snapped in two, and hid the broken end by tucking it into an open space beneath the baseboard.

Maybe, he reasoned with his five-year-old mind, if no one could telephone to tell him his mother had died, then she'd still be alive.

"I'm sorry," he said, slowing the car.

Ellen, her eyes wide with fear, was visibly trembling as Michael parked the Audi at the side of the road.

"I know I was driving like a maniac," he said, sounding contrite. "I'm sorry I scared you."

Ellen bit her lower lip and said nothing.

"It's just that you're *so beautiful*, Ellen. You make me *crazy* and I can't control my emotions." He tried to look as pathetic as a little lost puppy. "I've never felt like this before and I don't know what to do about it. Can you forgive me?"

His words began to have their desired effect. As her trembling eased and calm returned to her terrified eyes, he continued soothing her with his sexy voice.

"You're everything I've ever wanted in a woman, Ellen. Naturally, I was disappointed when you rejected me..."

"Rejected you? I didn't reject you."

"Then I misunderstood. When you asked to leave, you broke my heart. I thought you didn't want to be with me..."

Now he had her. The old carrot-and-stick routine worked every time.

"Now that I've found you, I couldn't bear the pain of parting. But it's only for a little while, isn't it? We'll see each other tomorrow for dinner, won't we? You're fixing dinner for me tomorrow night, aren't you?"

"Yes," she said.

"You've made me happy again," Michael beamed. "I feel like the luckiest man in the world."

Ellen smiled. Any trace of fear that might have remained would soon be forgotten.

"Buckle your seat belt," Michael said. "I'm going to drive you home—sanely, this time. No more speeding, I promise."

Ellen looked relieved. Her fear was gone now, and she thought she was safe. But the seeds of fear had been planted, buried under a thin layer of topsoil where Michael would nourish them with BS until the seeds sprouted and the time came when her fear was ripe to harvest.

The old carrot-and-stick routine. Desire and fear. Love and hate. The oldest trick in the book.

And it still worked wonders.

CHAPTER SIX

Wesley emptied the ashtray and opened a fresh pack of Camel Filters. Instead of another cigarette and an umpteenth cup of black coffee, he knew that what he really needed was to eat a big breakfast at the greasy spoon around the corner from the station house and then go home to his empty apartment for an hour or two of sleep.

But he also knew he couldn't afford a good night's sleep until the killer was caught.

Three murders in as many weeks, each with similar MOs. The victims were all young women between the ages of nineteen and twenty-six. The murder weapon was a keen-edged blade, an expensive knife perhaps. Or possibly a scalpel—utilized with the surgical precision of a modern-day Jack the Ripper.

The third victim—one Glenda Rose Williams, discovered last night in the park—had been dead five days, according to the autopsy report. And that made three murders in less than three weeks.

"A murder epidemic," the deputy coroner had commented as he dropped a preliminary report off in Wesley's office just before dawn.

"What are we dealing with here, Doc? A sicko? A pervert? What kind of person would cut a woman up and leave her remains to rot?"

"Obviously some kind of psychopath who preys on lone women for kicks. Evidently, none of the victims put up much of a struggle. Maybe that's why he picks on women instead of men."

"Did any of the victims know their assailant?"

"It's possible, I suppose. More likely, though, the perpetrator stalked each of the women and then took them by surprise when they least expected an attack. Each victim was almost instantly killed with a single, clean incision of the ascending aorta, and the succeeding slash wounds seem excessive and quite unnecessary. Tom, those girls were already dead when the killer began practicing his bastardized surgical technique on other parts of their bodies."

"You're saying a doctor did it?"

"Not a licensed physician. A first-year med student, perhaps. Or, possibly, an apprentice meat cutter. Maybe even a chef or a butcher. Someone who knows how to handle a knife and understands basic anatomy. Certainly not your average street thug, but not a skilled surgeon, either."

"A butcher? A *real* butcher? The kind who works in the meat department of a grocery store?"

"Could be. Or someone who's had experience as a meat packer. A man who isn't afraid of blood. A man who knows how to control his knife when slicing through flesh and bone. Maybe just a hunter who dresses deer during hunting season."

"Shit. It could be practically anyone then, couldn't it? I thought we might narrow this down because of those precision cuts you mentioned in each of your autopsy reports. I was sure the killer had to be a surgeon—or at least an M.D."

"Definitely not a surgeon, Tom. Definitely not a trained physician. Could be a veterinarian, maybe. Could even be a member of a satanic cult, I suppose. There's a hint of ritualistic pattern in the murderer's method, but there's pattern to any serial killer's method, isn't there? Doesn't necessarily mean the killer's part of a cult, does it?"

Wesley leaned back in his chair and lit a cigarette. "Want some coffee, Doc? I'll make a fresh pot."

"No thanks. I'm heading home now to get some sleep, and I certainly don't need another cup of coffee. You been to sleep yet?"

"Not yet. I waited up for your report."

"Figured you did. That's why I dropped it by on my way home."

"I appreciate it, Doc."

"But now that you've seen my report, Tom, go home and get some shut-eye yourself. You can't catch a killer when you're asleep on your feet, you know."

Can't catch a killer when I'm asleep in bed, either, Doc, Wesley wanted to say.

After the doctor left, Wesley went over the autopsy report again. Then he went over the previous reports and outlined similarities on a page in his notebook.

The first victim—Elizabeth May Singer, age twenty-two—was stabbed to death in a condominium parking garage two-and-a-half weeks ago. She'd been visiting a girlfriend in one of the apartments and left to go home around eleven-thirty at night. Her body was found near her car in a corner of the garage the next morning. No evidence of sexual molestation, though her clothes had been slashed to shreds. Purse, car keys, and jewelry were untouched by her assailant. Probable motive for Ms. Singer's murder: unknown.

JoAnn Green, a twenty-six-year-old secretary, turned up dead in a dumpster behind her apartment on the village's east side a week ago Tuesday. A bag lady, looking for aluminum cans in the garbage, found the woman's bloody body at five-forty-five Tuesday morning, but didn't report it to the police until three hours later. By then, another resident of the building discovered the body while taking out trash on his way to work. Time of death: between midnight Monday and dawn on Tuesday. Motive for murder: unknown.

Then Glenda Rose Williams, age nineteen, died from similar stab wounds sometime between Friday night and early Monday morning. Her body, however, wasn't discovered until just last night when Lenny Johnson decided to take a leak in the park bushes.

Two things stood out:

(1) Motive.

Most of the killings Wesley had investigated over the past ten years as Willow Woods' chief homicide detective had proved to be simple passion killings—usually a spouse killing an unfaithful husband or wife in a rage of righteous jealousy. One or two murders had also occurred during convenience store robberies, but those were few and far between. Though part of a large metropolitan area, the village had always seemed like a quiet suburban community untouched by the usual forms of big-city violence—until now.

Now there'd been three killings in less than three weeks in a town that normally averaged fewer than five killings in an entire year, and the motive seemed to be neither jealousy nor robbery.

What would motivate a man to kill a beautiful young woman, cut her body to shreds, and then simply discard the remains like a worn-out pair of shoes?

Had there been evidence of sexual assault, Wesley might have understood a rapist's warped reasoning for killing his victims to eliminate the only witness to his crime, but none of the women had been touched below the waist.

Obviously, rape wasn't the killer's motive. So what was? Revenge?

Was the killer getting back at all women for something a former girlfriend had once done to him?

Christ, I hope not, Wesley thought. *If that's the case, then no woman is safe in this town until the killer is caught.*

And that brought him to the other thing that stood out like a sore thumb and kept Wesley from going home and getting even an hour of much-needed sleep.

(2) Frequency.

The first killing had seemed an aberration—an anomaly—in the small town of Willow Woods. The killer could have been a visitor—a person merely passing through on his way somewhere else—who saw the victim as a random target of opportunity.

But the second killing indicated the murderer might be a resident either of the village of Willow Woods or one of dozens of adjacent bedroom communities— villages and towns that existed primarily to supply personnel for the hundreds of factories and warehouses being built up along the interstate beltline—instead of a transient from one of the crime-ridden skyscrapers or housing projects of the inner city. The third killing confirmed it in Wesley's mind. The killer lived right here in Willow Woods.

Who the hell is this maniac? And where will he strike next?

There'd been more than a full week between the Singer and the Green murders. But Glenda Rose Williams was stabbed to death only four or five days after JoAnn Green—and that, Wesley feared, meant another killing could happen any day now.

Or, most likely, any night.

And it was up to Tom Wesley to find the killer and stop him, before the nut could kill again.

Danny was asleep on the couch when his mother came home.

"Where have you been?" Aunt Suzi demanded as Mom stepped through the door. "I've been worried sick!"

"After dinner we went dancing, Suzi. I guess I lost track of time. I'm sorry. I should have phoned."

Danny became half-awake. Though he could hear the adult conversation, his mind wasn't completely functional. He fought to wake up the rest of the way, to push the cobwebs of sleep from his consciousness.

"Danny almost died," he heard Aunt Suzi tell Mom. "I mean, he did die..."

"What! Where is he?"

Danny heard his mother's footsteps running toward him, felt his mother's hand on his forehead testing for fever.

"He'll be alright, Sis. The policemen said he'll be fine."

"Policemen?"

"Danny had stopped breathing and I didn't know what else to do. I was scared, Sis. I called the police and two policemen knocked on the door before I even hung up the phone. It was like a miracle, Sis. They got Danny breathing again..."

"You're sure he's okay?" Danny felt his mother shaking him. "Danny! Wake up!"

Danny tried. His eyes blinked open, but the sandman must have weighted the lids with a ton of sand. He couldn't keep his eyes open no matter how hard he tried.

"Danny!"

"Poor kid's exhausted, Sis. He wanted to wait up for you, and I let him. But twenty minutes ago he curled up and fell asleep on the couch. Maybe you should carry him up to bed and tuck him in. I don't think he'll wake up again before morning."

"Tell me what happened," Mom said. It sounded like she was crying.

Danny drifted in and out of sleep as Aunt Suzi tried to explain. The next thing he knew, it was morning. He could see dust particles floating in streams of bright sunshine. He was in his room, in his own bed. Mom must have carried him up and tucked him in while he was asleep.

"Mom?"

"Good morning, sleepy-head," his mother said as she came into the room. "How do you feel?"

"Hungry," Danny said, rubbing sleep from his eyes.

"Want some corn flakes?"

"Can I have Cocoa Puffs?"

"Sure." Mom opened his dresser and took out underwear and socks. "Need help getting dressed?"

"I'm a big boy now," Danny said, slipping out of his pajamas. "I can do it myself."

Mom selected pants and shirt from the closet. "Don't forget to wash your hands and face, big boy," she reminded sternly. "I don't want to see dirt in your ears either. Think you can clean your ears all by yourself, too?"

"Uh huh."

When he went downstairs he was surprised to see Aunt Suzi sitting at the kitchen table.

"I'm cutting classes today," Aunt Suzi said. "I only have two classes on Friday, and I haven't cut either this semester."

Aunt Suzi was in grad'ate school. She read a lot, and Mom said Suzi was real smart. When Aunt Suzi grew up, she wanted to be an electrical engineer. Danny thought it was funny to have to go to school to learn how to run electric trains. He thought it even funnier that Aunt Suzi wasn't grown up yet. She looked grown up, didn't she?

"You're cutting classes today, too," Aunt Suzi said. "Your mom's calling the day school and telling them."

"Kindergarten too?"

"We're all staying here today, Danny. Just to make sure you're okay."

"I can't get through on the phone," Mom said from the living room. "The line's dead."

"It worked fine last night," Aunt Suzi said.

Danny thought about telling his mother about the broken cord, but decided not to say a word. He didn't want to be punished for destroying the telephone.

But breaking the phone jack had worked, hadn't it? Since no one could call to say she'd died, Mom was still alive. In a way, Danny reasoned, he'd been responsible for saving his mother's life.

He smiled with satisfaction. Then he filled his bowl with Cocoa Puffs and cold milk, and promptly forgot about the phone.

"You look terrible," Leonard Johnson said as he arrived at the office and saw the unshaven Wesley's bleary-eyed face.

"I've been up all night," the lieutenant said, lighting a cigarette. "I cleared your temporary transfer with the chief."

"Thanks."

"Don't think I'm doing you a favor, kid. I need help on this case, and you're the only one I could get transferred. You'll probably hate me before the night's halfway over, because I'm going to work your butt to the bone."

"I see," Johnson said, wrinkling his nose at the stale cigarette smell in the room. "We're the only two on the case?"

"Ellis and Peters from Violent Crimes are assigned to back us up. But we're the investigators on this one."

"Don't you have a homicide squad?"

Wesley laughed. "It's a small department, kid. You know the village can't afford more than one full-time homicide dick. I was lucky to get you on loan for two weeks."

"Two weeks?"

"That's all. We've got two weeks to crack this case or the chief will turn it over to County. Once the sheriff's department takes jurisdiction, you go back to patrolling a beat and I get to follow the county boys around with my thumb up my ass."

"Jesus!"

"Here," the lieutenant handed the rookie three file folders. "These are the autopsy reports on our victims. Read 'em and weep."

Johnson pulled up a chair and went over the reports. "Same modus operandi," he quickly concluded. "A psycho serial killer?"

"Looks like it."

"Have you checked with the mental hospitals? Maybe a patient escaped..."

"There's the phone," Wesley pointed. "I'm going to make another pot of coffee while you make the calls. Let me know if you get lucky."

Ellen rang the doorbell six times before Mrs. Galbraith answered.

Annie Galbraith, Ellen's nearest neighbor, was eighty years old and hard of hearing. Though she owned a hearing aid, she seldom used it.

"My phone's out of order," Ellen shouted. "Can I come in and call the telephone company?"

"Of course, dear," beamed the old woman, happy to have company. "Come in and I'll make us some tea."

Annie's home was immaculate. Ellen suspected the octogenarian of cleaning and dusting twice a day.

"I can't stay for tea today, Annie. I need to make several calls, if you don't mind. Then I've got to get right home. Danny might be sick and I don't want to be away longer than necessary."

"Oh? That's too bad. What's wrong with the boy?"

"Probably just a cold," she lied.

She called the phone company first. The repair service promised to schedule someone to check the line as soon as possible. "Do you have an inside wire maintenance plan?" asked the service representative. "Bell is not responsible for repairs inside your home unless you have an inside wire maintenance plan."

"I don't know," Ellen admitted.

The service representative explained that deregulation allowed customers to choose their own repair service for inside wiring. Residential customers could choose a Bell maintenance plan for a small monthly charge. But, if Ellen had neglected to purchase the plan prior to the need for repairs, the phone company would charge $17.00 for the first fifteen-minute period and $11.00 for each additional fifteen-minute period, plus cost of material, plus a $12.50 service charge. Depending on the problem, Ellen could be billed fifty to a hundred dollars for the repair of her phone. "Of course, if you have our maintenance plan," the representative said, "we'll repair the problem for no additional charge."

Ellen couldn't afford fifty to a hundred dollars tacked onto her next month's bill. But what could she do?

"We'll have a repair person look into the problem and notify you if the inside wiring needs work," the representative suggested. "Then we can quote you estimated repair costs and you can decide if you want Bell to do the work or if you want to try an independent contractor. Is there a working phone number where you can be reached?"

Ellen gave the woman the Galbraith number. "You can leave a message with Annie Galbraith. She lives right next door."

Ellen used Annie's phone to call the day school and Danny's

kindergarten teacher. She called Evans Surgical Supply and asked for a day of sick leave. Then she called Blake Blades to cancel her date with Michael Thompson.

"Mr. Thompson's out of the office," a secretary said. "Do you wish to leave a message?"

Ellen did. She said she wouldn't be able to keep their dinner date that evening. She promised to phone Michael on Monday. The secretary read the message back and asked if Ellen wanted to add anything. Ellen said she'd talk to Michael on Monday and give him the details then.

When Ellen hung up the phone, Mrs. Galbraith came from the kitchen with two cups of tea on a silver tray.

"What a nice surprise," the old lady said. "I'm so glad you came to visit with me."

Ellen didn't have the heart to refuse.

CHAPTER SEVEN

Michael was surprised to see a pretty blonde woman—instead of Ellen—behind the reception desk at Evans Supply.

"Where's the usual girl?" he asked.

"Ms. Lester's not here today," said the blonde. "Can I help you?"

Michael let his eyes wander to the woman's left hand. A gold wedding band and matching diamond decorated her ring finger.

"I don't think so," Michael said. "When will Ellen be back?"

"She should be in on Monday. Are you a friend of hers?"

"You might say that," Michael smiled. "Have a good day, Miss."

"TGIF," the blonde said, returning the smile. "Have a good weekend."

"I intend to," he said, exiting through the door to the parking lot.

Why wasn't Ellen at work? he wondered. Surely, he hadn't kept her out so late that she needed the day off work to recover.

Perhaps she stayed home to prepare tonight's dinner?

Yeah. The way he'd worked on her emotions last night had paid off. Ellen was home cleaning the house, planning the menu, making sure everything would be perfect during their little tête-à-tête tonight.

Ellen was malleable, and Michael considered himself a master manipulator. He'd mold the raw material of her psyche the way school children sculpted dolls out of papier mâché.

And then he'd play her like a puppet on a string.

Michael would use Ellen to reach Lane Evans. How? He wasn't sure yet of the details. But after tonight—after he played Ellen the way a first-chair violinist played his instrument at a symphony concert—Ellen would do anything he asked. And once he'd captured the Evans account, Michael would have enough clout with Blake to take on Wayne Gillespe.

And then, positioning himself as the president of Blake Blades, Michael could manipulate the old man and eventually take over the company.

He'd already acquired a sizable chunk of Blake stock. Investing his salary, commissions, and bonuses, Michael now controlled eighteen percent of Blake's common.

At twenty-four, Michael Thompson was the third largest shareholder in the Blake Blades Corporation. By the time he turned twenty-five, he expected to own the company.

Michael parked his Audi in the stall marked "Reserved for Vice President of Sales." Then he entered the sprawling Blake Blades manufacturing complex and rode the elevator up to his second-floor office.

"You have a few messages," his secretary said, handing him a half-dozen pink "While You Were Out" slips.

Michael took the messages into his private office and glanced through the stack. When he saw the one from Ellen Lester, his face flushed with anger.

"Sally, get your ass in here!" he shouted to his secretary.

Sally Foster came to the doorway holding a steno pad in her trembling hands. "Yes, Mr. Thompson?"

"You took this message from Ellen Lester, didn't you? What else did she say?"

"Why, nothing, Mr. Thompson."

"This is it? 'Cannot keep dinner date. Will phone on Monday.' Didn't she say anything else?"

"No, Mr. Thompson. I read the message back to her to make sure I heard her correctly."

"Get Ellen Lester on the phone. She's listed as E. Norman in the book."

"Right away, Mr. Thompson."

While Sally dialed Ellen's home, Michael paced nervously back and forth in front of his desk. Something was wrong, very wrong. He needed to know what.

"I get no answer at that number, Mr. Thompson," Sally said sheepishly. "Shall I try again later?"

"Yes, dammit. Keep calling."

This shouldn't be happening, Michael knew. He'd made all the right moves, hadn't he? *What the hell had gone wrong?*

As he paced, Michael went over the plan again in his mind. Step by step he rehashed the details, worrying over anything he might have missed. Everything was in place and on track. Everything, that is, except Ellen Lester.

He'd been so sure that Ellen was ripe; she'd responded perfectly to each machination, even inviting him to her home for dinner this evening. Obviously, she needed him as much as he needed her.

No, he concluded. It wasn't Ellen that was out of place. Something else must have intruded to ruin his plans. Frustrated and angry, Michael Thompson reached for the vase of flowers on his desk and flung it across the room. The crystal vase shattered to pieces and the floral arrangement scattered on the carpet like beheaded dandelions spewed helter-skelter from the rotating blades of a power lawn mower.

"Is everything all right, Mr. Thompson?" Sally asked, rushing into the room. "I heard a noise..."

"Everything's *fine*," Michael said, feeling suddenly back in control. "Clean up the mess, will you? Then," he smiled benignly the way kings smile when pardoning prisoners from the gallows or guillotine, "take the rest of the afternoon off and have a good weekend. I won't need you again until Monday."

"But what about Ellen Lester? I haven't been able to reach her."

"Don't worry about Ellen," Michael said. "I'll take care of her all by myself."

"Another dead end," Johnson said as he hung up the phone in disappointment.

"No escapees from nut wards? No recent releases of violent criminals from the state pen, either. I already checked." Wesley ran his fingers through his tangled hair. "Looks like we've got a psycho killer on our hands and no leads."

"Uh, Lieutenant," Johnson said, wrinkling his nose while searching for the right words. "Don't take this wrong. But you're beginning to stink."

"This whole damn thing stinks," Wesley said. "It—"

"No, that's not what I meant. I wasn't talking about the case.

I was talking about you—you, personally. You smell like a dirty ashtray filled with day-old cigarette butts."

"You saying I need a bath?"

"And a change of clothes. How long have you been wearing that same suit?"

"Two days."

"How long since it's been to the cleaners?"

Wesley sniffed his armpit. "I see your point, kid," he said.

"Let's take a break, Lieutenant. I'll drive you home so you can shower and change clothes. Then I want to run by the Norman house and check on Danny. I've called there three or four times and don't get an answer. Maybe the kid had a relapse."

"What could we do if he did?"

"I don't know," Johnson said. "But I feel responsible for him, somehow."

"Kind of like the Chinese feeling responsible for cheating death once they've saved a person's life? You gonna be responsible for everything the kid does from here on out?"

"Maybe."

Wesley sniffed his armpit again. "Okay, Lenny. Let's go and get it over with. I can't win an argument with B.O. and karma both conspiring against me, can I?"

"King me," Danny said.

Ellen feigned surprise that her son was winning the game. But she always let him win at checkers and Danny knew it.

But he liked to win anyway.

Today Danny felt like a king himself. Mom had stayed home from work and spent the whole day doing whatever Danny asked. She'd read him stories, let him watch cartoons on TV, and played all his favorite games.

She was trying to make up, he suspected, for leaving him alone last night.

Danny was beginning to understand the way guilt motivated adults to do things they wouldn't otherwise want to do. Like play checkers with a five-year-old. Like let the five-year-old stay home from kindergarten and day school.

Children under six have no conscience, and guilt was a

meaningless abstraction to the boy. But he was always alert for things that would get him what he wanted from the world around him, and Danny's primary world was his mother.

He hated the other world that existed outside this house, outside the warm and comforting embrace of the four walls he called home. Here he was king. Out there he was nobody. He couldn't understand his mother's insistence that he venture out into that other world where he felt at the mercy of people and things he didn't know. He hated sharing with other children, hated and feared those children because they called him "cry baby" and beat up on him and because they wouldn't share with him any more than he with them.

The unknown was a scary place.

Danny had enough scary places right here in his own house, but they were only scary when he was alone. When he had his mother around to protect him, Danny wasn't scared of anything.

Not even the dark. Or the monsters under his bed.

Danny knew his mother felt guilty if things happened when she wasn't around to protect him—like last night when he "died."

Death was another concept Danny's mind couldn't grasp completely. Death, he surmised, meant something like the way he felt when mother wasn't around: Alone, abandoned, and scared.

Death was when someone left and never came back.

Last night Danny had been scared his mother would die. He'd worried that she'd leave him and wouldn't ever come back.

The way his father had left him.

But his father wasn't dead, Mom said. Though, for all intents and purposes, his dad might as well be dead. Danny didn't like thinking of his father. Yet, Danny knew, the ghost of Robert Daniel Norman was something he could use to his advantage. Mom felt guilty every time Danny mentioned his father leaving; and when Mom felt guilty she went out of her way to make up for Danny being without a dad.

"I win!" Danny said, seeing a move where he could jump all of Ellen's remaining checkers with his king.

"You're just too smart for me," Ellen said. "You beat me every time we play."

"Let's play again," Danny urged.

Ellen smiled with resignation as she set up the board for another game.

Wesley felt almost human again.

Clean-shaven and wearing fresh clothes, he was aware how bad he must have looked and smelled before.

"Like death warmed over," Johnson had remarked.

"Better?" he'd asked after emerging from the shower.

"Much better," Lenny claimed.

There were lights on in the Norman house when they parked outside. "Someone's home," Wesley noted. "The place is lit up like a Christmas tree."

They rang the doorbell and waited. Johnson looked nervous.

Was Lenny worried about Danny's health? Wesley wondered. Or was he nervous about seeing Aunt Suzi again? When Suzi opened the door, Wesley knew the answer.

She was wearing a white blouse instead of the yellow sweater. Her hair was tied back in a ponytail with a rubber band holding it in place.

She reminded Wesley of a bright-eyed schoolgirl—a sixteen- or seventeen-year-old—opening the door for her date. Her eyes really did light up, Wesley mused. The moment she saw Lenny her whole face became one big, beautiful smile.

And Lenny, Wesley noted, was smiling back at her like a lovesick puppy with his tongue hanging out.

"We wanted to make sure Danny wasn't having aftereffects from last night," Wesley told the girl. "How's the kid doing?"

"Who is it, Suzi?" a woman's voice called from the next room.

"Come on in," Suzi said, holding the door open all the way. "You can see for yourself."

Danny was sitting on the living room couch with a handsome-looking woman, a checkerboard between them. From the looks of the board, the woman was a lousy checker player.

"Ellen, these are the police officers who saved Danny's life. Officer Johnson and Lieutenant... I'm sorry, I can't remember your name."

"Lieutenant Wesley," Tom offered.

"Gentlemen, this is my sister Ellen."

Ellen stood and extended her hand. "I don't know how to thank you enough for saving my son's life," she said. "Danny's all I have in the world."

Danny, sitting on the couch with a puzzled look on his face, stared up at Lenny as if he wanted to ask a question.

"You okay, sport?" Wesley asked, tussling Danny's hair. "You remember us, don't you?"

"What happened to his policeman's un'form?" Danny wondered.

"I'm a detective now," Lenny replied. "Detectives wear regular clothes so no one knows were cops."

Danny tried to digest this information, but obviously he found it too hard to swallow.

Wesley took out his badge and handed it to Danny. "We're still policemen," Wesley said. "But if we want to catch criminals, sometimes we have to hide our uniforms and work undercover. If the criminals knew we were watching them, they'd run away and we'd have to chase them. Wouldn't we? This way we can sneak up on them and maybe nab them in the act."

"You still have a gun?" the boy asked.

Wesley smiled. "Yes, Danny. Both of us carry guns. But we can't show them to you." He leaned down and whispered in the boy's ear. "We don't want the criminals to know we have guns, do we?"

"I'm not a crim'nal," Danny logically concluded. "You can show me your gun."

"But we don't know who might be watching, do we? What if a criminal drove by and glanced through the window?"

Danny glanced nervously at the bay window. A car, its headlights cutting through the twilight outside, drove past the house slowly.

"Is that a crim'nal?" Danny asked, pointing at the car.

"Could be, Danny," Wesley whispered.

"Aren't you gonna go catch him?" the boy wondered.

Wesley laughed. "Sure, sport. But first I've got time to play you a game of checkers. Think you can beat me?"

"Sure," Danny said, forgetting about the car.

"I haven't played checkers since I was a kid myself," said the detective. "Let's see if I remember how."

The red Audi drove around the block, drove slowly past the Norman house two additional times, and then sped off into the night—barely missing a black cat that happened to saunter across the residential street only moments before.

That cat, saving all nine of its lives for another day, never realized how lucky it was that the Audi driver's attention had been diverted.

Michael Thompson's mood after seeing another man in Ellen's living room was such that, had he then noticed the cat, he surely would have aimed his bright-red Audi straight for the defenseless animal's glowing eyes—and taken great pleasure in stomping the accelerator all the way to the floor.

Ellen was pleasantly surprised at the way Danny had instantly warmed to the detective. Danny didn't seem to mind when the man beat him two out of three games, though that quickly wore off. Now Danny didn't want to play checkers anymore, demanding the detective tell him a story instead.

"What kind of a story would you like to hear?" the Lieutenant asked.

"A story about how you catch crim'nals," the boy insisted.

Ellen wondered when the man would run out of patience. Danny could be quite demanding, she knew, and few men had the fortitude to put up with a five-year-old for very long.

But Wesley actually seemed to be enjoying Danny's company!

He has to be married, she told herself. *I bet he has two or three kids of his own at home and gets plenty of practice putting up with their antics.*

Does Danny look up to Tom Wesley as an authority figure because the man's a cop? she wondered. *Or does Danny look up to the man as a father figure?*

Both, she concluded. The man was certainly the right age for a father figure—about five or six years older than herself, she guessed. His hairline hadn't yet begun to recede, and the worry-lines in his clean-shaven face said more about his character than about his age, and the mixture of aftershave and tobacco odors he exuded smelled rugged and masculine, rather than perfumy and revolting.

Ellen felt strangely excited by the man's presence in her home. There *he* sat, not more than an arm's length away from where *she* sat, and it made her aware of her own sexuality.

And his.

Last night Michael had reawakened Ellen's long-dormant thoughts of complete womanhood, rekindling a flame inside Ellen that was warm and glowing and ready to be fanned into a raging fire.

And now Ellen could feel that fiery heat rising from between her legs, warming her whole body, making her hot. The palms of her hands felt suddenly sweaty.

She fought to control her fire, to dampen the fierce flames before they became all-consuming. The last time she'd felt those flames, she'd been badly burned.

Damn you, Bob Norman, she thought. *Damn you to hell!*

Ellen stood up and hurried to the kitchen. Tears filled her eyes and smothered the flames before they could do any real damage.

"Hi, Sis," Suzi greeted Ellen from the kitchen table where Suzi and Officer Johnson sat sipping colas. "Something wrong?"

"No," Ellen lied. "I think an eyelash is irritating my eyes. Maybe if I splash water on my face the lash will wash out."

Ellen went to the sink and ran cold water from the tap. Then she cupped her hands under the faucet and splashed icy water on her face.

"Did you know that Lenny takes classes in police science at the university?" Suzi asked. "Can you believe we go to the same school and haven't met before?"

"It's a big campus," Lenny said, smiling fondly at Ellen's sister. "But now that we know each other, we'll probably run into one another all the time."

"You really think so?" asked Suzi hopefully.

Ellen tore a paper towel from a roll above the sink. After drying her hands and face, she quickly straightened her hair. Then she joined the pair at the table.

"You can count on it," Lenny said, sliding closer to Suzi to make room for Ellen.

Ellen noticed that Suzi didn't seem to mind his closeness. In fact, Suzi seemed to be enjoying it.

And, for the first time in her life, Ellen felt jealous of her sister.

Laura Godwin was a junior History major. She'd made the Dean's list every semester for the past two years because she spent Friday nights at the library doing research, rather than partying with her roommates. But this Friday was a rare exception when Laura reluctantly bowed to peer pressure and joined the party. It proved to be a fatal mistake.

Laura, because she looked closer to twenty-one than twenty, had volunteered to make the first beer run. But the owner of the liquor store directly across the street from her dormitory asked to see an ID, and Laura had to walk almost a mile before she found a convenience store that didn't bother to card her.

Laura was on her way back to the apartment with a twenty-four pack of Budweiser when she decided to take a shortcut down a dark alley. The beer was heavy and she hoped to save half a block by using the alley instead of the street.

Though she read the daily newspapers and listened to nightly news broadcasts on television, Laura only paid attention to national and international events and skipped over local reports. Nothing important ever happened in Willow Woods, did it? Why waste valuable time?

But now she recalled that one of her roommates had recently mentioned something about a young woman's murder in a nearby park, and now Laura racked her brains to remember the gory details. Maybe walking down a dark alley wasn't such a good idea after all.

It was certainly spooky back here. The sounds of traffic from Third Avenue reached into the alley, but streetlights, headlights, and storefronts couldn't penetrate a solid wall of brick buildings on either side of the narrow passageway.

Suddenly, Laura felt claustrophobic. Fenced in. Trapped.

Fear filled her mind with all kinds of horrible possibilities.

Laura Godwin had lived a sheltered life. Her father was a lawyer—a prominent corporate attorney with strong political ties to the Statehouse—and Laura had grown up without knowing hunger, material want, or personal fear.

But now—feeling out of her element, dangerously alone and isolated—she knew Daddy wouldn't be able to help her if some weirdo suddenly popped up from behind a garbage-filled dumpster and tried to rape her. Or something worse.

Laura peered into the darkness ahead of her and couldn't see a thing.

Suddenly the case of Budweiser weighed a ton in her hands. If she planned to get out of this alley alive, she knew in her heart, she'd best abandon the beer and make a run for the street.

Thank God I'm wearing Reeboks, she thought.

But before Laura could set down the case of cans, reason intruded and told her she was being silly. If she returned to the dorm without the beer, her roommates would want to know why.

And when she told them the truth, she'd become the laughingstock of the whole campus.

You can lie, her mind said. *You can tell them you were carded every place you went. You don't need to say anything about leaving the beer in an alley because you were scared.*

Laura stopped walking and set the beer on the ground.

Was that a footstep behind you? she asked herself. *Did you hear it? Or was it just your imagination?*

Laura didn't dare turn around. She knew she should run, but her feet felt rooted to the spot—glued to the macadam with debilitating fear.

Her bladder felt fuller than full and she had an overwhelming urge to urinate.

And then, unable to believe this was really happening to her, she did turn around.

Something cold cut through the layer of skin beneath her left breast, passed through part of a lung, and penetrated her heart before she could muster a scream.

As Laura Godwin died, she irrationally worried about two things over which she had absolutely no control.

Her bladder was about to let go and she would soon soil her pretty lace panties.

Blood had already started to spurt from the hole in her chest and was splattering the brand-new, pristine-white Reebok running shoes Daddy had bought her for her birthday, and Laura Godwin was the kind of girl who didn't want to be found dead wearing dirty underwear, or dirty shoes, but this time she just couldn't help it.

CHAPTER EIGHT

Ellen had insisted they stay for dinner. "It's the least I can do for the men who saved my son's life," she'd said. "Please stay."

Unfortunately, she'd served spaghetti.

And, right now, the pasta wasn't sitting too good in Wesley's stomach—because the dried blood splattered on the dead girl's once-white shoes looked an awful lot like Ellen's homemade spaghetti sauce.

"You okay, Tom?" the coroner asked.

"Yeah. Fine."

The coroner shook his head. "Same MO. Caught the girl by surprise, stabbed her in the heart, and cut her up after she died. Opened her up like a can of sardines. Then the bastard dumped her body behind a row of garbage cans and left her to rot."

"Who found her?"

"A bum by the name of Pete Williams. Claims he sleeps it off back here every night. Tonight he came across a full case of Budweiser in the alley and killed two cans before he noticed blood on his fingers. Then he saw there was blood all over the place and called the police."

Wesley's stomach churned at the mention of blood. He was having a hard time keeping the bile in his throat from erupting in a gusher.

"Williams is over there in the police van," the coroner pointed. "Want to hear the story from the horse's mouth?"

Wesley swallowed. "Maybe I better," he said.

Pete Williams was in his early sixties. He had solid silver hair, but strands of red were scattered through a week-old growth of beard that stubbled his jaw. He looked scared.

"I didn't do it," he repeated again and again. "I didn't do it."

"Did you see who did?"

"I didn't see nothin'."

Wesley took two cigarettes from the pack in his shirt pocket and offered one to Williams. The bum's hands were shaking so badly that he dropped the cigarette twice before getting it to his mouth.

Wesley flipped the lid on his lighter, rolled the wheel against flint, and lit both cigarettes. Then he snapped the lid closed and dropped the lighter back in his pocket.

"Look, Williams," he said. "I know you didn't kill that girl. Your hands aren't steady enough. Whoever made those cuts had complete control of his faculties."

Williams dragged on his cigarette and thought about that. "I ain't always been a drunk," he said.

"Even if you used to be a brain surgeon," Wesley said softly, "you couldn't cut that way today. You can't even walk straight, can you? How the hell could you cut straight? No, my friend. You didn't kill that girl. But maybe you know who did."

"I already tol' you. I didn't see nothin'."

"Yeah. Well, it is pretty dark back here, isn't it?" Williams took another drag from the cigarette.

"I want you to tell me everything that happened from the moment you entered the alley. Think you can remember?"

"I tol' them other cops."

"Tell *me*. I'm in charge of this case."

Williams slowly thought about that. His muddled mind had difficulty keeping things straight. He needed a drink in the worst way.

"Gimme a beer," he said. "You gimme a beer, an' I'll tell ya all I know."

"I can't do that, Pete."

"You're the man in charge, ain't ya? You can do anything you want, can't ya? Get me one of them beers, an' I'll spill the beans. Otherwise I won't tell you diddlysquat."

Wesley realized his mistake. Instead of trying to befriend the old drunk, he should have intimidated the hell out of the bastard. Once Williams knew he wouldn't be charged with murder, he wasn't about to cooperate without a bribe.

Wesley shook his head. Lack of sleep had dulled his senses. He'd already made one mistake. He couldn't afford to make another.

"I'm going to read you your rights, Peter," he said. "Then one of the nice policemen will drive you to the station and book you on a drunk and disorderly charge. After you've sobered up, well talk again. Okay?"

"Hey! You can't do that to me!"

"Sure I can. I'm the man in charge, remember? I can do anything I want."

"Wait a minute. Can't we talk this over?"

"I'm listening."

Williams took a last puff of his cigarette and flipped the butt out the door.

"I was panhandling on Third Street," he began. "Nickels, dimes, quarters. When I finally got enough to buy a bottle, I came back to the alley and broke the seal."

"Keep going."

"I got this place, see. Over there under the loading dock behind Grogan's fish market. Smells pretty bad, but the smell keeps people away."

Wesley glanced at the wooden platform behind Grogan's Market.

"All the comforts of home," the cop said.

"Hey, it's a roof over my head when it rains. There's a crawl space under the platform that stays warm and dry, an' I don't gotta pay no rent, either."

"All the comforts of home, and none of the responsibilities."

"Exactly. I was headin' for my hidey hole when I stumbled over this box an' fell flat on my face. Didn't mind fallin' so much—I fall all the time—but I dropped my bottle an' I heard it break. A whole night's work down the drain!"

"Enough to make you cry, isn't it?"

"You bet. Made me madder'n hell. I got up and gave that ol' box a kick, an' that's when I heard the cans. I know what a full can sounds like. Figured I'd hit the jackpot when I tore into that case and found all the cans full."

"Then what'd you do?"

"I popped open a can an' drank it."

"Right there?"

"Yeah. Right in the middle of the alley. Drank the whole thing and opened another."

"Then what?"

"Then I carried the rest of the cans back to my hidey hole."

"And?"

"And that's when I saw I had blood on my hands."

Wesley lit two fresh cigarettes and gave one to Williams. "Go on," he said.

"I got scared. I thought it was my blood. Maybe I'd hurt myself in the fall. I checked my body all over and couldn't find where I was bleedin'. Then I saw the Budweiser case was soaked in blood, gooey an' sticky an'…"

"And that's when you called the police?"

"Naw. First I lit a match an' looked around. When I saw there was lots of blood on the ground, I knew I wasn't safe in the alley until someone checked things out. *That's* when I went over to the greasy spoon on the corner an' asked the waitress to call you guys."

"You didn't see the body?"

"Didn't need to. All that blood had to come from somewhere, right?"

Wesley exhaled a lungful of smoke. "Any idea who might have done it? Did you see anybody hanging around or notice anything unusual? Anything out of place?"

"Nope. I've been out on the streets all day. When I came home, the alley was dark as the dickens—the way it always is. Only thing different was the case of beer that tripped me up. An' the blood, of course."

Wesley left Williams in the van and went to find Johnson. The rookie, he discovered, was helping Forensics comb the alley for clues.

"Anything interesting turn up?" he asked.

"Nothing. We've gone through the dumpsters and garbage cans, but all we've found so far is lots of garbage. Looks like the killer followed the girl into the alley, cut her to pieces, stashed the body behind those empty fifty-five-gallon drums, and left."

"What'd you find out about the girl?"

"Laura Godwin, student at the university. Just turned twenty a week ago. Money and IDs still in the purse. Keys, too. Killer didn't touch the purse, so robbery wasn't a motive. Looks like the same M.O., doesn't it? Some nut case who gets off on killing young women."

Wesley sighed. "The guy might be crazy, but he's crazy like a fox. He's in and out before anybody sees him, doesn't leave prints, doesn't leave a single clue. Sometimes I think the bastard's deliberately thumbing his nose at us."

"What do you mean?"

"Four killings in three weeks. No serious attempts to hide the bodies. I think the bastard's thumbing his nose at the police and saying, 'na-na, catch me if you can.'"

"Oh, come on, Lieutenant. You can't take this personally. The killer's bound to slip up sooner or later."

Wesley ground his cigarette beneath the heel of his shoe. "Maybe you're right, kid. Maybe..."

Suddenly, bright lights hit Wesley's eyes and he couldn't see.

"We're talking with Lieutenant Thomas Wesley, Chief Homicide Investigator for the Willow Woods Police Department," a woman's voice said. "Lieutenant Wesley, do you have any idea who's responsible for these grisly murders?"

Wesley blinked. A microphone suddenly materialized in front of his face.

"Turn that damn thing off!" Wesley growled.

"We're live from the crime scene," the woman said as the lights shifted to focus on her face, "where another young woman was brutally butchered tonight by the Mad Slasher of Willow Woods. Once a sleepy little village on the edge of the city, Willow Woods has entered the spotlight because a madman—a serial killer—has already murdered four lone women. Tonight's victim is Laura Godwin, twenty, an honor student at the local university, and daughter of Arthur Godwin, senior partner in the prestigious law firm of Godwin, Goldwyn, Samuels, and Spielberg. Lieutenant Wesley, is anyone safe in Willow Woods?"

The lights hit Wesley's face again. He didn't know what to say.

Then the lights went out. The woman handed her microphone to one of the men holding minicams.

"I'm Sheila Meyers," she said, extending her hand to Wesley. "Sorry we didn't have more time, but we wanted to go live at the tail-end of the ten o'clock news and we only had two minutes."

Wesley glared at the woman. "Who gave you permission?" he growled.

"The first amendment," the woman said. "We cover the news. And Laura Godwin's murder is big news."

"You know the dead girl?"

The woman laughed. Sheila Meyers was a bottle blonde who reminded Wesley a little of Veronica Lake in an old Warner Brothers B-movie.

"I know the girl's daddy," Sheila Meyers said. "He's a rich and powerful man, Lieutenant. You've heard of Art Godwin, haven't you?"

"No."

"Don't you people out here in the sticks ever watch 'People Profiles' on the ten o'clock news?"

Wesley indignantly answered, "Some of us have to work at ten o'clock, Ms. Meyers."

"You really *don't* watch the news...?"

"No."

The woman pushed a loose strand of hair away from her eyes. "My God, man. Then you've got troubles you don't even know about yet."

"Troubles?"

"With a capital T. When Arthur Godwin finds out you let his little girl get killed in your hick town, he'll not only go after your badge, he'll want a piece of your hide—and he'll get it."

"I take it Godwin's a politician."

"Not a mere politician, Lieutenant. A *political force.* Arthur Godwin is the real power behind the state government. When he pulls the strings, the governor dances a jig and sings Godwin's tune. You better catch this killer quick, Lieutenant. Or you can consider yourself lucky if Arthur Godwin only busts you down to patrolman—directing traffic at Third and Main during rush hour in the rain—while Godwin goes after his daughter's killer by himself."

Michael Thompson watched the news at midnight, having recorded the program earlier on his DVR.

Now that he was back in control again, he felt on top of the world. Nothing would stand in his way. Nothing.

Especially not that dodo cop on the news. What a bozo!

That dumb cop just stood there—saying nothing and staring into the camera like he'd been caught with his pants down.

"Is anyone safe in Willow Woods anymore?" Michael chuckled. "Not with a cop like that on the job, that's for sure."

Michael laughed aloud. Then, just to make sure he didn't jinx himself, he rapped his knuckles three times on the wooden end table next to his couch.

Michael Thompson was the only one in Willow Woods who was absolutely sure he had nothing to fear.

Ellen was glad Susan had agreed to stay the weekend. After the policemen left and Danny was tucked into bed and ready for sleep, Ellen and Suzi stayed up and talked the night away, like two teenagers at a slumber party.

"What a gorgeous bod!" Suzi said with a gleam in her eye. "Did you catch Lenny's tight buns? I bet he jogs and works out with weights to have an ass like that. I wonder what he looks like with his clothes *off.*"

"You're terrible," Ellen chided.

"Come on, Big Sister. I saw the way you ogled his partner. You're just as terrible as me, aren't you?"

"No."

"You're lying, Sis. And you're blushing, too."

Ellen clapped her hands to her cheeks. "I am not!"

"Since when did you become Miss Goody Two Shoes?"

"Since... since Bob."

Ellen felt Suzi's scrutinizing stare. "You can't forget him, can you? Even after all this time, you can't forget him."

"I've tried."

"Big Sister, that man messed your mind up real good. You need to let go of your memories. Find someone who'll take your mind off Big Bad Bob."

"Like who?"

"How about Michael? You had a good time last night, didn't you?"

Ellen smiled. "Yes," she said. "I enjoyed the dinner. And the dancing. But Michael scares me. I can't explain why, Sis. Something about him reminds me..."

"Of Bob?"

Ellen grimaced. "I know I'm being foolish."

"Yes, you are. Michael isn't anything like your ex-husband."

Ellen knew Suzi was right. Bob was big—six-foot-four and two hundred-sixty-five pounds—a virtual giant compared to the diminutive Ellen. Michael was medium height, medium build—a much better match.

But, still, there was something about Michael that bothered her. He came on too strong, too fast.

Last night, with the music and the wine going to her head, Ellen had felt herself swept off her feet by Michael's aggressiveness, his self-assurance, his insistence, his *need*.

She'd discovered herself wanting to please *him* more than she wanted to please *herself,* and that scared her.

In the early days of her marriage, Ellen had wanted to please her husband by doing everything he demanded regardless of consequences.

It was irrational, she knew, to let herself be used the way Bob had used her. Now, distanced from the man by divorce and years of regret, she acknowledged the irrationality of her actions. And that was what scared her—if it happened once, it could happen again. She could find herself swept off her feet and made a slave by her emotions.

"When will you see him again?" Suzi asked.

"Michael?"

"Who else? You are going to see him again, aren't you?"

"I don't know," Ellen said.

"Well, I think you should. It'll do you good to get out of the house—away from Big Bad Bob and all the memories he left behind in this house."

"Maybe you're right."

"Of course I'm right. You should have seen yourself last night, Sis. You looked positively radiant. You haven't seemed that happy since..."

"Since I married Bob?"

"There you go again, thinking about that bastard. I was going to say 'since your senior prom.'"

"I went to the prom with Bob."

Suzi threw up her hands. "Let's change the subject," she said. "Okay?"

"Okay."

"What do you think of the way Danny took a liking to Lenny's partner? Danny's usually shy around strangers, but the two of them seemed to hit it right off."

"I still can't believe it."

"What I can't believe is Danny losing at checkers and not throwing a fit."

Ellen laughed. "He doesn't like to lose, does he?"

"He didn't mind tonight."

"No, he didn't. But he won the last game fair and square. I watched."

"The kid's learning."

"Having a man to learn from helps," Ellen said. "Danny's at that age when he needs a man around all the time, not just to learn checkers but to learn other things, too. Too bad he's married."

"Who?"

"Lenny's partner."

"Is he married?"

"He must be."

Suzi grinned. "I knew it," she smirked. "I knew you were hot after Tom Wesley's bod. You don't fool me, Big Sister!"

"His bod has nothing to do with it," Ellen said, pretending to be offended. "I'm only interested in his mind."

"If that's true," Suzi said, "then it doesn't make any difference, does it?"

"What?"

Suzi's grin widened. "If you're only interested in the man's mind," she taunted, "then it doesn't matter if he's married. Does it?"

Ellen didn't know if she dared answer.

CHAPTER NINE

"You had any sleep?"

"Not yet, Doc."

The coroner sadly shook his head. "You can't do those women any good, Tom," he said, pointing at the autopsy reports on Wesley's desk. "They're already dead."

"Four are dead. But the fifth victim, whoever she may be, is still alive. I can't sleep till I get the killer, Frank. I've got to find this nut and stop him before he kills again."

"You're not going to do it without sleep. Go home, Tom. Get some rest. Come back later and look at those reports with a fresh eye. Maybe you'll see something then that you can't see now."

"All I need is one solid lead I can follow up on—an eyewitness, a fingerprint, a semen sample, a blood type. Goddammit, Doc, I need something that'll point a finger at the killer!"

"Maybe this will help," Doctor Frank Monroe said, handing Wesley a photograph of a butcher knife. "That's one of Blake Blades Best, part of an expensive cutlery set. I measured the entry wounds on each of the victims and compared them to various cutting instruments for size and shape similarities. The killer used a Blake Blade on each of his victims."

"You sure?"

"As sure as I can be without having the actual murder weapon in my possession. Wound margins are well defined—the length, width, and depth easily measured—in stabbings like these. Although the depth of a stab wound doesn't necessarily reflect the total length of the blade, characteristics of the entrance wound perforating the chest wall will show that the lateral corner is blunted and the medial corner is acutely angled. By comparing wound tracks in all four victims, I'm able to get a good idea of the size and shape of the instrument. Fortunately for us, Blake Blades uses a patented size and shape that's distinctive. I can say, with some degree of certainty, that all four women were killed with a butcher knife from a Blake Blades cutlery set."

Wesley stared at the photo and smiled. "Thanks, Doc. It's a start, something to follow up on."

"I wish I had more, Tom. Blake sells thousands of those cutlery sets every day. Tracing the murder weapon won't be easy."

No, Wesley thought after the doctor left, *it won't be easy.*

Wesley leaned back in his chair and lit a cigarette. Early morning light was starting to stream through the windows and he thought he could hear the day shift banging lockers next door.

The corporate headquarters of the Blake Blades Company was located out on the beltline, wasn't it? Maybe it'd be worthwhile paying them a visit, finding out what stores in Willow Woods carried Blake cutlery sets. Then he and Johnson could go around to all the stores and... and what? Would it do any good to go around to the stores and ask sales clerks if they remembered someone suspicious buying Blake Blades Best knives?

Probably not, but at this point, Wesley was ready to grasp at straws.

Danny liked cartoons, especially Road Runner cartoons, and Saturday mornings were normally spent with both eyes glued to the television screen.

Danny loved the expressions on Wile E.'s face when the coyote realized he'd chased the Road Runner past the edge of the cliff and was about to fall. Then *Zoom! Splat!*

It never occurred to the five-year-old to question how someone could be falling hundreds of feet to their doom one minute, and be alive and well and again chasing the Road Runner the next. Part of the enjoyment of cartoons was the absence of reality—reality never intruded to spoil the fun.

Why couldn't life be like that?

Danny wanted to believe it was, but he had a growing suspicion that life was far more complicated than he could imagine.

Tiring of the insane antics of make-believe animals on TV,

Danny searched for his coloring book and crayons. Then he flipped through the book until he found a page that wasn't full of scribbles.

"What'll I draw?" he asked himself aloud.

Danny didn't like to simply fill in the outlined spaces with different colors. Coloring between the lines wasn't any fun. Instead, he drew a stick man. Then he drew a large silver star on the stick man's chest.

"That's Lieuten't Wesley," he said, sounding incredibly pleased with his work.

Danny had had tons of fun last night listening to the policeman's exciting tales of cops and robbers. He couldn't wait to tell the kids at school—especially that bully Johnny Radcliff—that he'd had a real policeman in his very own home, teaching him how to catch crim'nals.

For almost an hour, Danny fantasized about catching criminals and putting them in jail where they belonged. He became a "master detective" helping Wesley and Johnson chase crooks from one end of the living room to the other.

Finally, his attention span exhausted, Danny forgot about cops and robbers. He went into the kitchen and hounded his mother into a game of checkers.

"What're you doing here on a Saturday?"

Michael looked up from his desk. "Working," he said.

Wayne Gillespe slipped into the chair next to Michael's. "You after my job?" Gillespe asked half-seriously.

Michael laughed. "Sure I am, Wayne. Someday you'll want to retire, and I hope I can fill your shoes."

Gillespe seemed satisfied with that. He visibly relaxed in the chair and casually crossed his legs.

Body language, Michael thought. *My answer put him at ease.*

"Seriously, Mike. What *are* you doing in the office on a Saturday?"

Michael bristled. Did the bastard know how much he hated that name? Had Gillespe deliberately used the familiar just to get Michael's goat?

He's just trying to be friendly. Forget it. He didn't mean any harm. He didn't know. How could he know?

Michael handed Gillespe a stack of three-by-five cards, some with business cards stapled to them. "Telemarketing," he said. "I can reach executives directly on Saturdays. Nine out of ten bosses work on Saturday mornings, but their secretaries don't. With no one in their offices to screen calls, I can get right through and pitch the decision maker directly."

"Ingenious," Gillespe said.

Michael noted from the tone of voice that the man meant it. It wasn't just a meaningless compliment. Gillespe was truly impressed.

Careful now. Don't let it go to your head.

"I got the idea from you, Wayne. You work Saturdays, don't you?"

"Saturday mornings."

"Mister Blake works Saturdays, too. Doesn't he?"

"He's a regular workaholic. 'Top management has to put in extra hours—extra sweat—if a business wants to be successful,'" Gillespe said, voicing one of Bill Blake's favorite phrases.

"Exactly," Michael agreed.

Gillespe twisted nervously in the chair. "Well," he said, uncrossing his legs. "I'll let you get back to work then. I was just passing by and saw the door open. I must admit, I was surprised to find you sitting there."

"Glad you stopped by, Wayne." Michael stood and extended his hand. "It's always a pleasure to talk with YOU."

They shook hands and smiled. Gillespe's grip was weak, hesitant. He carefully avoided looking into Michael's clear-blue eyes, afraid of what might be reflected there, as if he truly believed eyes were the window to the soul.

"Be seeing you," he said half-heartedly, and quickly hurried from Michael's office.

After Gillespe left, Michael laughed. *Gotcha, Wayne,* the Master Manipulator chortled. *Gotcha good!*

Michael knew that Gillespe's Saturday morning office appearances were more show than substance. The man never did any work on the weekends, but he had to put in an appearance to please the nearly-puritanical work ethic of Bill Blake. Blake always noticed such things, keeping track of who was there and who wasn't. So, as the president of Blake's company, Wayne Gillespe was *expected—required!*—to occupy his office until mid-afternoon on Saturdays.

Michael, on the other hand, though he was now the Vice President of Sales, didn't have to answer to the old man for his whereabouts on the weekend, but only for increases or decreases to the bottom line.

Michael was glad he didn't have to worry about production—or distribution, financing, personnel, or any of the other mundane things Gillespe had to contend with daily—to keep the company profitable. Those were the kinds of things an MBA like Wayne Gillespe thought were important, but Michael knew differently.

The only thing that *really* mattered to a man like Bill Blake was the amount of bottom-line profits he put in his pocket. Michael understood—and Gillespe didn't —that intrinsic human worth was nothing more than a myth, a fairy tale made up to obscure the truth. One person's value to another person was predicated not upon his goodness—whether that meant good looks, good reputation, good education, or good behavior—but solely upon his ability to deliver what the other person wanted most. Michael had, unfortunately, learned this lesson the hard way, but it was something he'd never forget.

Unlike Wayne Gillespe, who'd been born to upper middle-class parents and raised with middle-class morality, Michael Thompson was the product of an inner-city, single-parent household. His father had been an uneducated machinist who committed suicide when a multinational conglomerate acquired the local factory and laid off half the workforce. After his unemployment benefits ran out, Ted Thompson had tried to find work as a day-laborer, but even minimum-wage temporary work was unavailable for a semi-illiterate man with no marketable skills. Bills piled up, the Thompsons were eventually evicted from their apartment and forced into welfare housing, and—when Lisa Thompson told her husband she was pregnant and there'd soon be another mouth to feed—Ted took a short clothesline out to the alley behind the housing project, climbed to the top of a nearby utility pole, tied one end of the clothesline to a metal spike protruding from the side of the pole and the other end into a tight knot around his neck, and jumped.

He had no insurance, of course. He left his wife and unborn son a legacy of debt, disillusionment, and despair.

Michael's mother had been a pretty woman once, but she had no way to maintain her looks after Michael was born. Her diet consisted mostly of carbohydrates, heavy in starches and full of calories. With an infant son to lug around, she found it easier to stay at home and didn't get out much and didn't try to exercise at all. By the time Michael Thompson entered kindergarten, Lisa was almost a hundred pounds overweight.

And Lisa hated herself for the way she looked.

Aid for Dependent Children and State Welfare Services paid the rent and put food on the table, so Lisa Thompson spent the days of her life watching television soap operas and bemoaning her fate. Luck had conspired against her, she reasoned. If only she hadn't married that no-good Ted Thompson, if only she hadn't gotten pregnant and been saddled with an infant son, Lisa might have been like one of those beautiful women she saw on the daily soap operas—married to a rich man who supplied all her material needs while she daringly flirted with handsome hunks behind her husband's back.

There was never enough money for anything more than the bare necessities (a large-screen color TV and monthly cable service were considered necessities), and Lisa impressed on Michael early in life the importance of money. If they had money, she claimed, they could get out of the dump in which they lived to go places and do things like other, normal, people. They could own nice clothes, a fancy automobile, and a big house, and they could eat steak and chocolate cake every day, if they wanted.

But luck, she said, had turned against them. "Your father's to blame," she told him often. "And you're just like your father!"

The more she said it, the more she came to believe that it was true. Ted Thompson had been responsible for all her bad luck, and Michael was, somehow, responsible for her luck turning from bad to worse.

"What good are you?" she liked to ask her son. "I feed you and clothe you, and what do you give me in return? *Bad luck!* That's what you give me. *Nothing but bad luck!*"

She made little Mikie feel like a jinx, a Jonah. She made him wish he'd never been born.

When he was six he tried to commit suicide by cutting his wrists with a table knife. The knife was so dull that he had to saw back and forth ten times before the blade penetrated the outer layer of skin. Finally, he gave up in disgust.

He couldn't do *anything* right. He was such a jinx that he couldn't even kill himself!

Even at school, kids called him "Jinx" and "Poison" and avoided him like the plague. Michael's mother had told her neighbors that she thought she'd been hexed by the boy and the boy's father. The rumor, of course, spread through the projects like wildfire.

Little Mikie Thompson became the local pariah, the butt of cruel jokes.

The other kids refused to let Mikie join in any of their games. No one wanted a jinx on their team, and he had to learn sandlot baseball by covetously observing his classmates from the sidelines.

Michael became a careful observer of the subtleties of human interplay.

Then, when he was eight, a profound thing happened to change his life. It was a beautiful spring evening, the sun was just setting in a fiery display of reds, yellows, and pale blues off to the west. Michael was sitting on the cracked back steps of the housing project's cement-block main building where he could watch the other kids from a "safe" distance. In order to jinx them, they'd somehow determined among themselves, Jonah Mikie needed to be closer than a car length. The effects of his terrible curse, they firmly believed, diminished with distance. Imagine his surprise, then, when a group of children—boys and girls close to his own age—cautiously approached the Jonah and invited him to join them in a game of tag.

Of course, he agreed immediately. At last! He was being accepted by his peers.

And then—when he asked "Who's It?"—the terrible truth hit him like a ton of bricks.

"Why, *you* are!" cried out a nine-year-old boy who was the leader of the pack. "You're already poison! You're already It!" The kids ran, scattering over the lawn and keeping their distance, taunting him with, "Catch me, if you can!"

Michael ran after them. Tears stung his eyes as he chased first one, then another, of the taunting, squealing shadows through the fading twilight.

Out of breath, unable to tag even one of his tormentors, Michael was about to give up. It was pitch black now, and no one could see. It was useless to continue the chase.

He sat down in the darkness and wept silently to himself. What a cruel joke! The kids had used him to make the thrill of the chase more exciting—adding real danger to the game by choosing a jinx for an It. If he got close enough to tag one of them, then that person would be jinxed in real life.

It was more than just a game they were playing; they were playing for keeps.

Michael heard a noise off to his left—footsteps on the dry grass. He didn't dare breathe.

Someone was coming toward him in the dark, unaware that he was close enough to reach out and...

"Gotcha!" he yelled as he grabbed for the small figure that had wandered into his clutches like a fly into a spider's deadly web.

The girl shrieked. Michael could smell her fear as her bowels let go.

"Gotcha!" he yelled again. "Gotcha good!"

The girl struggled to get away, but Michael wouldn't let her go. "You're It, now," he said. "You've got the jinx, not me."

"Noooooo," she wailed. "Take it back. I can't have it."

"Sure, you can," Michael insisted. "I gave it to you. It's all yours." He released his grip. "You gotta tag somebody else to get rid of it. Go on. Catch someone. You catch someone and you'll give him the jinx instead of keeping it."

The girl stopped sniffling.

"Go ahead," he said. "Pass it on to someone else." The girl stood still for a moment. Then she reached out and slapped Michael's arm.

"Got you back," she said, scampering away. "Mikie's It," she yelled. "Mikie's It, looks like shit, Jinx, Sphinx, Rinky Dinks."

"I'm immune," Mikie called after her. "You can't jinx me back, I'm immune."

"No, you're not," shouted someone else. "She used the magic words on you."

"What magic words?" Michael demanded.

"Jinx, Sphinx, Rinky Dinks," chorused several voices from the darkness.

"That's not fair," Michael complained.

"Nothing's fair in love and war," came the chorus, taunting from the darkness. "Mikie's It, looks like shit, Jinx, Sphinx, Rinky Dinks."

Mikie's rage was uncontrollable. He ran through the dark, jousting with windmills.

"I'll kill you!" he promised. "I'll kill you all!"

Fortunately for those children that night, Michael Thompson gave up the chase before he caught anyone.

Later, in his room, where he lay on his bed crying softly, he heard the nine-year-old ringleader call out "Allee allee alisin! Alls in free!"

The game was over, but, for Michael, the game never ended.

There had been an instant after he'd tagged the girl when he'd felt freed of his curse. For more than a minute, he'd managed to pass the jinx on to someone else.

Someone else had known desperation and despair for a change.

The girl had been scared half to death when Michael had leapt from the darkness to touch her. He remembered with fondness her shrieks, her trembling, her smell.

He'd gotten rid of it then, hadn't he? Even if it was only for a moment, he'd really passed it on and been rid of it.

And then, incredibly, she'd passed it right back. Michael knew now that he could rid himself of his jinx. It was possible to pass it on to somebody else. But only if he could keep that somebody from tagging him back. And next time, he'd know to use the magic words, too: Jinx, Sphinx, Rinky Dinks.

It wasn't until years later that he discovered the rest of what he needed to do to change his luck.

CHAPTER TEN

Michael turned fifteen, but the curse stayed with him. It wouldn't leave him again, not even for a moment.

It had followed him through elementary school and middle school, but by the time he reached high school, it finally began to weaken—but it wouldn't die.

It's only a silly superstition, Michael told himself again and again. *There's no such thing as a curse. Or a jinx.*

Sometimes he even believed that—almost.

His mother, a vile and bitter woman in her late thirties, never let him forget that he was to blame for the miserable life she endured. If it hadn't been for Michael, she might have remarried and lived a life of luxury, had other children, and been happy.

Instead, she claimed, she'd sacrificed *everything* for her son. And what did she get in return? Nothing but bad luck.

Michael was old enough now to see that his mother was simply a pathological liar—a pathetic person who found it convenient to cast blame on others in order to alleviate her own guilt, and find imaginary reasons that would absolve her of responsibility for her own choices.

Michael's mother had never worked a day in her life, nor did she intend to. She'd married Ted Thompson because Ted had promised to support her and provide her with a home and all those luxuries she'd seen advertised, in full color, on television. Ted had a good factory job at that time that paid better than union scale, and she saw him as the lesser of two evils: It was either marry Ted Thompson or get a job, and she certainly didn't want to get a job.

Her parents had supported her while she was growing up, but her father had insisted she get a job and move out of the house as soon as she had graduated from high school. She'd moved out all right, living with a succession of young men who provided bed and board in exchange for her company. But she refused to find a job.

Each of those men had, in turn, tired of her. Not one had ever mentioned marriage, though Lisa herself had mentioned it constantly. And then, when she was almost twenty-five and her latest lover was about to throw her over for a nineteen-year-old, Lisa began to look around desperately for someone to take care of her. That's when she met Ted Thompson in a bar.

Ted Thompson was a loner, a shy man in his late twenties who preferred the simplicities of fishing or hunting over the complexities of contemporary society. His factory job—tending a string of greasy, noisy machines—suited his personality quite well and satisfied what meager aspirations he had in this life. Ted was perfectly happy going to work every day in the hot, impersonal atmosphere of an industrial plant where he kept busy doing menial labor and nobody ever got on his back. He went to work, drew his paycheck, had a few drinks on Friday night at the local bar with some of his co-workers, and spent Saturdays and Sundays alone in the woods during hunting season or angling along a riverbank during trout season. What more could a man ask for from life?

Then he met Lisa Ellers, and she showed him all he'd been missing.

He felt flattered when she offered to leave her former boyfriend and move into the small apartment Ted rented near the factory. They lived together for two weeks before she suggested they might want to make the arrangement more permanent—or she'd think about leaving.

A month later they were married. It proved to be an amicable relationship for both of them until Ted lost his job, and the money began to run out.

Never once did Lisa offer to help with the expenses. Never once did she look for a job.

And, once, when Ted suggested such a thing, Lisa swore she'd surely leave him if he so much as brought up the idea again.

"If you can't support your wife," she argued, "then you aren't much of a man. Are you? I thought you were a real man when I married you. But I was wrong!"

When their creditors repossessed the color television, Lisa lit into him again.

"What good are you?" she'd start in on him and wouldn't relent for days. "You can't even keep the finance company from coming into your own home and taking away the furniture and TV. My TV, for chrissakes! What'll I do without a TV to watch? I never should have married you. I've given you the best years of my life and for what? *What*? For *nothing*!" She spat those words in his face like a cobra spitting venom. "Everything's been taken away from us and there's nothing left. Do you hear me? There's *nothing left*!"

A week later they were evicted from the empty apartment. Public Aid found them temporary housing in one of the projects. And then Lisa discovered she was three months pregnant.

"My life is ruined," she shouted at her husband every morning between bouts of morning-sickness while holding her head over the commode. "*Ruined*! And it's all your fault. *Your fault*!"

That's when Ted decided to climb the utility pole at the end of the alley, and end their relationship the only honorable way he knew how.

But it didn't end there for Lisa Ellers Thompson. Feeling betrayed, she blamed her husband for all her misery, all her troubles and woes. Frightened and bitter and too far along in her pregnancy to legally have an abortion, Michael's mother carried her baby to term with nothing but hatred in her heart.

Michael couldn't deny that his mother had indeed suffered. The way she told it, she'd lived through hell to give him birth and provide him with the bare necessities of life.

And now, she continued to remind him daily, he owed her a huge debt that he needed to repay.

So he didn't complain a bit when she farmed him out, first during summer vacation and after school, to do odd jobs for anyone in the neighborhood who would pay for his time. Anything, he reasoned, had to be better than sitting at home with his mother and watching game shows on television—especially when being bombarded by his mother's bitter remarks that cut through his heart as if she'd deliberately stabbed him with a sharp knife.

That's when Michael discovered that his neighbors, though knowing about the jinx, were willing to overlook their own superstitious natures—willing to chance being jinxed—if the price were right.

Cheap labor made such risks seem worthwhile. He mowed lawns, shoveled snow, reshingled roofs, cleaned out eaves, rooted drains, painted exteriors and interiors, trimmed hedges, swept floors, and washed cars. And all for slave wages that his mother spent on snacks she'd gobble down while watching television.

Word soon spread that the underage kid would literally work for peanuts. Though too young to be legally hired at minimum wage, local businessmen offered Michael's mother a dollar an hour—under the counter and without withholding taxes or social security—for the boy's help in their stores during inventory periods. Some even offered as much as a dollar and a quarter an hour, which was ten cents less than they usually paid illegal immigrants, most of whom didn't speak English and couldn't understand written instructions, in order to do the same job.

Roger Horton owned a half-dozen inner-city grocery stores where he charged food stamp customers inflated prices for dietary staples like bread, milk, and fresh meat. One of Horton's stores happened to be located less than a block away from the housing project where Michael and his mother lived, and Horton offered her a discount on food if Michael would work nights restocking the shelves. She agreed, and Michael went to work for Horton—from nine to midnight every weeknight and six to ten on Sundays.

It was an experience Michael would never forget.

Roger Horton himself had begun in the grocery business as a stocker and bagger at one of the major supermarket chains when he was just sixteen, working long hours for little money until he became assistant manager at nineteen. Horton, though a high school dropout, had an aptitude for figures that soon made him invaluable to upper management. Before he turned twenty, Horton was put in charge of the chain's regional inventory management system where he had access to information regarding profitability margins for each type of produce, each cut of meat, each case of canned goods.

When Horton discovered how much money the chain made, he asked for a raise. Instead of an increase in pay, upper management offered him a cash bonus, based on Horton's ability to increase the profit margin for certain commodities.

Horton did it by analyzing turnover rates, eliminating slow-moving items in favor of increasing the buy on high-turnover goods, and thereby doubling the wholesaler's discount. Gross profits increased twenty percent.

Horton got his bonus, though it was far less than he thought he deserved, so he quit the chain and started his own store with the money he'd earned and managed to save.

Horton's first store was a hole-in-the-wall corner grocery that made most of its profits from cigarette and lottery ticket sales. Though he stocked a full line of brand name canned goods, his prices weren't competitive with nearby supermarkets. He might have lost his shirt and gone out of business if it hadn't been for the fresh meats he sold from a deli freezer. Nearly everyone who came into the store to buy meat, he discovered, bought other things, also: potatoes, bread, tomatoes, mushrooms, even three-pound cans of coffee. His meat department was surely worth its weight in gold.

Horton hired Angelo Scorcisi, an out-of-work alcoholic who'd once been a master meat cutter, to select whole sides of beef which Horton could buy in quantity from a food locker. Then Angelo would cut steaks, ribs, roasts, and hamburger to sell in the store, attracting customers from far and wide.

As the store prospered and Horton grew rich, he was able to expand to other outlets. He opened five more stores in inner-city neighborhoods, filling a market niche that chain supermarkets considered too risky.

Horton kept his overhead low, his per item profit high, and organized each store's layout so shoplifting remained at a minimum.

Only once did an armed robber try a stickup. Horton pulled his own gun from the cash drawer and shot the thief twice in the chest. Word went around that Horton wasn't a man to mess with, and holdup artists avoided Horton's place like the plague.

Roger Horton had just turned thirty when fifteen-year-old Michael Thompson began working for him.

"You work hard, keep your nose clean, and someday you'll be just like me," Horton told the boy. "Fuck off and I'll fire you so fast your head'll swim."

Though Michael had grave doubts that hard work and a clean nose would transform him into a successful businessman, he was pleasantly surprised that Horton thought he might have a chance. Surely, Horton must know about the jinx. Or did he?

One night when Horton and Michael were alone in the store, the boy asked: "Mr. Horton, why'd you hire a jinx like me? Aren't you afraid I'll bring you bad luck?"

Horton laughed long and hard. "I don't believe in any of that superstitious nonsense, Mike. Luck is something we make for ourselves by looking for opportunities and taking advantage of every opportunity we find. I hired you because I needed someone to stock shelves and take inventory, but I couldn't afford to pay regular wages. Quite frankly, you're an opportunity to save a few bucks on payroll."

"Oh," Michael said, sounding disappointed.

"Looking at it another way, though, this is an opportunity for you, too. If you pay close attention to what I tell you, you'll learn the ins and outs of the grocery business even earlier than I did. Who knows? Maybe, if you apply what you learn and look for the right opportunities, you'll be a millionaire *before* you're thirty."

"Are *you* a millionaire?" Michael asked innocently.

Horton didn't laugh at the question. "Almost," he said. "I've got most of my money tied up in inventory and I'm still paying off high-interest loans, but I figure my net worth comes close to a million. Maybe more. I don't know for sure."

"Gee," Michael said. "I never met a millionaire before."

"Millionaires put their pants on the same way you and I do, Mike, one leg at a time. Everything I own I've had to work for, earning a penny here, saving a dollar there. It all adds up." He paused to survey the shelves, walked over to the cake mix section and aligned boxes.

"The chains check stock with computers because it's quicker and easier," he said. "But, because of computers, chain managers've lost touch with day-to-day buying patterns. They see product numbers on printouts and don't know what any of those numbers mean in real life. They've forgotten that the only numbers that matter are the bottom-line numbers on a profit and loss statement. Don't forget that, Mike. Don't forget what numbers really mean."

Michael didn't know what Horton was talking about.

Six months later, Horton showed Michael how to figure a profit and loss statement.

Each day he'd learned more and more about the business, wanting desperately to prove himself to this wise man who was the first person ever to treat Michael like a human being. Horton seemed delighted by Michael's progress and even gave the boy a daily bonus that Horton claimed was much better than a raise.

Michael was allowed to take home any of the canned goods that were damaged or dented, any of the milk or bread that hadn't sold by the expiration date, and any scraps of meat that Angelo Scorcisi had left over that wasn't ground up for hamburger filler or sausage stuffing.

Michael's mother considered such bonuses lucky windfalls. It was her due, she said, after all the bad luck she'd had to endure in the past.

Now she let Michael spend as much time as he wanted at Horton's, certain that the boy would bring home more and more goodies. If Michael cut school to work in Horton's back room, it was fine with her. She couldn't care less what the boy did with his days as long as he kept putting food on the table and money in her pocket.

One afternoon, when Michael was playing hooky from school, Horton introduced his protégé to Angelo Scorcisi.

"Show the boy," Horton told the old man. "Show him your craft. Teach him everything you know." And the old man did.

The phone in Michael Thompson's office broke the silence, shocking Michael from his reverie.

Michael looked at the dial on his watch. Eleven-fifteen. Who could be calling at this time on a Saturday? Only one way to find out.

"Michael Thompson," he said as he brought the phone to his face.

"Thank God, you're still there," said a nervous Wayne Gillespe, his voice high-pitched and shrill. "I don't know what to tell Bill. Maybe you can think of something."

"Whoa. Calm down. Take a deep breath and count to ten."

Michael heard Gillespe do as he was told.

"Okay, Wayne. Now start over again, slower this time. What happened?"

"It's the police," Gillespe said. "They want to see our records."

Michael smiled to himself. If Gillespe was this worried about showing the cops corporate records, then maybe the man had something to hide. Was Gillespe doing something illegal? Was Bill Blake?

Michael couldn't imagine Blake skimming from his own company. That left Wayne Gillespe, his hand caught in the till.

Michael was pleased at the panic in Gillespe's voice. He sensed an exploitable weakness—an *opportunity* to put the man at a disadvantage.

Michael pounced.

"Whatever it is, Wayne, you've got to tell Bill. It can't be that bad, can it?"

"Yes, it can." Wayne's voice was trembling.

Gotcha! Michael almost said aloud. Instead, he said, "Then tell me first, Wayne. Give me all the gruesome details. I'll break the news to Blake as diplomatically as possible."

"I knew I could count on you to help, Mike. We're all in this together, aren't we?"

Again, involuntarily, Michael winced at the familiar use of his given name. "Listen, Wayne, stop beating around the goddamn bush and tell me what the police are after. I can't help unless I know everything you need to hide."

"Hide? How can we hide anything from the police?"

Michael felt his patience wearing thin. "Damn it, Wayne. Tell me what the police are looking for, won't you? What records do they want to see?"

"Why, our sales records, of course. They want the names and addresses of all accounts within a fifty-mile radius of Willow Woods."

"What the hell for?"

Gillespe hesitated. Then his voice, panicky and filled with fear, said, "Those women the newspapers claimed were killed, Mike. They were killed—butchered—by a *Blake* knife from a set of Blake Blades Best Cutlery."

"Where are the police now?" Michael interrupted, feeling panicky himself. "Are they here? In your office?"

"On the phone, Mike. They want to come over this afternoon

and look through all our records…"

"So let them," Michael said, forcing himself to sound calm. "What's the big deal? They can't put us in jail for selling knives, can they?"

"I don't think so."

"When do they want to come?"

"Three o'clock."

"Tell them to see me and I'll have our sales records ready. If they think the killer bought one of our knives, I'll help the police pursue that idea in any way I can."

"But what'll I tell Bill?" Gillespe worried. "How can I tell him that one of his knives was responsible for killing… how many women?"

"I don't keep track," Michael said, his mind busy on how to throw the police off his trail. "It's unlucky to count past thirteen."

CHAPTER ELEVEN

When Johnson arrived at the police station shortly before three to start his afternoon shift, he discovered that Wesley had fallen asleep sitting in his chair behind the desk. The lieutenant, bent over in the chair with his head on the desktop and spittle drooling from his open mouth, looked almost as innocent and vulnerable as a newborn babe.

"Rise and shine, Lieutenant," Johnson said. "Wake up and smell the coffee."

Wesley stirred, knocking papers from the desk to the floor.

"You ought to try a bed sometime," Johnson quipped. "It's supposed to be better for your back."

"What time is it?" Wesley mumbled.

"Almost three."

Wesley snapped erect. "God! We have an appointment at three. Draw a car from the motor pool and I'll meet you in the parking lot."

Twenty minutes later, they parked in front of the main entrance at Blake Blades. Michael Thompson met them at the door, introduced himself as Vice President of Sales, and escorted the policemen up to his second-floor office.

"Quite a place you have here," Wesley said, looking around in envy. "My office is smaller than that storeroom over there."

"That's a coat closet," Thompson said, amused.

"A coat closet? Really? I'm glad we're using your office instead of mine then."

Thompson offered chairs to the detectives and took a seat himself behind a massive mahogany desk that was stacked high with file folders.

"What exactly are you looking for?" he asked. "Wayne Gillespe wasn't very specific, so I decided to pull out only the invoices for the past two years. We can start with these, if you like. If you need anything else, just ask."

"Do you mind if I smoke in here?" the lieutenant asked. "I don't see an ashtray."

"I'll get you one."

While Thompson was out of the room searching for an ashtray, Wesley pulled a file from the middle of a stack and thumbed rapidly through the folder's contents.

"What are we looking for?" Johnson asked his partner.

"Needles in a haystack," Wesley mumbled.

He returned the folder to its place in the pile as soon as he heard Thompson's footsteps approach the office.

"Thanks much," Wesley said when Thompson handed him the ashtray. "Smoking's a dirty habit, but I can't seem to quit. You don't smoke, do you?"

"Very seldom," Thompson said.

"You're the Vice President in charge of Sales?" asked the lieutenant, lighting a cigarette. "I expected someone older."

Thompson smiled. "If your partner is old enough to be a detective, then I guess I can be a corporate vice president. Can't I?"

"Sure. How old are you, by the way?"

"I'll be twenty-five next June," Thompson answered, seeming a bit irritated by the question. "Did you come here to learn my age, Lieutenant, or do you want to see what's in these files?"

"I'm sorry." Wesley stubbed his cigarette out in the ashtray. "I was just curious about you, Mr. Thompson. Getting to be a vice president of a big company before you're twenty-five isn't easy, is it?"

"No, it's not."

"Didn't think so. Johnson and I couldn't do it, that's for sure. You must have started with the company when you were very young and gradually worked your way up the ladder. Right?"

"Actually," Thompson said, "I'm relatively new with this company. I started a year or so ago as a field sales rep. When the previous V.P. of Sales retired, Bill Blake thought I was the best man for the job."

"Where'd you work before coming here?"

"I was a buyer for a supermarket chain. I traveled around a lot. Why?"

Wesley lit another cigarette. "If you're new to the area, then you probably don't know who handles Blake cutlery locally and who doesn't. Or do you? I thought maybe you could save us some valuable time. We don't have time to wade through all those invoices. That'll take us forever."

"No, it won't," said Thompson, looking relieved to get down to business. "Everything's filed by zip code. Here," he handed a folder to Wesley, "is the transaction file for Willow Woods. Here's Garden Springs. Here's Trillium Trail."

Wesley and Johnson split up the folders and jotted down names and addresses of stores as rapidly as possible. No sooner did they finish with one folder, then Thompson gave them another.

Checking all the outlets in a fifty-mile radius looked like an impossible task. Every department store, discount store, bridal boutique, and hardware store in the area stocked Blake cutlery.

"I noticed," Wesley said, lighting a fresh cigarette from one he'd smoked down to the filter, "that you're listed as the salesman on most of these invoices. Does that mean you service the accounts personally?"

"Of course he does," said an unexpected voice from the doorway. "Michael's the best salesman I have."

Thompson quickly got up from behind his desk and introduced Bill Blake and Wayne Gillespe to the detectives.

"Wayne's worried about bad publicity," Blake said, taking Thompson's chair. "Tell me, Lieutenant, is it true those women were killed with one of my knives?"

"It appears like it," Wesley said.

"And you think you'll uncover the killer's identity by checking out each and every one of the tens of thousands of people who've bought Blake Blades in the past year? It won't work, Lieutenant."

"Why not?" Wesley asked.

"Because," Bill Blake said, "Blake Blades are bought as wedding gifts, anniversary gifts, birthday gifts, Christmas gifts. Nine out of ten people who own our cutlery sets don't purchase our knives themselves. They receive Blake cutlery as gifts. Do you understand what I'm saying, Lieutenant?"

Wesley looked defeated. "I'm not sure," he answered. "Would you be kind enough to elaborate?"

"The chances are, Lieutenant, that this killer—if he indeed uses one of our knives—received that knife as a gift from someone else, someone who quite likely lives halfway across the country. Going around to stores in the vicinity of Willow Woods and asking merchants if anyone suspicious bought Blake Blades Best will prove futile. Have I made myself clear?"

"You're saying that the killer didn't buy the knife he uses on his victims? He got it as a gift?"

"Precisely," said the Chairman of the Board of Blake Blades, Incorporated. "I'll stake my reputation on it." He puffed up his chest proudly, looking at Wesley eye to eye. "None of the fine people who buy Blake Blades would use a Blake knife to kill another human being. Such an act, Lieutenant, would be considered a sacrilege."

Michael had to admire the old man's bullshit ability. Blake sounded as if he actually *believed* what he was saying.

Who knows? Maybe he *did*.

Too bad he had to show up and spoil the elaborate smokescreen Michael planned to use to mislead the police. Thompson was sure he could have kept the cops busy for months—made them run around in circles like cats chasing their tails—locating all the people who'd purchased Blake cutlery in this area of the country.

It would have been fun to send the police off on a wild goose chase, while Michael continued to play tag without fear of interference, wouldn't it?

Why couldn't Gillespe keep his mouth shut?

This morning on the telephone Gillespe had agreed to let Michael handle the whole matter—dealing with the police first, then telling Blake the details as diplomatically as possible. But Wayne must have panicked over the thought of adverse publicity. As president of Blake Blades, Gillespe knew Blake held him responsible for maintaining the company's impeccable image. If that image were ever tarnished, Gillespe would be out of a job.

Blake had hired Wayne Gillespe to be a figurehead president, a do-nothing sycophant with the right family and social connections to enhance the company's prestige. Gillespe's credentials were impressive, and Bill Blake used Gillespe's image to make up for Blake's own lack of education and social grace. Michael and Blake were a lot alike, maybe even too much alike, while Wayne Gillespe was odd man out.

Blake had built this company up from a small fabricator of precision surgical instruments—such as scissors and scalpels for the medical professions—into a corporate giant that also controlled a considerable corner of the consumer market, by using other people's money, other people's talent and brains, other people's blood, sweat, and tears, then throwing those other people to the wolves.

Michael could certainly appreciate that. It was the way the world worked, and he'd long ago accepted the fact. But Wayne Gillespe was naive. He didn't realize when he was being used, that he, too, was expendable. Until today.

Today Gillespe must have thought about it and realized that he was vulnerable to the vagaries of the marketplace—realized that his only value to the company consisted in enhancing the company's reputation in the eyes of the consumer.

And if the company's reputation was tarnished by adverse publicity, then Blake had no reason to keep Gillespe on as a figurehead, but every reason in the world to make him into a scapegoat.

If Blake Blades' status-conscious customers thought of the high-priced cutlery sets as instruments of death favored by serial killers, they'd boycott the product and buy other brands. Then Wayne Gillespe would be as useless to Bill Blake as a diaphragm to a pregnant woman.

So Gillespe had gone to Blake and told him about the police and their suspicions. What else had Gillespe told Bill Blake?

Gillespe had that smug, righteous look on his face that Michael hated with a passion. Wayne thought he was better than everybody else because he'd been lucky—lucky enough to be born into a wealthy family that loved him and pampered him and gave him everything he ever wanted, and expected nothing in return.

Whatever else Blake and Gillespe had discussed in Blake's office before coming down here, it had restored Gillespe's confidence in his invulnerability. Gone now were the fear and panic Wayne had displayed this morning on the telephone.

Wayne Gillespe seemed assured that he would keep his job. Did that mean that Gillespe had set Michael up to be the scapegoat?

Michael glanced furtively at Bill Blake. Blake and the police lieutenant were discussing ways to track and trap the killer without alerting the public. Michael listened while Blake suggested a solution that seemed to satisfy the detective. It sounded like a good idea. But was it?

"I'll advertise in the local newspapers that we will sharpen, free of charge, any Blake Blades Best knife that's owned by an area resident. They need only bring the knife here to the factory, we'll sharpen or replace the blade in less than an hour, and the customer's cutlery set will look good as new again. While they're here, however, we'll ask them to complete a marketing survey that'll tell us how they acquired their Blake Blades, how often they use their set, how satisfied they are with our product—you know, the usual information. We'll ask for their names and addresses, of course. If you like, you can be the person who hands them the survey."

"How long before you run the ads?" the lieutenant wanted to know.

"I'll get our marketing department started on it first thing Monday morning. The ads will start in Tuesday's newspaper and we'll run them for a week. Maybe we'll even squeeze some money from the budget for radio and TV air time."

"It's worth a try," Wesley agreed.

Blake smiled and offered the lieutenant his hand. "I'm glad we could find a way to help the police, after all," Blake said. "Keep me posted, will you? Let me know if you learn anything else about the killer and his methods."

"I'll do that," said the lieutenant, shaking hands. "Thanks for your help."

Michael escorted the detectives back to their car. "Thanks for your help too, Mr. Thompson," Wesley said at the door.

"Don't mention it," said Michael, hoping the cops wouldn't notice how much his palms were sweating as he shook hands with each of them and wished them luck.

"Whadya think?" Wesley asked his partner.

"Another dead end," Johnson said, starting the car. "We'll never muster enough manpower to check out all the stores. And I seriously doubt if the killer'll bring in the murder weapon to have it sharpened, even for free. He'd have to be stupid to do that, and I don't think he's stupid."

"Crazy, but not stupid," Wesley mumbled. "Yeah."

They rode in silence up the entrance ramp to the expressway. Johnson edged the car into traffic and merged with the flow of Saturday-afternoon shoppers hurrying home to have supper and watch television.

"He's hiding something," Wesley said at last.

"Who?"

"Thompson."

"What?"

"I dunno."

"Why do you think he's hiding something?"

Wesley rolled down the window and reached for a cigarette. "Thompson's name was on almost all the invoices. He's been around to each of those stores and talked with the owners. He could have given us inside information, if he'd wanted to, but he didn't want to."

"That's it? You think he's hiding something because he didn't offer inside information on his clients? Don't you know that salesmen protect client information from cops the way lawyers do? They volunteer nothing, and you've got to drag it out of them."

"Then why'd Thompson offer to show us the files in the first place?"

"Maybe he was afraid we'd get a search warrant and see the files anyway," Johnson ventured.

"Uh uh. He wanted us to think he was being helpful. Why?"

"Most folks want cops to think they're being helpful. Keeps us from suspecting them, they think."

"Right."

"It doesn't work, though."

"Nope."

"The reason it doesn't work," Johnson added, "is because we naturally suspect everybody anyway."

"Right."

"People sense that, you know, and it makes them nervous. Sometimes they act like they have something to hide even when they don't."

"Uh huh."

"You hungry, Lieutenant? How about stopping for a sandwich and a cup of coffee?"

Wesley took a last puff from his cigarette and threw the butt out the window. "I could use the coffee," he said. "But only on one condition."

"What's that?" Johnson asked.

"You radio in first and let the dispatcher know we'll be on break."

"Roger that," Johnson said, and picked up the microphone from under the dash.

Michael thought Blake's suggestion to the lieutenant was brilliant one-upmanship. Not only was it a superb community relations gimmick that would please local customers and placate the authorities at the same time, but Blake saw it as an opportunity to minimize normal personnel expenses by utilizing police officers to conduct the routine marketing surveys he'd already scheduled for next week. The marketing department had designed, placed, and paid for area newspaper advertisements more than a month ago. The first insertion—offering free sharpening for Blake Blades Best Cutlery customers—was set to run on Tuesday.

Blake had pulled the proverbial wool over the lieutenant's eyes. Michael had to hand it to the old man. When it came to manipulation, Bill Blake was more than a master—he was a Grand Master!

That worried Michael a little. Playing games with fools like Wayne Gillespe or cops like Lieutenant Wesley posed no threat to Michael. He knew he could out-manipulate *them* in a minute. But Bill Blake was different.

Blake had reminded Michael of Roger Horton the minute Michael met the man. Though they were worlds apart in their outward appearance, Blake and Horton were exactly alike in their hearts. They were *liars.*

Not only did they constantly lie to others, but they lied to themselves all the time, too—the way Michael's mother lied to everyone, herself included.

From the very first, Michael had seen obvious similarities between Blake and Horton. But never before had he perceived that they were no different than his very own mother—cruel, heartless, selfish, avaricious *liars*.

Michael felt himself growing agitated at the revelation. Was it because Blake reminded Michael of Horton that he'd set out to take over the company and ruin its founder, or was it because Blake reminded Michael of Mother?

It's the jinx that's making you think this way. The jinx is coming back. It doesn't stay gone long anymore, does it? It keeps coming back quicker and quicker. Better get rid of it again.

Michael's agitation was rapidly reaching crescendo. He could hear his heart pounding in his head.

Do it.

Do it.

Do it.

DO IT!

DUH-DO IT! DUH-DO IT! DUH-DUH-DO IT!

Instead of returning to his office, Michael walked to a display case in the lobby and selected an eleven-inch butcher knife from a set of Blake Blades Best Cutlery.

He didn't have long to wait. Fifteen minutes later, Wayne Gillespe exited the elevator and headed across the lobby toward the front door.

Michael followed him from the building and into the parking lot.

Gotcha! Michael thought as he stalked Gillespe to the secluded garage where the company president had the privilege of parking his car.

Gotcha good!

CHAPTER TWELVE

"Suppose I could take tomorrow off?" Johnson asked Wesley between sips of his coffee. "I've worked ten days straight without a break, and I need some time for rest and relaxation."

Wesley choked on his coffee. Johnson thought for a moment the lieutenant was about to spit up and spray coffee all over the table.

"Did I hear you right?" the lieutenant asked after swallowing again. "Tell me you didn't say what I thought you said."

"You heard me right. I'm asking for a day off. Tomorrow's Sunday. There's a movie I'd like to see at one of the mall theaters."

"Cop picture?"

"No. A comedy."

Wesley lit a cigarette, though this part of the restaurant was clearly marked as a non-smoking section.

"I can't let you do it, kid. I need your help tomorrow. We're in the middle of a homicide investigation, for chrissakes."

"Look, Lieutenant. Department regulations are specific: Willow Woods officers cannot work ten consecutive days without one day off for R and R. The department headshrinker claims we'll go bananas if we stay under pressure more than ten days in a row. Why don't you take the day off too, and we can double date to the movies?"

"Oh, I see. You've got a date to go to the movies?"

"Not yet. But I thought maybe I'd ask Susan Lester." Lenny grinned. "You could ask her sister."

Wesley flicked the ashes from his cigarette onto the floor. "Later, Lenny. After we catch the killer. Okay?"

"She likes you, Lieutenant. Susan's sister likes you."

"She's a divorced woman with a kid. I don't have time to get involved. Especially not with a woman who's got another man's kid."

"Oh, c'mon. You and Danny had a great time last night."

"Okay, so I get along better with kids than adults."

"Then ask the kid to the movies, why don't you?"

"Can't do that."

"Why not?"

"Because I've got work to do. And so do you, Romeo. Susan Lester will have to wait until we catch this killer and put him away in a nut house."

"I don't get tomorrow off?"

"Neither of us gets a day off until this case is under wraps."

Lenny slowly shook his head. "You need a day off worse than I do," he said. "You're pushing too hard, Lieutenant. Slow down, or you'll wind up in the nuthouse before the killer does."

Wesley ground his cigarette butt into the floor with the heel of a shoe and lit up another. "What's that supposed to mean?" he asked.

"You smoke too much, for one thing. You don't get enough sleep, and you don't eat right, either."

"So?"

"So, according to a psychology course I took at the university, that makes you a prime candidate for either a heart attack or a mental breakdown. Maybe both."

"Know what I think? I think you're trying to use some of that college psychology on me so I'll give you tomorrow off," Wesley smirked. He took a puff on his cigarette and blew smoke at Johnson's face. "You get too big for your britches, sonny, and I'll send you back to patrolling a beat."

"Go ahead. At least then I'll be able to take a day off once in a while."

The waitress brought Johnson's sandwich and refilled both coffee cups. She gave Wesley's cigarette a dirty look, but didn't say anything. The restaurant was half-empty, and she wouldn't risk losing a tip unless someone complained about the smoke.

Johnson wasn't worried about a tip. "You ought to give those up," he said. "You'll live longer."

"If I wanted someone to tell me how to live my life, I'd get married again," Wesley said. "Shut up and eat your cheeseburger."

"Then maybe you ought to get married, Lieutenant. It might improve your disposition."

"Sure."

"'Course, no woman in her right mind would even go out with you—much less marry you." Johnson speared a French fry with his fork. "Ellen Lester'd have to be crazy to go with you to the movies."

"Lay off, Lenny."

"C'mon, Lieutenant. It doesn't have to be tomorrow. I'll work tomorrow. The next day, too. But you need to take a break, have some fun, *live* a little. Don't tell me you like being a workaholic?"

"No. But I don't like seeing innocent women cut to pieces, either. I feel *responsible* for those women, Lenny. I should have been able to prevent their murders, but I had no way to do that. All I can do now is try to catch the killer before he kills again—before more innocent victims turn up dead—or I'll never be able to live with myself. If I drive myself too hard and kill myself in the process, then so be it. But I'm going to get that bastard before I die, Lenny. I'm going to get him and put him away."

Johnson shoved his half-eaten cheeseburger aside. "You can kill *yourself*, if you want. Just don't take *me* with you."

"Fair enough," Wesley said, dropping his cigarette into his coffee cup, where it sizzled and sent up a puff of smoke before going out. Wesley pulled a five-dollar bill from his pocket and shoved it under the saucer.

"You want tomorrow off to go to the movies? You got tomorrow off. Go to the movies and have a great time. Eat some popcorn for me, while you're at it. But, come Monday, you're back in uniform, buster."

He kicked his chair out of the way and headed for the door.

"Goddamn kids," he muttered barely loud enough for Johnson to hear. "Doesn't anyone take responsibility seriously anymore?"

Wayne Gillespe inserted a key in the automatic garage door opener and waited impatiently for the lift mechanism to complete its noisy task. Normally, one of the employees did this for him—delivered his car to the front door, part of the presidential perks that went with the prestige image Blake so carefully cultivated for Gillespe. But on Saturdays, when none of the hourly employees were around,

Gillespe was forced to fend for himself.

This section of the garage had four bays to house company-owned cars. Another section, much larger, was where the half-dozen leased delivery vans that the company used for area deliveries were parked on weekends. Blake Blades also leased several trucks and semi-trailers, but they were parked down at the loading docks in back of the warehouse.

As the overhead door ground to a screeching halt, Gillespe entered the large bay and searched the wall for a light switch. It was darker than hell in the garage. Where the fuck was that damn switch?

Gillespe felt uncomfortable in the dark. Even as a child he'd slept with a nightlight burning in his room, and he'd never been forced to come to terms with anything he couldn't see.

Wayne Gillespe had a very vivid imagination, and now his imagination had a chance to work overtime. In the dark, he imagined he heard someone behind him, sneaking up behind his back.

Where's that damn light switch? It's got to be around here somewhere!

Gillespe's fingers probed the wall the way a blind man probes a sidewalk with his cane. Wayne's nerves were all on edge and his armpits were sticky with sweat.

He'd been nervous ever since eleven o'clock this morning when that police lieutenant had telephoned and asked to look at company sales records. When Wayne learned that the "Mad Slasher" used a Blake Blades Best knife to carve up women victims, he'd felt sick to his stomach, for he felt his neatly-ordered world collapsing on top of him.

Murder was something foreign to Wayne Gillespe, a rare disease like cholera or AIDS that might touch ordinary people but never came anywhere close to touching humanity's elite. Wayne and his family had spent generations carefully distancing themselves from the contaminating infections that afflicted the lower classes. Money and an almost incestual elitism kept his kind conveniently isolated from the everyday concerns of humanity.

Wayne Gillespe had other things that he worried about, more important things—like being late for the dinner party his wife was giving tonight for members of the museum's Board of Trustees. Wayne and his wife had been nominated to the board for their

generous contributions to the museum's acquisitions fund, and
tonight's dinner would virtually assure them seats as trustees.
Social dinners cemented friendships and established alliances,
and the Gillespes were honored that no one had ever refused an
invitation to one of their parties.

Wayne's world was far different from the mundane world of
Lieutenant Wesley, or Michael Thompson, or even Bill Blake. Yet,
Wayne was aware how fragile his own world could be. He couldn't
afford to have his spotless reputation tarnished by even a hint of
corruption, and murder was the most vile corruption of all. His
friends, he knew, would never understand. Wayne would be guilty
by association. He could hear the gossip already:

"The Mad Slasher uses Blake Blades to cut up his victims."

"Isn't Wayne Gillespe president of the Blake Blades Corporation?"

"Yes, he is."

"Shouldn't we avoid Wayne until the Slasher is caught? In case
the Slasher is someone Wayne knows, I mean."

"It might be a good idea. We don't want to take chances. We
wouldn't want the Slasher to come after us, would we?"

"Maybe we shouldn't buy Blake Blades Cutlery either."

"Of course not. Having it around the house would only remind
us of our own vulnerability."

"We could be next to be murdered."

These voices were what had worried Wayne most of the day.
They were what had made him go to Bill Blake and tell the old man
that Michael Thompson promised to take care of everything, that
Wayne had the utmost confidence in Michael, and, if something
went wrong, Michael was entirely to blame—Michael, not Wayne.

Wayne wanted to wash his hands of the whole affair, but Blake
didn't see it that way. Blake saw, instead of the police investigation
having a negative impact on his product line, a way of turning
the ensuing publicity into a positive advantage. Blake Blades
Corporation would assist the police in hunting down this killer—a
man who was surely insane, but who nevertheless appreciated
quality.

It proved, once again, that Blake Blades Best Cutlery was
recognized as the best blade on the market, even by certifiable
lunatics. Handled correctly, Blake claimed, all publicity could be

reframed and prove valuable, even bad publicity.

Wayne didn't argue with the old man. Relieved that Blake himself was taking charge, Gillespe accompanied the old man to Thompson's office and confronted the police.

He'd worried needlessly. Now, however, he was scared.

There really is someone behind me in the dark. Isn't there?

His hand, still fumbling for the light switch, found what his fingers were searching for. With a flick of the wrist, he flipped the switch, and blinked his eyes as bright overhead fluorescents flooded the bay.

Turn around quickly. See who's there.

Wayne spun on his heels and saw neither hide nor hair of whoever had been behind him.

Nerves, he thought. *It's just my nerves making me imagine things.*

He opened the Lincoln Continental's door and got behind the steering wheel. A twist of the key, and the car's engine roared to life.

Everything's all right, now. All my worries are over.

Wayne snapped the transmission lever into drive, eased off the brake, stepped on the accelerator, and cruised out of the garage.

"Nothing to worry about," he told himself as he parked just the other side of the garage door. "I'm home free."

He left the car to idle, with the car door wide open and the headlights on, while he returned to the garage to switch off the fluorescent lights and close the overhead door. He reached the light switch, flipped it down with a fingertip, and threw the world into darkness.

It would take a minute for his pupils to adjust to the dark. A few seconds more and his night vision would kick in. He could already see some things out of the corners of his eyes. Lots of shadows, mostly.

One of those shadows looked like it was moving. He knew it had to be an optical illusion.

Suddenly, he heard a car door slam shut. Then the Lincoln's taillights brightened, becoming blood-red glowing embers as if someone had stepped on the brakes prior to putting the car into gear. The backup lights lit up. *Someone's stealing my car!* Wayne thought. *Some sonofabitch is stealing my company car!*

The engine revved. Then the bright-red taillights dimmed as foot pressure on the brakes decreased, but the backup lights remained brightly lit. Tires squealed as the heavy car, gunned in reverse, re-entered the garage and headed straight for an astonished Wayne Gillespe, who desperately tried to get out of the way at the very last second—and couldn't.

The rear bumper hit him first—caught him midway between knees and ankles—and shattered his leg bones.

He cried out in pain as the trunk rammed into his hips, smashing his testicles and fracturing the pelvic bone into thousands of tiny fragments, squeezing his buttocks tight against the garage wall until built-up pressure made the capillaries of his eyes burst and blood gushed from his nose and mouth and ears and rectum.

Wayne Gillespe was too dead to notice when Michael Thompson stepped from the car and looked down at the bloody mess on the floor of the garage.

Gotcha!

CHAPTER THIRTEEN

"Wiped completely clean," the evidence technician told Wesley. "I dusted the doors, steering wheel, gear shift, glove box, you name it. The only prints I could find were the victim's."

Wesley nodded his head. "Pull the car in and ask the state boys to try. Maybe they'll come up with something we missed."

"Waste of time, Lieutenant."

"Do it anyway."

Wesley knew the state police crime lab had state-of-the-art equipment, similar to that used by the FBI, which could bring out partial latent prints that dusting often overlooked. Maybe they'd get lucky and find something.

"The victim's a male Caucasian, age fifty-two, crushed to death when the back end of this fancy car pinned him against the garage wall," said the coroner. "The impact broke half the bones in the man's body."

"At least he's not another Slasher victim," sighed Wesley. "How long's he been dead?"

"Two, maybe three hours."

Wesley looked at his watch. "That'd place time of death between six-thirty and seven-thirty, wouldn't it?"

"Approximately."

"Hey, Lenny!" Wesley shouted over to his partner who was examining skid marks on the gravel outside the garage. "What time'd we log out to eat?"

"Six twenty-seven."

"We saw Gillespe alive at six o'clock, Doc. He was still breathing when we left here around six-fifteen."

"You talked to the victim today?"

"Yeah."

"About the Slasher?"

"Yeah. You think there's a connection?"

"Could be. I'm too old and cynical to believe in coincidence anymore."

Wesley scratched his chin. "Doesn't match the M.O.," he said.

"Course not. The Slasher isn't stupid."

Wesley mulled that over in his mind. "No," he said at last. "He isn't stupid. But, if the Slasher killed Gillespe to cover up a connection with Blake Blades, then it was a stupid move on his part—the first real mistake he's made."

"Mistake?"

"Yeah, Doc," Wesley smiled. "He just let me know that I'm closer to catching him than I thought I was."

Michael slowed the Audi to sixty. He'd been doing ninety—racing in and out of traffic on the expressway like a lunatic—until the thought crossed his mind that a cop might stop him and give him a ticket.

And that, in his present mood, he couldn't allow. He'd very likely kill any cop that tried to stop him with the knife he'd taken from the display case and hadn't had a chance to use on Wayne Gillespe.

It was important to use the knife, but not on a cop. Oh, no. If he killed a cop, he'd be in big trouble. He'd intended to use the knife on Gillespe, but he didn't dare take the time. After he'd vented his nervous energy by pinning the man to the wall with the car, it didn't seem like such a good idea to stick around and stab him too.

But now he knew it was absolutely necessary. Gillespe was dead, but killing him hadn't removed the jinx.

Michael had tagged Wayne Gillespe fair and square. He'd caught the man in the dark and tagged him good, but he hadn't used the knife, nor had he said the magic words. It was the combination of magic instrument and magic words that passed the jinx on to someone else—not for long, not for forever, but long enough for Michael's luck to change. Without the jinx sitting on his shoulders, he had the opportunity to take advantage of any luck that came his way.

Horton had shown him how to take advantage of opportunities, and Michael hadn't forgotten; Angelo Scorcisi had shown him how to make magic with a blade, and thereby change his luck.

"In the old days—long before Rome ruled the world—men knew there was magic in metal," Scorcisi had told the teenaged Michael Thompson. "So they fashioned fine instruments from heat-treated metal and, like a magic amulet, carried those instruments on their persons to ward off evil. Even in my father's day, before he left the old country to come here to America, men knew that there was a magic in metal that attracted luck like a magnet. All the men in the old country carried stilettos in their pants pockets because knives are said to be magical."

"Really?" an enthralled Michael had asked.

"Really," the old man said. "That magic is even present in metal chalices Catholic priests use for communion. If you touch your lips to the metal, it is said to bring luck."

"Gosh!"

"But the most magical metal is in a honed blade. Like a broadsword, for example. Even, I believe, in a cheap knife like this one." Scorcisi held up one of the butcher knives he used to trim gristle and fat from meat. "A honed edge is the only protection against the Evil Eye, my father used to say to me. And he was right."

The old man had loved to tell stories, and Michael loved to listen.

"When I'm not working—when I don't have a honed blade in my hand—the Evil Eye often sneaks up and hexes me. If I drink too much when I'm not working, it's because I've been jinxed by the Evil Eye."

"You've been jinxed by the Evil Eye?"

"Many times."

"What is the Evil Eye? Maybe I've been jinxed by it, too."

"The Evil Eye," the old man had explained, "is the eye of a young and pretty woman. Only she isn't really pretty. Nor is she young. She makes you think she is, though, but she's really an ugly old hag who's hexed you into believing she's beautiful. She can mesmerize you in the blink of an eye, turn you into her willing slave, make you believe whatever she wants."

"Geeze!"

"Some people say the hag's been around forever, making fools out of men since the time of Adam and Eve. The only way any man can protect himself from her is to touch metal when he sees her. But, after she gets her claws on a man, he's already jinxed. Touching metal don't do no good."

"Isn't there any way to get rid of the jinx? Ever?"

"Only temporarily," the old man had claimed, to Michael's bitter disappointment. "You can pass her hex off onto someone or something else through the honed edge of a metal blade."

Michael learned later that the old man had only been pulling his leg—laughing, behind his back, at the boy's gullibility. "You gotta watch out for young and pretty women, Mike," he'd warned Michael with a wink. "You never know when one'll hex you with the Evil Eye."

But what Angelo'd said about magic metal left a lasting impression on Michael. At last, Michael knew how to rid himself of the jinx, if only temporarily.

Sometimes he didn't believe in the jinx at all—knew it was just a silly superstition. Luck was something men made for themselves, and Michael learned to manipulate people and events to make his own luck. At other times—when things went wrong and there was nothing he could do about it, when he felt as if he were himself being manipulated like a pawn in a chess game—he blamed his impotency on the Evil Eye.

It was the Evil Eye that had jinxed his father, wasn't it? And Michael, too?

Michael's mother had never said what it was that jinxed him. She'd simply blamed him—and his hapless father—for her own bad luck.

Wasn't it possible, instead, that the Evil Eye was to blame? Of course not. The Evil Eye didn't exist. It was just a silly superstition.

The rational Michael Thompson—the master manipulator who lived in the real world and who'd worked harder than anyone else to become vice president of a major corporation before he was twenty-five—knew such things as evil eyes, hexes, jinxes, and other kinds of superstitious malarkey existed only in the minds of people who couldn't cope with the way the world really worked. They were the little "white" lies people made up to absolve themselves for their own functional failures in life.

But the other Michael Thompson—the man who'd once been an

impressionable boy who'd grown up without a father and without siblings in a household of hate—couldn't help but believe those lies he'd learned as a child. When the rational Michael faced stressful situations that filled him with anxiety and an overriding fear of failure, he reverted to that other Michael, and looked around for someone else—or something else—to blame for his sea of troubles.

It's not my fault, Michael would tell himself. *I was jinxed.*

Rational Michael, of course, refused to accept that explanation. One half of his mind blamed itself, while the other half sought ways to absolve itself of blame. Both halves battled constantly for control. Tonight, the rational Michael was out of control. And it was the other Michael, the irrational Michael Thompson, who was driving the Audi—up one street and down another until he had crisscrossed the Village of Willow Woods, until he found what he'd been looking for all over town.

His fingers felt for the knife on the seat beside him. He parked the car at the curb and waited.

Peggy Shannon worked the three-to-eleven shift at Taco Bell every weekend. Tonight had been slow for a Saturday. Time seemed to stand still after the dinner crowd thinned around nine. The last two hours had dragged by like they'd never end, but now she was on her way home—four more blocks. Then she'd be able to kick off her shoes, put her feet up, and breathe a sigh of relief.

She planned to sleep late tomorrow, maybe until noon or one o'clock. Then, at three, she'd have to be back at Taco Bell.

Peggy worked weekends because she'd soon need the extra money. She was nine weeks pregnant and unmarried. How much longer, she wondered, could she hide it from her boss?

Monday through Friday, from nine to five, Peggy was a clerk-typist at Crawford Insurance. Dick Crawford, her boss, was the baby's father. Unfortunately, Dick was married. He and his wife had three lovely children.

"You're twenty years old and your life is already a mess," Peggy said to herself. "You're not seriously thinking of keeping this child. Are you?" Of course she was.

Tired, preoccupied with her thoughts, Peggy paid no attention to the man who emerged from a red Audi parked at the curb. She was almost home now. One more block and she'd reach the alley behind her third floor apartment. Then she'd slowly climb the three flights of dark stairs, take the key ring from her purse, and locate the backdoor key—the large silver Kwikset key—insert it in the lock, open the door.

She turned into the alley. The man from the red car followed closely behind her.

Peggy reached the first rung of the wooden stairway that snaked up the rear of the old brick building. She'd complained to the super about the poor lighting just yesterday, but nothing had been done to replace the burnt out bulbs on the second- and third-floor landings. Tonight, she noticed with chagrin, the first- and fourth-floor bulbs were burnt out too. The staircase was pitch black.

Someone could trip and break their neck, Peggy thought as she felt for the step with the toe of one foot. *Or a pregnant woman might fall and induce a miscarriage.*

She pushed that thought from her mind.

Peggy was about to brave the second step when she heard a noise not three feet behind her. Without thinking, she turned to see who was there.

Then she remembered the man from the red car. She couldn't see him in the dark, but she knew it had to be that nice-looking man in his early twenties who'd followed her home.

Peggy Shannon drew in a quick breath that would have erupted in an ear-splitting scream if her lungs hadn't been punctured by the point of a butcher knife before her last breath could be expelled. As she died, Peggy heard a strange hissing sound as air escaped through the hole the knife wound had left in her chest.

CHAPTER FOURTEEN

"I tried to telephone," Lenny explained, "but I didn't get any answer."

"We've a problem with the telephone," Ellen said. "The phone company promised to check the line."

She led him to the living room couch and offered to make a pot of coffee.

"I didn't wake you, did I?" Lenny wondered. Ellen's hair was wound around pink plastic rollers. She wore a faded housecoat over a flannel nightgown, and her face had the rosy glow of freshly scrubbed flesh.

"Danny did that hours ago," she laughed. "It's early to bed and early to rise with a five-year-old in the house. He's had us up since seven."

"No aftereffects from the other night?"

"He's perfectly normal."

"Glad to hear it," Lenny said. "He had me worried."

Ellen smiled. "He's upstairs floating an armada in the bathtub while Suzi shampoos his hair. Why don't you read the Sunday paper and I'll let Suzi know you're here."

Lenny found the newspaper and read the comics section first. Then he picked up the front section and stared at the headlines: GILLESPE SLAIN BY SLASHER.

"Oh, shit!" he said aloud.

When Lenny had gone off duty shortly after midnight last night, Gillespe's murder had seemed totally unrelated to any of the others. How the hell had the newspaper come to a different conclusion? Had Lieutenant Wesley clammed up on Lenny last night, shut him out of the investigation completely? True, the two men said fewer than a dozen words to each other at the crime scene, and Wesley had remained mum during the drive back to the station, but Lenny hadn't thought it particularly peculiar. Not at the time, anyway. Now he had to wonder.

He scanned the article quickly, his eyes darting over the words, hunting for fresh information. There was nothing he didn't already know, no new evidence that linked Gillespe to the Slasher. Then why the headline? Was the newspaper grabbing at straws, or was there some late-breaking evidence the reporters or editors didn't have space to include in the article but that justified the sensational headline?

Johnson knew that headlines were often the last words to be set in type, composed after the story had already been cast in lead. Maybe there wasn't time to rewrite the article or add a sidebar. Or, just maybe, the headline was pure speculation, run for the sole purpose of selling papers and bolstering circulation.

What do you care anyway? Wesley took you off the case, didn't he? Johnson tossed the newspaper aside.

Today was his day off. He should forget about the Slasher and concentrate on having fun. If he didn't watch out, he'd become just like Wesley.

"Penny for your thoughts," Suzi said from the staircase.

Startled, Lenny jumped to his feet. He hadn't heard her come down the steps.

"How long have you been there?" he asked.

"A long time," she said. "I like spying on you, in case you didn't know."

"Really?"

"Really," she said.

She looked ravishing. Her blonde hair, freshly washed and brushed, glistened like corn silk in a sunlit field. Her body, evidently braless under a too-tight T-shirt, caused a constriction in Lenny's throat that took his breath away. He could feel his heart race wildly.

"I like looking at you, too," he managed to say.

She pirouetted for his pleasure. "Look all you like," she said.

He couldn't help but stare.

"Seen enough?" she asked finally.

"No," he said. "I could look at you all day and never see enough of you."

"Well, that's all you're going to get for now. Ellen and Danny will be down in a minute and I don't want to shock them. Ellen's becoming prudish in her old age."

"Prudish?"

"She thinks I'm a brazen hussy."

"Oh."

"I am, you know."

"What?"

"Brazen."

Before he knew what she was up to, she planted a kiss on his lips. Her mouth tasted of toothpaste. Then, before his senses recovered completely, she danced beyond his reach and smiled coquettishly. He noticed a blush on her cheeks and neck.

"Told you I was brazen," she said.

"Brazen enough to do that again?"

"Uh uh," she said. "I don't want it to become a habit."

"I wouldn't mind."

She searched his eyes to see if he meant what he'd said.

"I came over today to ask you to a movie," he blurted out. "Will you go to a movie with me?"

"Sure," she said. She didn't hesitate at all.

"Don't you want to know which flick?"

"It doesn't matter. I'll go to any flick you want to see. But only on one condition."

"What's that?"

"After the movie we go out for pizza and beer. I'll treat."

He grinned. "Sounds fair to me. The movie starts at three-fifteen."

"Good. We've time to grab a bite to eat before we leave. Want to help me raid the refrigerator?"

"Coffee should be ready," Ellen announced as she came downstairs holding Danny's hand.

"I'm hungry too," said the boy. "Can I have a san'wich?"

"Sure, Danny," Suzi said. "Peanut butter and jelly for everyone. Right?"

"Right!" Danny agreed as he pulled free of his mother's hand and ran to the kitchen.

Tom Wesley read the autopsy report on Peggy Shannon and blamed himself for allowing her death to happen. It was his responsibility to protect the citizens of Willow Woods, and he'd failed. But Tom Wesley wasn't about to give up. Oh, no. He'd catch the killer, sooner or later.

Better make it sooner, he told himself.

Tom knew he was missing something—something important—in the autopsy reports, but *what*?

His eyes itched from lack of sleep and the accumulated cigarette smoke that hung over his head like a cloud. He was too tired to see straight. He stared at the autopsy report and the words blurred on the sheet of paper. He needed sleep, and he knew it. His eyelids closed and he forced them open again. Time had run out for Peggy Shannon and her unborn child. For Wayne Gillespe. For Laura Godwin and Glenda Rose Williams and JoAnn Green and Elizabeth May Singer. Tom Wesley couldn't afford the luxury of sleep because he knew time was rapidly running out for the next victim, and the one after that, and...

Homicides were supposed to be one-time isolated events in the Village of Willow Woods. Crimes of passion or greed—they happened so seldom that Wesley spent months investigating each case, methodically gathering evidence to convict the killer in a court of law. There had never been a need to hurry. Once the perpetrator had committed his single act of violence—whether a momentary lapse of sanity or premeditated murder—the killer had no reason to kill again. Normally, except in the case of a robbery or rape, when a witness was eliminated, the perpetrator knew the victim before the crime.

Finding the killer was simply a matter of gathering evidence at the scene of the homicide, interviewing family and friends of the victim, and determining who was the most likely suspect. Anyone who had motive, means, and opportunity remained suspect until Wesley checked out their alibis.

Tom Wesley knew he'd been successful in the past not because he was a brilliant man or a master detective, but only because he'd been doggedly determined to learn the truth. He never gave up on a case no matter how long it took.

But this case was different. Willow Woods had never had a crazed serial killer running around town killing citizens at random before. With the murders of Elizabeth May Singer and JoAnn Green,

Wesley had taken the time to talk to acquaintances of both victims. Not one of the people he'd interviewed had sufficient motive for murder, and all had alibis that held up under scrutiny.

Tom had thought, early in the investigation, that the killer was a stranger to town—a transient, someone like Ted Bundy who went around the country killing women in different locales, one of which just happened to be Willow Woods. Then the killer would move on to some other place and kill again before moving on yet again.

Working under that assumption, Tom had asked police departments nationwide to send him information on unsolved murders in their jurisdictions. The response had been overwhelming. Hundreds, thousands, of envelopes had arrived in the mail from every state in the Union. It was depressing to think about: that murder occurred so often was bad enough, but the fact that so many murders remained unsolved even after years of police investigation seemed like a crying shame.

After reading five or six of those cases, Wesley had stacked the rest of the envelopes unopened in a corner behind his desk.

Even if the "Mad Slasher of Willow Woods" had killed elsewhere before coming to town, it would be impossible to learn his identity by backtracking through the autopsy reports in all those envelopes, wouldn't it?

Forget it. You don't have time. Concentrate on the autopsy reports of the local victims.

Tom Wesley forced his eyes to focus. He read through Peggy's report again, laid it aside, and began on Laura's.

What am I missing? he asked himself again and again.

With that question foremost in his mind, Tom Wesley fell asleep in his chair.

Michael Thompson felt great. When he awoke around noon, he showered and shaved. Then, dressed in an expensive suit, he drove to Willow Woods' best restaurant for a sumptuous Sunday after-noon champagne brunch.

He was himself again. While he ate voraciously, with his body and mind focused on the smell and taste of the food, the sights and sounds of the busy restaurant simply disappeared. He was aware of nothing but the delicious food being shoved into his mouth on the pointed tines of a silver fork—and the knife he held in his other hand.

Michael loved the feel of finely crafted metal. The heft and balance of precision instruments allowed him conscious control over his actions. As a child, his mother had served only foods like bean soup and vegetable stew which were eaten with a spoon. Hamburgers and hot dogs were considered finger food, requiring no utensils. It wasn't until he'd grown up that he learned, for the first time, how to hold a knife and fork in his hands.

Michael finished his meal, wiped his mouth with a linen napkin, and called for another bottle of champagne. This was a day of celebration for Michael Thompson. Free once more from the horrible hex that had haunted him all his life, Michael was back in control of his own destiny.

That other Michael—the frightened child who was often victimized by pernicious happenstance—had gone away again.

It was the other Michael that had jinxed Michael's mother, wasn't it? And it was the other Michael that had, up until the time Michael became a teenager, clouded Michael's mind with its hated presence. Now Michael was rid of him. But only for a little while.

The waiter brought a new bottle of champagne and Michael nodded approval. At eighty-five dollars a bottle, it was the best brand in the house. Only the best was good enough for the *real* Michael Thompson.

Michael sipped his champagne, luxuriating in the expensive taste of the wine and the bubbly fizz that tickled his tongue.

By the time he left the restaurant, Michael Thompson was already legally drunk, but still in control.

Suzi ordered another pitcher of beer.

Lenny, feeling lightheaded, didn't want another pitcher, but Suzi insisted.

"You trying to drink me under the table?" he asked, half-seriously.

"I am, if it'll get you to loosen up," she admitted. "Are you always this uptight?"

"You think I'm uptight?"

She nodded. "Not as much as you were when I came downstairs and found you reading the newspaper. I thought my 'brazen hussy' routine might cheer you up, but obviously it didn't."

"You mean it was all an act to cheer me up?"

"Disappointed?"

"Sure, I'm disappointed."

"You like brazen hussies, do you?"

"I..."

Suzi's eyes twinkled mischievously. She deliberately arched her back to thrust her breasts against the too-tight T-shirt.

"Does this turn you on?" she asked.

Lenny felt himself blush.

"Well, I got your attention, at least," Suzi said. She, too, was blushing.

Lenny smiled. He couldn't help but like this girl. Maybe he liked her too much. He wanted to take her in his arms and hold her close. He wanted to embrace her, to feel those pointed breasts of hers pressed against his chest, those luscious lips of hers on his mouth. He wanted to immerse himself in Susan Lester, body and soul, so he could forget about the murders, and the serial killer that was still on the loose in Willow Woods. His mind had been preoccupied with the Slasher since reading the headlines in this morning's paper. Though he'd been looking forward to seeing the movie and spending the day in Suzi's company, he discovered he couldn't concentrate on anything but the killings.

And then, while driving from the movie to the pizza parlor, he'd heard the latest news on the car radio. A woman named Peggy Shannon was found dead behind her apartment building, another victim of "The Mad Slasher of Willow Woods." That made him think of Tom Wesley, diligently pursuing the killer all by himself, when Lenny should be helping him.

Lenny felt guilty. He was torn between his duty as a police officer and this woman he knew he could easily fall in love with.

"Hey, you!" Suzi waved a hand in front of his face. "Did I lose your attention again? You seem a million miles away."

"Sorry," he said.

"If you want to take me home..."

"Maybe I should. I'm not good company tonight."

"I hope you weren't put off by my 'brazen hussy' act. Did I embarrass you?"

"No."

"Then what did I do wrong?"

"Nothing."

"I must have done something wrong."

He looked into her eyes and saw the traces of tears. Did she think she wasn't attractive because he hadn't paid her enough attention?

"It isn't you," he said. "It's me."

"You're not gay, are you?"

Lenny laughed and shook his head. "I'm not gay," he said.

"Want to take me home and prove it?" She stuck her chest out at him.

"This is just part of your act, isn't it? Has to be. Ellen and Danny are home."

"I'm not staying at Ellen's anymore. I have my own apartment."

"Oh?"

"I went to Ellen's to babysit on Thursday. She asked me to stay the weekend because of what happened to Danny. But I don't live with my sister. I don't live with anyone, Lenny. I'm an independent woman, in case you haven't noticed."

"You're serious? You're inviting me to—"

"To stay the night with me. If you want to, that is."

"I want to," Lenny said. He reached for her hand and squeezed it.

Suzi leaned across the table and kissed him. Her tongue snaked into his mouth and explored.

Breathless, she whispered, "I finally got your complete attention, didn't I?"

CHAPTER FIFTEEN

Sometime during the night, colliding air masses became a massive storm front that passed through three states and dumped four inches of much-needed rain over the entire area, including the Village of Willow Woods. Roads flooded as storm sewers overflowed, and Monday morning traffic was a mess.

Johnson had investigated three accidents before ten o'clock, minor fender-benders without injuries. He was on his way back to the station to write reports when he drove past the entrance to the park and stopped the car.

The torrential downpour continued unabated, and his cruiser's windshield wipers—worn, with portions of the rubber rotting to pieces—made it dangerous to drive. He decided to pull over and wait for the rain to lessen.

Johnson radioed in that he was taking a ten-minute break. He gave his location and asked the dispatcher to confirm the time.

As soon as he killed the motor, windows began to fog. He immediately turned the engine back on and hit the defroster switch, but fog continued to form on the side windows. When he tried to wipe it away with a sleeve of his uniform, condensation left smears and streaks on the safety glass.

"Damn," he whispered.

He opened the door, got out of the car, and went around to the trunk. He searched through a box of emergency equipment for the clean rags that were supposed to be standard issue for department cruisers. Flashlight, spare batteries, plastic evidence bags, rubber gloves, first aid kit, everything else was there, but no clean rags.

In his hurry to dress, he'd neglected to add a handkerchief or Kleenex to the normal accessories he'd stuffed in his pockets earlier this morning. He had his keys, his billfold, a handful of change, but nothing to wipe windows with.

Slamming the trunk, he looked around for something, anything, to use on the windows. Then he remembered trash containers, filled with newspapers, at the other end of the park where the benches were. Surely, he'd find a dry newspaper he could use in one of the metal waste containers. It'd be worth the walk, if he did.

Outfitted in departmental rain gear, Johnson began slowly trekking through the park. Puddles of water pooled on the path, and he detoured around them as well as he could without trampling down the grass or invading fenced-off flowerbeds.

His regulation spit-shined boots were soaked by the time he reached a row of wooden benches lining the far side of the park. Off to the right he saw several trash containers, one of which had a metal cover. Inside, there was bound to be a discarded newspaper or two. Crumpled newspaper cleaned glass without streaking, his mother had once claimed. He hoped she was right. If she was, he'd remember to tell her the next time he saw her, when he brought Susan Lester home to introduce to his parents.

Thinking ahead too far, aren't you? One date and you're already thinking about introducing her to Mom and Dad. What if last night was only a fluke? A one-night stand? What then?

Johnson remembered the near-perfect tenderness and passion of last night, and he decided it was more than just a one-night stand for him. For Susan Lester, too. She'd begged him to stay the night, and he had stayed until four this morning. Then, allowing himself barely enough time to run by his own apartment where he had to shower, shave, and shine his shoes before donning uniform and rain gear and reporting for duty at five-forty-five, he'd kissed her goodbye and promised he'd call her later this afternoon. And she'd promised to wait for his call. It wasn't a one-night stand. No, sir.

Johnson found a dry newspaper and slipped it inside his raincoat.

He'd been thinking about Suzi all morning: the fine features of her flawless face, the delightful curves of her luscious body, the sweet sound of her melodious voice. She'd certainly gotten—and managed to keep—his undivided attention last night. Hadn't she? And she still continued to hold his attention.

He hadn't once thought about the Slasher, until the moment he saw the bushes where, less than a week ago, he'd discovered the decomposing body of Glenda Rose Williams, and thought he saw—

No! It's an illusion! It's gotta be an illusion! The rain is playing tricks on my eyes!

Lenny rubbed his eyes and looked again.

Half-hidden by those same bushes, less than ten feet away, was the unmistakable silhouette of a woman's body.

Instead of investigating on his own, Rookie Patrolman Leonard Johnson ran through the rain for the police cruiser he'd left with its motor running on the other side of the park.

This time he had enough sense to radio his discovery to the dispatcher immediately, and waited impatiently for Lieutenant Wesley to show up with a forensics team, dreading what he knew they'd find.

The deputy coroner's office was a small cubicle to the far rear of the Willow Woods Health Department laboratory complex, occupying that part of the Willow Woods Memorial Hospital basement not devoted to the hospital's huge physical plant. A labyrinth of plumbing and heating/air conditioning pipes and vents made cyclic gurgling, hissing, whistling and banging noises in the background, and all that incessant noise grated greatly on Wesley's already frazzled nerves.

He wasn't allowed to smoke in the building either, so all Wesley could do while waiting for Frank Monroe to finish an autopsy was to pace impatiently back and forth in front of the door to the examination room, silently urging the doctor to hurry.

The County Coroner was an elected politician, not a physician, and the coroner's office was located downtown in the new courthouse building, far away from the smell of formaldehyde and the company of corpses.

This morning, at about the same time that Johnson was discovering another body in the rain-soaked park, Tom Wesley was attending an emergency conference on the top floor of the courthouse. Called by the state's attorney, the meeting brought together law enforcement officials from all over the state to better coordinate efforts at apprehending the "Mad Slasher of Willow Woods."

Besides Wesley, the elected coroner and the chief of police, the state's attorney had invited the county sheriff, a deputy superintendent of the state police, and a representative from the governor's office.

Citizens were worried, the politicians had explained. These killings had gotten way out of hand and something had to be done *immediately*. If Willow Woods police couldn't catch the killer, then other law enforcement agencies would step in and get the job done fast. The prosecutor demanded action, and he wanted it now.

The chief politely reminded the state's attorney that Willow Woods had sole jurisdiction of the case. Unless or until a victim turned up outside the corporate boundaries of Willow Woods, the "Slasher" investigation would remain the chief's responsibility. He'd be happy to accept assistance, but he wouldn't tolerate intervention. He refused to relinquish control to anyone else.

The governor's man said the chief was full of shit. It didn't matter who caught the killer, did it? What mattered was putting the so-called Slasher permanently out of commission. The state police were better equipped to handle the case than a two-bit local municipality. If Willow Woods police didn't apprehend the killer within the next twenty-four hours, the governor would simply declare a state of emergency in Willow Woods and the state police could legally step in and take over.

Wesley had listened to their arguments without saying a word. Who headed the case was unimportant to Tom Wesley. Who got credit for the collar—whether the Willow Woods chief of police, the state's attorney, the sheriff, the state police, or the governor himself—made little difference, as long as publicity-hungry politicians stayed out of his way and let him do his job. But he knew they wouldn't, especially not the governor's man.

His name didn't ring a bell at first. Maybe it should have, but Wesley's mind had been too tired at ten o'clock on a rainy Monday morning to make the necessary connection.

But now, pacing back and forth in the morgue, it was perfectly clear why the governor's man wanted control of the case.

His name just happened to be Arthur Godwin, the rich and influential father of Laura Godwin, the Slasher's fourth victim.

Wesley knew payoffs had already been made, promises given,

political markers called in. The meeting at the courthouse was a sham. The governor had already committed to pulling the plug on the Willow Woods police force and placing the state police in charge of the investigation, with Godwin in control, and there was nothing Wesley could do about it—except catch the killer while he still had a chance.

Lenny Johnson completed the accident reports and turned them in to the desk sergeant before the end of his shift. Ellis and Peters from the violent crimes unit, assigned to back up Wesley's homicide investigation, had also asked Johnson for a written statement concerning the discovery of the body in the park. Lenny dropped the statement off at their office on his way out the door, and drove to the morgue to learn the results of the autopsy, as soon as Monroe finished his postmortem examination.

Because of the rain, the deputy coroner had ordered the body photographed, then bagged and brought to the morgue before vital evidence was washed away, if it hadn't all been washed away already.

Lenny had never been to the morgue before, though he'd seen pictures of the place during his training at the police academy. He had to ask directions at the hospital desk, then descend in a service elevator marked "Staff Use Only." When he reached the basement, he took the corridor to his right. Eventually, he reached the Health Department complex and found the deputy coroner's sanctum sanctorum.

He was surprised to find Tom Wesley in a small office next to the examination room.

"What are *you* doing here?" Wesley growled.

"Same thing you are."

"Didn't you get off duty at three? Don't try to tell me you're working a double shift, because I won't believe you."

"I'm off duty," Lenny admitted.

"Then go home, kid. You don't belong here."

"I'll go home after I hear the autopsy results," Lenny said defiantly, sitting down at Monroe's cluttered desk. "Maybe I'll be able to add some detail to Doc's report. I discovered the body, you know."

"So I heard."

"Tell me, Lieutenant, did the Slasher kill Gillespe? The newspaper said the Slasher did it. How did they come to that conclusion?"

"Doc."

"Doc?"

"Yeah. Doctor Monroe thought there might be a connection."

"Is there?"

"Nothing definite."

"How'd the newspaper pick up on it?"

"They asked Doc if he thought the Slasher was involved. Doc said there was a remote possibility."

"Someone mention my name?" Frank Monroe wondered as he entered his office. "Cussing me out 'cause I took so long?"

"I've been cussing you the past two hours," Wesley said truthfully. "What's your verdict, Doc?"

"Killed with a knife," Monroe said. "Most likely one of the big butcher knives from a Blake Blades Best Cutlery set."

"Another Slasher victim?"

"Looks like it, Tom. But we can't be sure."

"Whad'ya mean?"

"Significant discrepancies in the M.O. There are cuts to the torso, but no tell-tale X-slices across each breast common to the other female victims. Plus, this victim has widespread contusions. None of the previous victims displayed contusions—disregarding Gillespe, of course."

"Contusions?" Lenny asked. "You mean bruises?"

"Big ugly welts," the doctor said. "Some were fresh at time of death. A few were at least a day or two older. Looks like someone beat her up before stabbing her. I took pictures. Soon as they're developed, you can see for yourself."

"What else, Doc?" Wesley prodded.

"She wasn't killed in the park. She was already dead when the killer dumped her body in the bushes."

"You sure?"

"Positive."

"How do you know?" Lenny asked.

"Lack of blood at the crime scene is one reason. Livor mortis, or postmortem lividity, is another. Despite some exsanguination, the settled blood in cutaneous and subcutaneous capillaries was congealed—completely fixed—at the time the body was moved from place of death. Moving a body from its original position after the fixation of livor mortis leaves some of the lividity in defiance of gravity in the disturbed body. I won't go into all the clinical details. Suffice it to say that the woman was beaten, then stabbed. Then, twelve to eighteen hours later, the body was moved."

"Were you able to ID her?" Wesley asked. "We couldn't find a purse or wallet at the crime scene."

"I faxed her prints to Washington. They came back with a match from a recent passport application. Her name's Joan Norman, maiden name Gould, married to Robert Daniel Norman. She and her husband own one of those fancy apartments over at the Willow Condominium high-rise across from the park."

"Norman? Mrs. Robert Daniel Norman? *Jesus Christ!*"

"Danny's stepmother?" Lenny wondered.

"You two know the victim?" Doc asked.

"Never met her," Wesley mumbled. "Has her husband been notified yet?"

"Not yet," Doc said. "I haven't had time."

Wesley picked up the phone. Instead of calling the victim's husband, he dialed the cab company and ordered a taxi.

"I'll tell him in person," he explained. "I want to watch the bastard's face when I break the news."

"You think Norman's the Slasher?" Lenny asked.

"It makes sense, kid. Mrs. Norman is the only victim who's married. Her husband wants to get rid of his wife without arousing suspicion, so he thinks up an elaborate scheme to hide her murder. All the other victims are just subterfuge to throw us off the trail. Can't you see how it all fits together?"

"What about Gillespe?"

"Maybe Gillespe was an accident. Maybe his death had nothing to do with the Slasher killings."

"Let me go with you, Lieutenant," Lenny said. "Forget about the cab. I've got a car. We can drive and be there in ten minutes."

"No way, kid. Go home, go to a movie, go to hell for all I care. You wanted off this case and you're off the case permanently."

"You might need backup."

"Forget it, kid." Wesley slid his arms into his raincoat. "This bastard's mine."

"But what if you're wrong?" Lenny demanded. "What if Norman isn't the Slasher?"

"Then I'll just ask him about the bruises. He beat her up pretty bad, didn't he, Doc?"

"Somebody did."

"Had to be him. Doc said she's been dead for eighteen hours or more. Don't you think it's strange Norman hasn't reported his wife missing?"

"Maybe he has," Lenny said. "We don't see a missing persons report until someone's been missing more than seventy-two hours. Let me call the station and check with the desk."

"No time to check now, kid. I've got a cab waiting." Before Lenny could argue, Wesley was out the door and halfway to the elevator.

CHAPTER SIXTEEN

Doctor Monroe kept Lenny from catching Wesley at the elevator. "We need to talk, Officer Johnson," was all the doctor had said, but it was enough to keep Lenny from leaving.

"Do you think Norman is the Slasher?" Lenny demanded of the doctor.

"I'm more worried about Tom Wesley than I am about the Slasher at the moment," said the doctor, offering Johnson a chair. "Sit down, son. I want to tell you a few things you ought to know."

"About the Slasher?"

"About Tom Wesley."

Lenny sat down. He looked at the doctor and said, "Well?"

"I think Tom's about to go off the deep end."

"What do you mean?"

"Did you see the way he looked when he left here? The look in his eyes? That wasn't the look of a rational man, was it?"

"No," Lenny had to admit. "He hasn't looked or sounded rational for days."

"I don't think he's had a good night's sleep in weeks. He feels personally responsible for catching this killer, and he won't be able to rest until he does."

"So?"

"So he's driving himself too hard, heading straight for a nervous breakdown. When the body needs sleep but the mind won't let it, the conflict causes severe stress. Eventually, something's got to give, to break down completely—either the body or the mind. I think Tom knows he's right on the verge of cracking, and I think he's going after Norman because, if he can convince himself that Norman is responsible for the Slasher killings, he's then solved the case and can reward himself with some much-needed rest."

Lenny said nothing. He didn't want to believe what the doctor's words implied.

"Tom's been on the edge of cracking since the day his wife and kids were killed in an automobile accident almost three years ago. He was driving, you see, and blames himself for their deaths. Wasn't his fault, though. The drunk who ran a red light and rammed Tom's car on the passenger side died in the accident, and Tom didn't have anybody else to punish."

"So he punishes himself?" Lenny said, as much a statement as a question.

"He survived. They didn't. Somebody's got to be punished, he figures, and who else is there?"

"Robert Daniel Norman. My God! He's transferring his own guilt to Norman, isn't he?"

"Couldn't say for sure. I'm a pathologist, not a psychiatrist. But Tom Wesley did walk out of here looking like a ticking time bomb of volatile high explosives about to blow sky high. If Norman says or does anything to set him off..."

"I get the picture, Doc. I'm going over there. Maybe I can reach Norman's apartment before Wesley frames an innocent man."

"I'm not so sure Norman's innocent, but if Wesley thinks killing the man will protect even one more woman from being butchered by the Slasher, then I am sure Tom wouldn't hesitate to shoot him on the spot. Execute the man without a trial, put an end to the killings once and for all so Tom can go home and get some sleep without worrying about the next victim. That's the way Tom's tired mind might reason, I'm afraid."

"I'd better hurry," Lenny said, heading for the door.

"Be careful, son," warned Frank Monroe. "I wouldn't like it if you came back in a body bag and I had to do an autopsy on you. I wouldn't like it at all."

Wesley hated the inconvenience of taxicabs. He felt trapped in the back seat, at the mercy of a driver who didn't give a shit while a ticking meter marked off miles and minutes with another *Click! Click!* like a time bomb getting ready to explode.

Maybe he should have taken Johnson up on his offer of a ride.

Wesley didn't dare drive himself. He hadn't dared to get behind a wheel of a vehicle since that grisly Sunday morning, three years ago now, when a drunk hurtled through a blind intersection and rammed into the passenger side of Wesley's car like a speeding bullet. Joyce had been sitting in the passenger seat, dressed up for church, holding six-month-old Sara in her lap. Tommy Junior had been in the back seat, but on the same side of the car as his mother, and Wesley could still hear his son's screams as the boy's bones broke and splintered. The screams had died in Tommy's throat as abruptly as they'd started.

Joyce didn't scream at all. The passenger door had crushed her and tiny Sara into a bloody pulp before she even knew what had hit her. The airbag hadn't helped at all.

The driver of the other car was crudely decapitated when his airbag hadn't inflated in time, and his head and neck were stuck halfway through his shattered windshield. Judging from the alcohol content in his bloodstream at autopsy, he never knew what hit him, or what he'd hit, either.

Wesley had walked away from the wreck with only a few scrapes and bruises, but no serious damage, except a broken heart and an aversion to driving an automobile that sometimes proved to be an inconvenience, but wasn't debilitating.

Wesley paid the taxi driver and added a five-dollar tip. He'd made it across town in almost record time, and Wesley was grateful.

Overhead, the condo high-rise towered twenty floors—the tallest building in Willow Woods. Rain beat against plate glass walls, and the entire building seemed shrouded by fine mist. The top floor looked lost in the clouds.

Robert Daniel Norman lived on the top floor. Wesley took the first elevator, punched a button marked "Penthouse," and watched silently as an indicator light marked off each floor during the elevator's rapid ascent.

The Willow Condominiums were a new addition to the village's skyline, built exclusively to accommodate wealthy residents. Wesley's annual salary wouldn't even qualify as a down payment on a one-room studio apartment on the second floor.

If he saved every penny he'd earned in the ten years that he'd been a police officer, he knew he still wouldn't be able to afford the down payment on a penthouse suite. The higher one went in this building, the more money one needed to spend to live there. Robert Norman had to be very rich to live on the topmost floor.

The elevator stopped, and the door hissed open.

Wesley walked out onto plush, gold-colored pile carpeting. The walls and ceilings were decorated with mirrors, giving the illusion of spaciousness to a small hallway that led to a single solid-walnut door.

Was there only one huge apartment occupying the penthouse floor?

Jesus Christ! Did Robert Norman own the whole floor?

Wesley discovered he was developing a dislike for the man even before he met him. After he rang the bell several times and then had to hold his badge in front of a camera lens next to the door for the disembodied voice that answered his ring to verify he was indeed a police officer, Wesley's dislike for Robert Norman intensified even more. And when the door swung open and Wesley met Robert Norman face to face, that dislike turned into instant hate.

Norman—a hulking brute that stood six-foot-three and weighed two hundred-and-fifty pounds if he weighed an ounce—was dressed in a light-blue polo shirt and navy-blue slacks. His rugged, more than moderately handsome face showed signs of premature aging, obviously caused by bouts with the bottle. His eyes were cloudy and bloodshot from heavy drinking over an extended period of time, and his gut sported the telltale bulge of a burgeoning beer-belly.

Robert Norman was a goddamn drunk! Not the kind of drunk who'd someday become a pitiful derelict like Pete Williams and live in the alley behind Grogan's fish market, panhandling on the streets for his liquid supper. No, Robert Norman was the kind of respectable drunk that would some Sunday morning, while returning from an all-nighter of fancy parties, run a red stoplight and ruin the lives of an unsuspecting family on their way to early church services— killing innocent women and children as well as himself.

"Yeah?" Norman asked, and Wesley could smell alcohol on the man's breath.

"Are you Robert Norman?" Wesley asked. "Are you married to Joan Gould?"

"Yeah. Joan's out, though. When she comes back, I'll tell her you're looking for her. If you want a contribution, you're out of luck for this year. We already got enough tax deductions."

"I'm here to see *you*, Mr. Norman. Do you mind if I come in?"

"I paid my parking tickets," Norman said. "Most of 'em anyway."

"This isn't about parking tickets. Please, may I come in?"

Norman shrugged his massive shoulders. "Sure," he said. "Why not?"

Wesley followed Norman into a tastefully decorated living room filled with expensive furnishings.

"Take a seat while I fix a drink," Norman said. "You want a drink? I got top-shelf stuff. Beer, too, if you don't appreciate good liquor. You name it, I got it."

"I'm on duty," Wesley said.

"So?"

"So I don't drink on duty. Matter of fact, I don't drink at all."

"You should. It relaxes you, makes you feel good."

"No, thanks."

"Suit yourself."

Norman mixed his drink at a well-stocked bar that lined one entire wall of the room. The opposite wall, Wesley noted, was solid glass, a floor-to-ceiling picture window that looked out over the village from a dizzying height. The view was spectacular.

Across the street was the park where Lenny Johnson had discovered Mrs. Norman's body. *Convenient*, Wesley thought. *Too convenient to be a coincidence.*

Wesley wanted to jump up and handcuff Norman right now, slap the cuffs on him and haul him down to jail where they could throw away the key—put the bastard away where he wouldn't harm anyone ever again—and then Wesley could go home and sleep for a week without a worry in the world. But, even as tired as he felt, he was still too good a cop to do that. First, he had to prove Norman was a killer.

It didn't matter in the eyes of the law that Robert Norman was a drunk who had the potential of killing innocent motorists on the highway. Nor did it matter in the eyes of the law that Norman was a wife-beater, which Wesley suspected the man was from the bruises on Joan Norman's body.

Nothing mattered unless Wesley could prove that Norman had

motive, means, and opportunity for slaying one or all of the victims that the Slasher had already killed, including Robert Norman's dead wife.

"Mr. Norman," Wesley began, "I'm afraid I'm the bearer of bad news. Your wife was found dead this morning in the park across the street."

Normally, Wesley would have broken the news that a man's wife had been murdered as gently as possible to spare the husband's feelings. But, in instances when the husband looked like a prime suspect, Wesley liked to throw death in the man's face and watch his reaction. If the husband were innocent, Wesley would know immediately from the shocked expression on the man's face.

Robert Norman didn't even blink.

"Did you hear what I said, Mr. Norman?"

"I heard."

Norman reached into an ice bucket and dropped two cubes in his drink. Then, before the ice had a chance to melt, he tipped the glass and downed the contents in one gulp.

He began to mix another drink.

"Don't you want to know how your wife died?"

"Not particularly. I figure you'll tell me sooner or later."

"She was beaten and stabbed."

Norman downed a second drink. Instead of mixing a third, he refilled his glass with straight bourbon.

"I'd rather you didn't drink that, Mr. Norman. You need to be sober to answer some questions about your wife. After you answer all my questions, you can drink all you want. Okay?"

"What kind of questions?"

"When did you see your wife last?"

"Saturday night," Norman said. "She left for a dinner party around seven-thirty."

"You didn't go with your wife to the party?"

"It was one of those artsy-fartsy affairs. Pink champagne and all that shit. She had to go because she's on some kind of board at the damn museum."

"She hasn't been home since Saturday at seven-thirty PM?"

"No."

"You've been home all the time?"

"Not all the time."

"I'll need to know where you were at the time of your wife's death, Mr. Norman. Can you tell me everywhere you've been since Saturday at noon?"

"Noon?"

"Noon on Saturday, Mr. Norman."

"I already tol' ya. She was still alive Saturday night."

"Regardless, I need to know your whereabouts since noon on Saturday. It's just routine, Mr. Norman."

Norman took a sip of bourbon.

"Mind if I smoke?" Wesley asked.

"I mind," Norman said. "Smoke ruins your lungs. Even secondhand smoke. I don't allow anyone to smoke around me 'cause I'm an athlete."

Wesley put his cigarettes and lighter back in his pocket.

"I used to be an athlete, anyway," Norman corrected. "Could have been a famous football star, only I fucked it all up by getting married."

Wesley said nothing. Let the man ramble if he wanted. Maybe Norman would slip up and say something self-incriminating.

This was the kind of police work Wesley knew and loved, listening to suspects tell their tales, waiting to catch the right suspect in the inevitable lie that wouldn't hold water.

Until now, Wesley hadn't had a single suspect, not one. Joan Norman's death, however, gave him the clue he'd needed.

She'd been badly beaten before being stabbed!

Wesley had seen cases like this before, hadn't he? Sure. Lots of them. Domestic disputes were the bane of police work. Most often, they were handled routinely by patrolmen. Sometimes, though, they got out of hand and the violent crimes unit had to step in. And, occasionally, someone got killed and Wesley inherited the headache. These days it was called "domestic violence," a polite euphemism for wife-beating. Usually, the perpetrator was an alcoholic—a man like Robert Norman, only not quite so rich.

Did Norman kill his wife?

He certainly fit the pattern. Even if Wesley had other suspects— which he didn't—Robert Norman would still be his *prime* suspect.

But is he the Slasher?

Wesley couldn't help but remember a case he'd investigated five years ago. It was his first case as a homicide detective, and it had etched an indelible impression on his mind.

A man had murdered his entire family—wife, two sons, and one daughter—making it look as if some stranger had broken into their house. But an autopsy showed the wife had been severely beaten several times prior to the night of her murder, and so had the kids. The man had claimed he'd been held captive along with the rest of the family, tied up and repeatedly beaten by assailants who hid behind ski masks and demanded money. When the man told them he didn't have any money, the assailants allegedly went berserk and killed the woman and three children—one at a time—beating them to death in front of the man's eyes. Then, he claimed, they'd left him tied to a chair and made their getaway.

Later, Wesley learned that the man had inflicted a few minor wounds on himself only to divert suspicion. A few scrapes and bruises, self-inflicted, made his story more plausible.

Why did the man do it? What could motivate a man to murder his own wife and three small children? The wife had threatened to take the children and leave. He'd been abusing them for years, smacking the kids, beating the wife. But she'd stuck it out, enduring the pain and humiliation, hoping he'd eventually change, but he didn't. And then she learned he was having an affair behind her back, and was beating his mistress, too.

It was the mistress who'd telephoned the wife and warned her about the man's increasingly violent nature. Realizing her husband was hopeless, the wife tried to take the kids and file for divorce. Her mistake was telling her husband her intentions, and he hit her—hit her so hard two of her incisors splintered. He didn't stop hitting her until she was dead.

Then, angry at himself for what he'd done, he took out his anger on his children, and, finally, on himself, before regaining his senses and realizing what he'd done. He knew then that he was in trouble—big trouble—so he made up a story to tell the police. And Wesley had swallowed it, hook, line, and sinker—until the man tried to kill his mistress, and she shot him through the gut six times before calling the police and spilling the beans.

Was this case similar? Was Robert Norman a violent man who

vented his own anger and frustration on women and children? Had Norman killed other women as a smokescreen to divert suspicion? Was his wife the intended target and the others mere camouflage for the real crime—the premeditated murder of Joan Norman? Or had he knifed them all—viciously stabbed and cut every one of his victims—because he couldn't help himself? Was he a cold-blooded killer? Or was he a psychopath who got his kicks by mutilating the dead bodies of helpless women? And how did Wayne Gillespe fit into the scheme of things?

As Norman rambled on about how his first wife interfered with his youthful athletic ambitions, Wesley became more and more convinced of Norman's guilt. The way Norman berated Ellen and Danny intensified the detective's dislike of this prime suspect, and nailing Norman became almost an obsession.

C'mon, you bastard. Make a mistake. Say something incriminating. I want to get this thing over with so I can go home and catch up on my sleep.

"The smartest thing I ever did was divorce that nobody Ellen Lester and marry Joan Gould," Norman was saying. He'd finished his bourbon and poured another. Wesley noted with disgust that Norman's face looked flushed, but he didn't sound drunk. His words never faltered, his tongue never slurred.

"Joan was the daughter of Winston Gould, the famous financier. Old Winston was the man who put up the money to build this building, you know. Hell, he financed half the real estate in the country. When he and his wife died in a plane crash, Joan inherited the whole shebang—real estate, bank accounts, stocks and bonds." Norman's mouth twisted up in a grin. "So, you see, I don't have to be an athlete anymore. Do I? Now that Joan's dead, I've got enough money to buy my own goddamn professional football team if I feel like it."

That's it! Bingo! That's what I was waiting for, you bastard. A motive for murder: money.

Now what about opportunity?

"Mr. Norman, what did you do after your wife left for her dinner party on Saturday? Did you stay home?"

"Hell, no."

"Where did you go?"

"Out for drinks. I met some friends at the country club and

we—"

"Would you tell me the names of your friends?"

"I don't remember."

"Just one name would be fine. Anyone who can confirm he saw you at the club."

"Can't think of any names," Norman said.

"How long did you remain at the country club?"

"Two hours, maybe three."

"Then where did you go?"

"Couple of bars."

"Which ones?"

"Logan's over on Fourth Street."

"Do you remember what time?"

"Must have been around midnight."

"What time did you leave there?"

"When they closed."

"Two AM?"

"Yeah."

"Then where did you go?"

"Home."

"Was your wife here when you got home?"

"I already tol' ya. She never came home from that damn party."

"Which party was that?"

"The artsy-fartsy shindig for the museum."

"Do you know where that party was held?"

"I can't remember names. Some bigwigs on the museum board. It was at their house over on Riverside Lane."

"Do you know what time she left the party?"

"You trying to trick me?" Norman asked, his eyes narrowing to slits. "I already tol' ya she never came home from that damn party. How the hell should I know what time she left there?"

"Think hard, Mr. Norman. Try to remember whose house your wife went to for dinner. It's important."

Norman took a swallow of liquor. "Gill-something."

"Can you recall the last name?"

"Hell, that *is* the last name. Gill-something-or-other."

"Gillespe?" Wesley asked, expectantly.

"Yeah. That's it. Gillespe. Mr. and Mrs. Wayne Gillespe."

Bingo! Wesley thought. He fought to control his excitement as the final pieces of the puzzle began to fit neatly together.

There wasn't any doubt anymore, was there?

Joan Norman and Wayne Gillespe, both murdered at different times on the same night. It had to be more than mere coincidence, didn't it?

Now to prove means, and he'd have Robert Norman dead to rights. Wouldn't he?

CHAPTER SEVENTEEN

Ellen was late for work on Monday morning. Danny had cried and whined, refusing to get ready for school. He'd complained about feeling sick and insisted his mother stay at home to care for him. At first, Ellen had believed the boy. Concerned that he might be suffering a relapse from Thursday night's brush with death, she checked his pulse and temperature and found them normal. His answers to questions about specific symptoms seemed too vague and elusive—one minute he said he had chills, the next minute stomach cramps, then nausea, then fever.

Her son was faking, Ellen decided. She'd spoiled him with incessant attention during the long weekend, and now he expected more of the same if he feigned illness. Once Ellen saw through his sham, she knew exactly what to do.

"You can stay home," she told her son. "But I have to go to work and earn money so we can eat. You like to eat, don't you?"

"Sometimes," Danny agreed.

"Then I've got to go to work. But I don't want to have to worry about you, Danny. Will you be okay at home all alone?"

"No," Danny said. "I need you to stay here with me."

"I'd like to, Danny, but I can't. So I'll have to lock you in your room to make sure you don't get into any trouble while I'm gone."

Danny's face turned ashen.

"Of course, if you feel well enough, you can still hurry and get dressed for school. The choice is yours, Danny. Either you go to school, or you can stay locked up in your room all day. Which will it be?"

"S-school," Danny whispered, his face still ashen.

At noon, Ellen had tried to phone Michael Thompson at Blake

Blades. Michael was out on sales calls, but his secretary offered to take another message. Ellen left her office telephone number and asked Michael to call her when he returned.

She was surprised to discover how disappointed she felt when she couldn't talk to him, surprised to learn how much she'd actually looked forward to hearing his voice. She was even more surprised that she felt excited when she thought about seeing him again.

She owed Michael an explanation for cancelling their Friday dinner-date, and that was the only reason she'd called him. Wasn't it?

And to offer a rain check for standing him up on Friday.

It was only fair, she told herself. After all, she had promised to cook him a delicious meal and she still owed him a meal. Didn't she? Of course she did! And after the meal? What then?

Ellen couldn't help but remember the thrill she'd felt the other night when there had been a man in the house—in *her* house. She remembered the warm wetness between her legs that made her want to—

Stop it!

Just thinking about it was enough to send tingles up and down her spine.

Stop thinking about it.

But she couldn't.

You're going to get yourself in trouble, Ellen.

All afternoon, as she greeted customers and performed the routine tasks she normally did every day at Evans Supply, her mind kept thinking about—

Stop it, Ellen. What's wrong with you?

Maybe nothing's wrong, she tried to tell herself. Maybe everything's right for a change. Maybe, after years of pain and hurt, I've begun to heal.

It was as if her body and mind had been chained—locked up in a prison of her own making—for seven whole years. And now, for the first time since she married Bob Norman and entered a nightmare world where pleasure was impossible, the chains were beginning to slip away.

Ellen had denied her own sexuality too long, however. And now she was confused and frightened and afraid to admit she still had feelings.

She'd once thought that Bob had beaten those feelings out of her entirely, scarred her badly enough that she'd never want to have intimacy with a man ever again. Intimacy required a certain amount of vulnerability, and Ellen couldn't allow herself to be vulnerable.

Not with a son to think about.

But it was precisely because she did have a son to think about—a son who needed a man around to teach him things a mother couldn't— that Ellen had to let down the defensive barriers she'd erected against Bob, and take a risk.

Don't lie to yourself, Ellen.

I'm not lying, she told herself. Danny needs a father, doesn't he? He needs someone to teach him discipline, someone who won't give in to his demands every time he cries, someone who—

Who doesn't let him win at checkers?

That, too.

Then why are you thinking of Michael Thompson? Why not think about Tom Wesley instead?

The answer was obvious to Ellen, but she didn't want to admit it—even to herself.

Michael Thompson had already shown his interest in Ellen. He'd wined her and dined her, and he'd touched her in ways she hadn't been touched in years. Michael had made her feel like a woman again—a *complete* woman. Michael had reawakened long-dormant sexual feelings that made Ellen want to be more than merely a mother. She wanted to be a lover, too. Michael Thompson left no doubt in Ellen's mind that he wanted *her*, and that excited her and made her want *him*.

Tom Wesley, however, hadn't shown even a passing interest. The cop seemed more infatuated with Danny than he was with Danny's mother. Why should she waste her time pursuing a man like that when Michael seemed like a sure catch?

Because you're attracted to Tom Wesley, that's why.

No more than I'm attracted to Michael, Ellen argued.

Then, shortly before five, while Ellen was cleaning off her desk to go home, Michael Thompson telephoned, and Ellen immediately forgot that Tom Wesley even existed.

Wesley felt his tight control slipping. Up until now, he'd managed— rather successfully, he thought—to mask his own emotions from the suspect. But now that he knew beyond a reasonable doubt that Norman was guilty, Wesley wanted to throw out the final bait, hook the bastard, and reel him in.

"Mr. Norman, you didn't seem the least bit upset when I told you your wife had died. If I'd just heard that my wife had been murdered, I'd be real upset. But you didn't even blink an eye, did you?"

Norman took a quick sip of bourbon. "It helps to be drunk," he said. "Can't feel a thing when you're drunk."

"I find that difficult to believe, Mr. Norman."

"I don't give a shit what you believe."

"Maybe you should, Mr. Norman. Your wife was killed with a knife from a Blake Blades Best Cutlery set. Do you own a Blake Blades Best Cutlery set, Mr. Norman?"

Norman's eyes narrowed to slits. If looks could kill, Wesley was a dead man.

"Get out of here," Norman said. "Get the fuck out of my living room. Get the fuck out of this whole damn building."

"Answer my question. Do you own a set of Blake Blades?"

"Get out of here or I'll throw you out," Norman threatened, clenching his fists.

"Know what I think, Norman? I think you do own a set of Blake Cutlery. Know what else? I think you killed your wife with a Blake knife, and I'm going to come back with a search warrant and nail you for it. I'm going to see you fry in the electric chair, you sick bastard. And when you fry, I can guarantee you won't be drunk—you'll be able to feel every single volt that shoots through your body."

Without warning, Norman's fist lashed out at Wesley's face and connected with the policeman's jaw. The impact knocked Wesley to the floor. Before he could recover his senses, the pointed toe of Norman's imported-leather loafer slammed into Wesley's ribs with the same force a football player would use to kick a field goal.

Realizing that Norman was fifty pounds heavier and several inches taller, Wesley knew Norman could kill him with one well-placed kick. Purely in self-defense, Wesley reached for his gun, but Norman kicked the .357 Magnum from Wesley's hand.

Disarmed, his mouth bleeding and his ribs on fire, Wesley waited for the next kick. If he was going to die, at least he'd die happy, because he'd now proven beyond a shadow of a doubt that Robert Norman was capable of violent assault—and, most likely, cold-blooded murder too.

Michael smiled as he hung up the phone. Ellen's explanation that her son had been ill came as a welcome relief. It was proof that the jinx was indeed responsible for making her cancel that date and why she'd rejected him on Friday. But now that the jinx was gone and Michael was back in control again, his luck had returned too, and Ellen had invited him to dinner tomorrow night. Perfect. Everything was back on track again, wasn't it? Ahead of track, even. With Gillespe out of the way, Michael was sure to become the next president of Blake Blades.

He hadn't planned to get rid of Gillespe on Saturday. It was one of those random things that happened when the other Michael was in charge—the other Michael who never planned anything. But the real Michael always saw what the other Michael did as an opportunity that could be turned to his own advantage once the jinx was gone.

Tomorrow night Michael would seduce Ellen Lester. He'd play with her like a toy, manipulate her until he got what he wanted. And then, when he'd used her up and grew tired of playing with a broken toy, he'd simply discard her—unless the other Michael interfered, and killed her.

Michael smiled. He was still smiling when Bill Blake telephoned to tell Michael the bad news: Blake was naming someone else to replace Gillespe as president of the company. Michael Thompson, it seemed, was out of luck.

Adrenaline pumped through Wesley's body. He made his move with lightning-like speed.

As Norman's next kick came straight for the cop's midsection, Wesley's hands snaked out and grabbed the leather-sheathed foot like a halfback receiving a lateral pass during the final quarter of the Super Bowl.

Wesley twisted the foot counterclockwise, and Norman fell to the floor.

Both men scrambled to get up. Norman, surprised by the sudden turn of events, seemed slow to recover. Wesley got to his feet first, slammed a fist into the man's beer belly, and knocked Norman back to the floor with a quick knee to the groin.

Where the hell did that damned gun go?

Wesley's eyes scanned the living room carpet for his Magnum. Had it slid under a sofa? A chair? Behind the bar?

Suddenly something plowed into his side with the force of a ten-ton truck.

"You sonabitch!" Norman screamed in rage. "I'll kill you with my bare hands!"

Wesley was thrown backward, the momentum of Norman's flying tackle sending both men hurtling hallway across the room. Wesley landed flat on his back with Norman's weight on top of him.

Off to the right, just beyond reach of his fingertips, Wesley saw the blue steel of his Magnum on the mauve carpet. Norman saw it too.

As Norman went for the revolver, the weight that kept Wesley pinned to the floor shifted its center of balance, and Wesley reached up with his free hand and grabbed the collar of Norman's polo shirt, and yanked.

What little balance Norman had was used against him. Wesley rolled quickly to the right, tugging on the shirt with all his might, utilizing the slight difference in height and weight to his own advantage. Norman fought to regain his balance and stay on top, but it was already too late. Wesley rolled out from under his adversary and leapt away. Norman, his reactions slowed by alcohol, tried to reach for the gun, but Wesley was faster.

Driving across town during the height of rush hour traffic in a blinding rain took four times longer than Johnson had expected. Though the wipers in his personal car worked much better than those in the squadrol, he still couldn't see five feet beyond the windshield.

Trying to maneuver through traffic without aid of siren or MARS lights seemed a nightmarish impossibility in this weather. He didn't even try.

He pulled up in front of the Tower, parked in a no-parking zone next to the entrance, and hurried inside. According to the directory in the lobby, Robert Norman lived on the top floor. Johnson caught an elevator, punched "Penthouse," and prayed he'd be in time to keep Wesley from making a mistake. As soon as the doors hissed open on the top floor, Johnson heard the sounds of a nasty fight coming from the open door at the end of the hall. Johnson ran.

Wesley's fingers tightened around gunmetal, his thumb drawing the hammer back—*click CLICK!*—to full cock. It was time to put an end to the nightmare once and for all.

Wesley had never shot a man before, not even in self-defense, but he'd seen his share of gunshot victims, and he knew what a .357 dum-dum could do at close range. It wasn't a pretty sight.

He thought about the women victims of the Mad Slasher. They weren't a pretty sight either, were they? Certainly not the way they'd been cut up. Norman deserved what he was going to get. In fact, it was better than the bastard deserved. Wesley's finger tightened on the trigger.

"Don't!" cried a voice from the doorway. *"Don't do it, Lieutenant!"*

Johnson, rain dripping from his wet-weather gear to the wool carpet, stood in the doorway with his service revolver drawn. The kid looked scared.

"I don't want to shoot you, Lieutenant," he said. "Put the gun away."

Wesley looked at the kid, then at Norman, then at the kid again.

"I mean it, Lieutenant."

"He's the Slasher," Wesley tried to say, but his mouth was full of blood. Norman must have knocked a tooth loose.

"Then cuff him, Lieutenant. Put the gun down and cuff him."

Wesley wavered.

Norman, looking scared, didn't make a move. If he had, Wesley would have squeezed the trigger without another thought.

"Lieutenant?"

Wesley lowered the gun.

"Did you read him his rights, Lieutenant?"

"No," Wesley mumbled, sounding foolish with his mouth full of blood. He slipped the Magnum into its holster and quickly pulled a pair of handcuffs from his belt.

"Mr. Norman," he said, enunciating carefully as he slapped the cuffs on Norman's wrists, "you're under arrest for the murder of your wife and six other victims."

Then he pulled a Miranda card from his pocket and read it, word for word, aloud.

CHAPTER EIGHTEEN

Michael knew he should leave well enough alone, but he couldn't help himself. He stormed into Blake's office and demanded to know why Blake had picked someone else to replace Gillespe.

"I need you in sales," Blake answered. "Company presidents are a dime a dozen, but good salesmen are worth their weight in gold."

That answer didn't satisfy him. The old fool tried to be patronizing, but Michael wasn't about to buy it. "I deserve to be president," he said flatly.

"Someday you will be," Blake said, smiling. "But right now I need you—the company needs you—in sales."

"I'll quit. I'll go somewhere else. How would you like it if I sold for your competition?"

The smile faded from Blake's face.

"I mean it," Michael said.

"I don't think so," Blake said, caution creeping into his voice. An expression Michael couldn't easily recognize replaced the lost smile on Blake's face.

"I can get a job anywhere," Michael said. "If you think I'm worried about a bad reference from Blake Blades, forget it. References don't mean diddly in sales."

"You're right, of course. A salesman who can produce doesn't need references."

"So what makes you think I won't leave?"

"If you do," Blake said, his voice cold, "I'll tell the police about you."

Michael tried to mask his shock. Did Blake know? Impossible!

Blake smiled. "I don't want to lose the best salesman this company's ever had," he said. "Remain here as my Vice President of

Sales, Michael. If you do, I'll keep my mouth shut."

Michael searched Blake's eyes for any hint of bluff. He decided Blake wasn't bluffing.

"And if I leave?"

"Then I'll have to go to the police. I don't want you working for the competition."

"Are you trying to blackmail me? Me?" Michael asked astonished. "With what?"

"You know with what, Michael. Do I have to say it? What if someone overheard?"

"It's after five. Your secretary has left along with everyone else in the office. You and I are all alone, Blake."

Michael saw fear suddenly flash in Blake's eyes as the realization they were all alone hit home. Blake knew Michael was a killer alright, Michael thought. Otherwise he wouldn't be worried about being alone with a disgruntled employee.

Not unless he knew that employee was the Slasher.

"What made you suspect?" Michael asked. He made his voice sound soft, honestly inquisitive, nonthreatening.

Blake didn't answer.

"Was it the cop? Was it something Lieutenant Wesley said when he was here? What tipped you off?"

Blake's eyes glanced furtively around the room.

"You aren't thinking about making a run for it, are you? You'll never get by me, Bill. Forget about the door and answer my question."

Michael watched Blake accurately assess the situation. He could almost hear the cogs turning in Blake's brain. Calculating. Evaluating. Deciding.

"Sunday's newspaper," Blake said at last, hoping to buy time through conversation. "The headline said Gillespe was slain by the Slasher. I—I'd already guessed you'd killed Gillespe to get the presidency. But when I saw that newspaper headline, everything suddenly made sense. You used Blake Blades sales samples to kill those poor girls, didn't you? You are the Slasher, aren't you? Oh God, Michael. Why'd you do it? *Why?*"

"You didn't go to the police?" Michael asked, avoiding Blake's question.

"No, of course not. You're the best salesman this company has ever had, Michael. If I went to the police, I'd lose you."

"You thought you could blackmail me, didn't you? That's really why you didn't tell the cops, isn't it? Be honest, Bill."

"No, Michael." Blake was flustered now, fishing for lies. "I only said I'd go to the police to keep you from leaving. I'd never turn you in, Michael. *Never.*"

"How can I trust you, Bill? How can I be sure you won't tell the police?" Michael opened his sample case and selected a nine-inch carving knife.

"I'll make you president of the company, Michael. I'll make you Chairman of the Board, if you want. Let's talk this over like sensible men. Okay? Don't be foolish. Michael? Michael! Put that knife down, Michael. I promise I won't tell. *You've got to believe me, Michael!*"

But Michael—the Michael that Blake had known before, the real Michael, the rational Michael—wasn't there anymore. In his place was another Michael, and in this other Michael's eyes Bill Blake saw madness. It was the last thing Blake saw before he died.

Robert Norman was questioned by the state's attorney for more than three hours before Norman's lawyer, a high-priced mouthpiece associated with Arthur Godwin's law firm, convinced the politician there was no solid evidence of Norman's guilt. If the state's attorney attempted to try Robert Norman for Mrs. Norman's murder, he'd surely lose the case.

"My client is a law-abiding pillar of the community," the lawyer argued. "Overcome with grief at the news of his wife's brutal slaying, Robert Norman—understandably—drank too much. Is that a crime? No, gentlemen, it isn't."

Then the lawyer went on to show that Lieutenant Wesley had violated Norman's constitutional rights by questioning Norman without benefit of counsel, had deliberately picked a fight with the grief-stricken man, had drawn his gun and tried to shoot the unarmed man—in Norman's own home, a home the lawman had entered illegally without a search warrant or an arrest warrant— and Norman obviously had no choice but to defend himself. This was a clear-cut case of police brutality, the lawyer claimed. And Robert Norman was as much an innocent victim of an overzealous and overworked police officer as his lovely wife had been an innocent victim of the Mad Slasher. It was ludicrous to believe, the lawyer argued, that Robert Norman was the Mad Slasher of Willow Woods. It was a waste of the taxpayers' time and money to pursue such an idea, and the state's attorney would look like a fool if this case ever came to court.

And, unless Lieutenant Wesley ceased harassing Mr. Norman, the lawyer promised to sue the Willow Woods Police Department, the state's attorney's office, and anyone else, including Tom Wesley, connected with the case. A fifty-million-dollar personal injury suit wouldn't begin to compensate Robert Norman for damages to his impeccable reputation, but it might make public officials think twice before harassing other private citizens who'd done no wrong.

"I should have shot the sonofabitch when I had the chance," Wesley raged after the district attorney dropped all charges against Robert Norman. "He's guilty as sin and he isn't going to get away with it. Somebody's got to stop him, Lenny."

"The judge refused to issue a search warrant for Norman's condo?"

"The judge wouldn't even consider it."

"Why not?"

"Insufficient probable cause. Norman tried to kill me, Lenny. And the judge says there's no probable cause to issue a search warrant."

"Norman claimed you tried to kill him first, and he was only trying to defend himself. I guess the judge believed him and not you."

"You don't believe me, either?"

"It doesn't matter who or what I believe, Lieutenant. What matters is who the judge believes."

"Damn politicians," Wesley mumbled, and stomped angrily down the courthouse steps and disappeared in the rain before Johnson could stop him.

Wesley spent the night in the park across the street from Willow Tower. Intermittent rain showers made the night miserable. Wesley moved a wet wooden bench into position, laid down on the bench, and kept a low profile, but he didn't sleep. He had a perfect view of Norman's condominium. If Norman went out anytime during the night, Wesley would be sure to see him, and then he'd follow the bastard, and nail him in the act.

Wesley's body ached all over, and the rain only made the aches and pains worse. His head throbbed. His lips were swollen. His lower lip had been split wide open, and he still tasted the coppery taste of blood when he touched his lips with his tongue. Norman had knocked two of his teeth loose, and another tooth was cracked. His whole mouth hurt like a sonofabitch. His muscles, unused to the work he'd put them to today, cramped and spasmed continually.

As bad as Wesley felt, he did feel good about one thing: Norman had to be feeling almost as bad.

Wesley remembered the look on Norman's face when he'd sunk his fist in the man's belly, then followed up with a knee to the crotch. That look alone made these pains seem worthwhile.

Wesley lit a cigarette and winced. The filter stuck to dried blood on his lips. It hurt when he tried to pry the cigarette free. The night passed slowly.

Thank God for sunshine, Johnson nearly said aloud. Tuesday turned out to be a beautiful day, weather-wise at least. Traffic flowed freely on surrounding expressways and on all the main arterial streets through the heart of town, and Johnson didn't have to investigate a single accident the entire morning.

Last night, after leaving the courthouse, Lenny had telephoned Suzi and asked her out for a cup of coffee. She told him she was already in bed and didn't want to get dressed again. But she offered to make him a cup of instant if he wanted to come over. Fifteen minutes later, he was sitting in Suzi's kitchen drinking instant coffee and unburdening his soul to a sympathetic ear.

"Wesley's gone off the deep end, and I don't know what I can do to help him. Tonight he tried to kill your former brother-in-law."

"Beautiful Bob? Why?"

"He thinks Norman is the Mad Slasher."

"Oh, Christ!"

"Could he be? You had a chance to observe him when he was married to your sister. What was Norman like back then?"

"Charming when sober. He conned Ellen into marrying him, really hooked her with his good looks and the way he treated her. He sent her flowers, took her dancing, made her feel like a queen.

But then, after they were married, he changed."

"Oh? How?"

"Bob started drinking. I suppose he'd been drinking just as much before they were married, but Ellen had never seen him drunk. When drunk he wasn't the same person that he was when sober. Instead of being charming, Bob turned rude and crude, mean and nasty. A big bully. He beat her up really bad a few times. Then he started playing around behind her back when Ellen got pregnant and she wouldn't let him touch her."

"Playing around behind her back?"

"Going out with other women. She was glad, actually, that he didn't stay home anymore. When he was home, he tried to hit her. I think he wanted her to lose the baby."

"Didn't he need to work? Didn't he have a job?"

"Beautiful Bob? Don't make me laugh. He was always too hungover to hold down a job for longer than a month. He got fired from every job he'd had, and finally no one would hire him."

"Then how'd he support himself?"

"Ellen supported him."

"She worked and he didn't?"

"When Mom died, Ellen and I became beneficiaries of a hundred-thousand-dollar insurance policy. I used my half to pay for college. Ellen gave her half to Beautiful Bob, and he spent most of it on booze."

"And that's why she left him?"

"Oh, no. Sis didn't leave him—he left her. You see, Ellen's sort of old-fashioned. She believed—still believes, I think—that marriage is supposed to be for life. Till death do you part and that sort of thing. If Bob hadn't filed for divorce, they'd probably still be married. Or maybe they would have killed each other by now, I don't know. Anyway, Ellen's money ran out, and Bob decided to take a hike."

"Not Mr. Nice Guy, is he?"

"Uh uh. But I don't think Bob could be the Slasher."

"Oh? Why not?"

"It just isn't his style. He's scared to death of knives."

Suzi had gone on to explain that Ellen once threatened Norman's manhood with a butcher knife, and Norman had backed off instantly.

"Any man would," Lenny had confided. "That doesn't mean he's afraid of knives. If you promised to tickle my balls with a butcher knife, it'd scare the hell out of me, too. I'd probably stay away from *you* after that, but I doubt if it'd make me afraid to use a knife myself."

"Should I get a knife and see what happens?" Suzi offered playfully, touching Lenny's lap with her fingertips. "Or would you rather I used something else to tickle your manhood?"

"Like what?" Lenny had asked.

"I'm open to suggestions," Suzi had said, opening his fly and slipping her hand inside.

Last night had been wonderful and this morning was wonderful, and Lenny was in love. Maybe not in love, he corrected, but definitely in lust.

And tonight he'd be seeing her again. Susan had invited him to dinner at her apartment.

"I hope you like microwaved pizza," she'd said, apologetically. "I'm a lousy cook, but I make a mean pizza in a microwave."

Lenny glanced at his watch. Thinking about food made him hungry, and he hadn't had time for breakfast before roll call at five forty-five. It was almost nine now, and the streets were quiet. He could afford to take a break.

His favorite restaurant was a small dinette, a greasy spoon with the best eggs in town, located just past the park. Since it was part of his regular patrol route, he drove slowly around the park on his way to the restaurant.

Twice now, the Slasher had dumped bodies in the park and Lenny kept his eyes peeled, just in case. He wasn't expecting to find another dead body—the Slasher would have to be stupid to do it again—but there was always the chance. He cruised slowly past the entrance, past the bushes, past the trash cans.

There! On one of the benches. Was that another body? Probably just a wino sleeping off an all-night drunk, but he couldn't tell for sure, not from the street. Johnson circled around the park. As he passed the bench a second time, he decided to stop.

Better check it out, he told himself. *Just in case.*

The body on the bench still hadn't moved. Was it a woman? A man? Stretched out on the bench, facing the opposite direction and partially obscured by trees, it was impossible to tell.

Johnson radioed his location to dispatch, got out of the car, and slowly approached the bench. He breathed a sigh of relief when he saw clearly that it was a man, not a woman—and then he recognized the suit. And, at the same time, he saw Norman's apartment across the street.

"Oh, shit!" Johnson said, reaching for his holstered weapon.

He couldn't miss. Even from this distance, from this angle, a .357 Magnum would penetrate the window and hit the target easily. All night Wesley had watched that top-floor window. And now, finally, Robert Norman stood directly in front of the window, making an excellent target. Several times in the last five minutes Norman had passed the window, but he hadn't stopped to look out. Wesley had waited for the perfect opportunity at a clear shot before firing. It'd be so easy to pull the trigger.

Wesley had come here last night to catch Norman in the act—to follow the monster as he stalked a potential victim or follow him to a dumpster as he tried to get rid of a Blake Blades Best Cutlery set in the trash, but Norman hadn't left his apartment all night. Did that mean Norman was innocent? Could the Slasher be somebody else?

Wesley wasn't certain anymore. Yesterday, he'd been so sure of Norman's guilt that he would have pulled the trigger without thinking twice, but today he couldn't do it.

Wesley's thumb eased back on the hammer. He lowered the muzzle and started to put the gun away. "Oh, shit!" someone said behind him.

Wesley rolled from the bench, his adrenaline kicking in as he brought the muzzle around. Fortunately, he'd been trained to hold fire until he could positively ID his target.

"Mexican standoff," he mumbled, lowering his weapon as he recognized the man in uniform. "How'd you know I was here, Lenny?"

"I didn't," Johnson answered. He kept his gun trained on Wesley's chest. "Are you crazy, Lieutenant?"

"I was, but I'm not now." Wesley slid the Magnum into its holster and locked the safety strap. "Put the gun away, Lenny, and I'll buy you a cup of coffee."

"You were going to shoot Robert Norman, weren't you? You wanted to kill him!"

"I couldn't do it, Lenny. Not in cold blood, anyway."

Johnson looked at Wesley's bloodshot eyes. "I'm going to report you to the chief, Lieutenant. You're not fit for duty anymore. You shouldn't be allowed to carry a gun."

"I won't fight you kid," Wesley said. He unbuckled his belt and removed his holstered weapon. "You want this?" he offered.

"Place it on the bench and back away."

Wesley did.

Johnson pocketed the piece, then holstered his own. "Okay, Lieutenant," he said. "First, you owe me a cup of coffee. Then I'll take you in."

Wesley smiled. It made his lips hurt to smile, but he smiled anyway.

"You driving?" he asked.

"Yeah," Lenny said, returning Wesley's smile.

"Then lead the way, Officer Johnson. And when we get to the car, don't forget to radio in that we're going on break."

"You going to bust me if I don't, Lieutenant?"

Wesley laughed. He hadn't laughed in a long time. It surprised him to discover how much it hurt to laugh, and how much more it hurt when he didn't.

CHAPTER NINETEEN

Johnson took the call on the way to the restaurant. All available cars were being dispatched to the Blake Blades corporate headquarters building on the outskirts of town. There had been another murder at Blake Blades, the dispatcher said. This time the victim was Bill Blake.

Wesley was surprised when Johnson asked him to ride with him to the scene, but he was even more surprised when Lenny handed him his gun back.

"You okay?" the kid asked.

"I could use some sleep, a change of clothes, a quick shower and shave. Other than that, I'm not sure," Wesley mumbled as he slid the holster onto his belt where it belonged. He'd felt, curiously, naked without it.

"You look like shit."

"I feel like shit."

Finally the kid asked the big question: "Why didn't you shoot Norman when you had the chance, Lieutenant? You could have killed him, but you didn't. Why not?"

"I'm a cop," Wesley mumbled. He didn't know what else to say.

"Yeah," Lenny agreed, sounding somehow completely satisfied with Wesley's answer.

"That why you gave me the Magnum back?"

"You offered me a second chance when I was the one who fucked up, Lieutenant. Today you gave Norman a second chance, didn't you? I thought maybe you deserved a second chance, too."

"Thanks, kid."

"I'm not a kid, Lieutenant."

Wesley laughed. "No," he said. "You're not a kid anymore. You're a cop—a real cop—a grownup cop."

The parking lot at Blake Blades looked full of cars. At nine-fifteen on a weekday, twelve hundred employees were already hard at work. The manufacturing complex literally hummed with activity.

Wesley noticed two state police cars parked at the main entrance. An unmarked state car and a Mercedes Benz bearing the name "Godwin" on its plates were parked in reserved visitor's stalls next to the two police cars.

Wesley directed Lenny to pull up behind the Mercedes and park there, deliberately blocking Godwin's exit route. Wesley then keyed the mike and radioed the dispatcher to report their arrival at the crime scene. "The state boys beat us here," he added. "Who called them out on a local?"

"They're taking jurisdiction," the dispatcher responded. "You're supposed to be their backup, Lieutenant. See a man named Godwin. He's in charge."

"Oh, Christ!"

"It just came down the pipe," the dispatcher said. "Governor's order."

"The chief okayed it?"

"The mayor did."

Wesley slammed the mike down without acknowledging the governor's order. He hated politicians with a passion.

Sally Foster, Michael Thompson's secretary, couldn't stop crying.

First Mr. Gillespe and now Mr. Blake. It was terrible—too terrible to think about. Who would be next? Mr. Thompson? No. Not Mr. Thompson. Sally wouldn't let anything bad happen to *him*. Never ever! Though Michael had shown no personal interest in his secretary, Sally was completely enamored of her boss. He was rich, good-looking, and the same age as she. How could she help but feel the way she did?

When he first came to the company as a field rep, Sally was one of six secretaries in the sales department, and her job—taking messages and confirming appointments for on-the-road salespeople—was a boring, thankless task. She hated each and every day she had to work.

Then, one day, she'd found a bouquet of flowers on her desk.

There was a card, too. A simple thank-you note from Michael Thompson. "For your efficiency," the card had said.

Other secretaries received flowers from Michael only occasionally, but Sally received them regularly. She began to go out of her way to do things for him—little things that weren't part of the job and that she'd never think of doing for anyone else—because he appreciated her efforts.

She suddenly discovered how much she looked forward to each day at work. Some days it was flowers that awaited her arrival. Other days boxes of chocolates. Almost always there was something waiting on her desk when she arrived at work. And she loved it!

And then, when Michael became District Sales Manager and acquired a secretary of his own, he'd specifically requested Sally Foster by name.

Michael proved to be a demanding boss, driving Sally almost as hard as he drove himself. But all that hard work and extra effort eventually produced really spectacular results. Sally was happy to have helped.

Sales increased two hundred percent in Michael's district the first month he was manager. Profits rose accordingly, and Sally received a decent bonus at Christmastime and a more-than-handsome raise when she passed her next annual review.

All this simply contributed to Sally's fierce loyalty to Michael Thompson. She was willing to do anything the man asked without question, without hesitation—anything. But Michael had never asked her to do what she most wanted to do for him. And now it looked as if he never would.

She should have guessed Michael would someday have a girlfriend. But he'd always seemed far too busy, too wrapped up in his work, to have time for an active love life.

Then, last week, Michael had asked Sally to make dinner reservations for two at an expensive restaurant.

On Friday, a woman named Ellen Lester had telephoned to cancel a dinner date with Michael. And Sally knew, from the way Michael had seemed so upset, that Ellen Lester was the one, the one Michael preferred. Sally was heartbroken.

Yesterday, the Lester bitch had called again. And as soon as Michael got the message, he called her back, ahead of all other calls—even the call from Mr. Blake.

That Michael had sent Sally home early on Friday and again yesterday, only served to confirm her suspicions. And this morning, despite the terrible news of Mr. Blake's murder, Michael didn't seem at all upset. In fact, he seemed happy! It had to be because of that Lester bitch, didn't it?

Sally concluded correctly, but for all the wrong reasons, that Michael must have another date with Ellen Lester scheduled for some time this evening, and that was why Sally Foster couldn't stop crying.

Blake's office was full of people. Any shred of evidence the killer might have left behind was already contaminated.

Wesley recognized Sheila Meyers, the TV reporter, interviewing Arthur Godwin in front of a minicam. Blake's bloody body was in the background, clearly visible for maximum impact on the television audience. It was almost enough to make Wesley sick.

Then he got a whiff of the dead man's odor, and he really was sick. Bile rose in his throat as he looked around for a nearby men's room. He didn't quite make it in time.

When a man dies, every muscle in his body—including the bladder and sphincter—simply lets go. Even the muscles that control eyelids and eyeballs. Without some kind of control by the brain, human muscles cease to function completely—until rigor mortis sets in, and then they stiffen up. But immediately after death, every muscle in the human body loosens. The eyelids pop open, the eyeballs roll up, the arms and legs collapse, and the bladder and bowels secrete.

In the enclosed confines of Bill Blake's office, the smell of day-old defecate was overpowering, nauseating.

Fortunately, Wesley hadn't eaten in three days. All that came out of his gaping mouth was a handful of spittle.

"Can't stand the heat, stay out of the kitchen," a state trooper quipped. Another trooper roared with laughter.

Wesley pulled a wrinkled handkerchief from his pocket and wiped his mouth and hands.

"Who found the body?" Wesley asked the troopers.

"You a reporter?"

Wesley showed them his ID.

"Blake's secretary," one of the troopers said.

"What time was that?"

"Eight-thirty, I think." He looked at the other trooper for confirmation.

"Yeah. Eight-thirty."

"They had to take her to the hospital," the other trooper said. "She couldn't stop screaming."

"Who reported the homicide?"

"How the hell do we know? One of the other employees, I guess."

Wesley's mouth was dry and his teeth hurt, but he continued to ask questions until he got answers.

At ten o'clock, the coroner arrived. It was the first time Wesley had ever seen the county coroner himself visit a crime scene. Deputy Coroner Frank Monroe examined the body while the coroner posed for pictures from the press.

Wesley watched Monroe make a preliminary examination. Then, after chalking the body's outline on the floor and taking pictures, the doctor bagged Blake's hands separately before placing Blake's entire body into a plastic body bag.

"Finished, Doc?" one of the troopers asked.

"Done all I can here," Doc said. "After you deliver the body to the morgue, I'll do a complete post mortem."

Wesley followed Monroe from the office.

"You look awful, Tom," Monroe said when he saw Wesley. "Go home and get some sleep."

"What'd you find out, Doc?"

"Stabbed. Looks like the Slasher's work. One stab wound, and two Xs cut deep into the chest. Blake's been dead for twelve to fifteen hours, but no one reported the body until about an hour ago. Can't tell too much until I take the body apart."

"Give me a full report when you're through?"

"You'll have to wait this time, Tom. I can't release anything until the coroner signs off on the official report."

"Since when?"

"Since you raised that stink last night with Norman. The DA wants everything routed through state and county before you get to see it. Looks like they want to shut you out, Tom."

"They took jurisdiction, Frank. Governor's edict."

"Then the burden's off your shoulders, Tom. It's their responsibility now. Why don't you go home and get some shut-eye?"

"Maybe I will."

"Want a lift home? My car's right outside."

Wesley looked back at the crowd of politicians, state troopers, reporters, and curious factory employees. He didn't see Johnson anywhere.

"Take me home, Doc," he said with a sigh. "I think it's high time I caught up on my sleep."

Johnson, because he was the only Willow Woods officer in uniform, found himself cornered by reporters demanding a statement.

"Why did the Slasher, who normally attacks women, kill Blake and Gillespe?" an insistent reporter inquired.

"Blake and Gillespe worked for the same company. What's the connection?" another asked.

"I'm just a beat cop," Johnson told them. "Why don't you ask one of the state troopers?"

"They won't tell us anything," said Sheila Meyers. "Where's your lieutenant... what's his name?"

"Wesley," one of the other reporters said.

"Yeah, Wesley. Where is he?"

"He's around," Johnson said.

But, no matter where he turned, Wesley was nowhere in sight.

"Where'd he go?" Sheila Meyers asked again later. "I can't find your lieutenant anywhere."

Sometime shortly after twelve-thirty, Blake's body was removed and the office sealed. Most of the reporters had already left by that time, and so had the politicians.

Art Godwin, however, couldn't go anywhere until Johnson moved his vehicle. Finally, Godwin sent a trooper to find the Willow Woods cop and order him to move his goddamn patrol car.

"Better move it," the trooper suggested. "You don't want to fuck with a man who tells the governor when to wipe his ass and when to drip dry."

"I'm waiting for my partner," Johnson said. "Soon as he shows up, we'll move it."

"I don't think you heard me, boy," the trooper said.

"I heard you, Smokey."

"You got a burr up your butt about somethin'?"

"Yeah. I can't find my partner."

"What's he look like? Maybe I've seen him."

Johnson described Wesley's wrinkled suit.

"Puke-face is your partner?"

"Huh?"

"Puke-face. Guy who threw up when he saw the stiff in there. Wrinkled suit, right? Looks like death warmed-over? Red eyes, hasn't shaved, needs a bath real bad?"

"You seen him?"

"Not since this morning. You sure he's still around?"

"Help me look for him. If we don't find him in five minutes, I'll go move the car."

After five minutes of scouring the halls and offices of Blake Blades, Johnson agreed that Wesley was nowhere around.

He went outside and moved the car before Godwin had a goddamn shit hemorrhage.

CHAPTER TWENTY

Wesley tried to sleep but his mind wouldn't let him. Obviously, Norman couldn't be the killer because Wesley had watched the man constantly for fifteen hours—during which time Blake had died at the hands of the Slasher.

If Norman wasn't the killer, then who was? Wesley still had the feeling that he'd missed something important. It gnawed at the back of his mind like a squirrel gnawing insulation from electrical wires up in the attic of an old house. Sooner or later it would gnaw through the insulation and start a fire.

Wesley knew he was close to an answer. Though Robert Norman had somehow managed to sidetrack him, Wesley felt it was only because he'd previously overlooked something he should have seen. Maybe it was time to go back to the beginning and start over from scratch.

Wesley got out of bed and took a long and leisurely shower. Now that the pressure was off, he found that he was thinking like a cop again, and he did a lot of thinking. While hot water pelted his aching body, his mind was busy reviewing everything that had happened up until now.

Elizabeth May Singer. Start with her.

He went through the list of victims twice, examining every detail he could remember. Then he started over again, beginning with Elizabeth May Singer, a third time.

But maybe it started before her, his mind suddenly said. *Maybe she wasn't the first. What if there were others elsewhere? Before the killer came to Willow Woods? Bingo!*

Wesley turned off the water and toweled himself dry. Though he nicked himself twice while shaving, it didn't hurt the way it usually did when the razor sliced his skin.

By the time he'd finished dressing, both cuts had stopped bleeding.

He telephoned for a taxi. Ten minutes later, Wesley was in his office going through the envelopes he'd stacked in the corner behind his desk.

Johnson found Wesley in the office, going through autopsy reports from other states.

"So this is where you disappeared to," he said. "Thanks for telling me you were leaving."

"I'm sorry. Doc gave me a ride home," Wesley apologized, looking up from his reports. "But I couldn't sleep. I think I'm onto something here, Lenny. Give me a hand, will you?"

"I'm off duty, Lieutenant."

Wesley looked disappointed.

"I've got a date," Johnson explained. "Otherwise I'd stay and help."

"I understand, kid," Wesley said.

"I don't think you do, Lieutenant."

"Look, Lenny. You did me a favor today and I'm grateful. If I'd followed your advice in the beginning and invited Ellen along on a double date with you and Ellen's sister, maybe I wouldn't have gone off the deep end the way I did."

Lenny couldn't believe his ears.

"You mean that, Lieutenant?" he said.

"With all my heart."

"Uh, Lieutenant," Johnson said, feeling suddenly generous. "Listen, why don't you join us for dinner? You look like you could use a break and I bet you haven't eaten today. Right?"

"No. But I don't want to intrude..."

"Don't worry about it. I'll call Suzi and see if she can get her sister to join us tonight. Danny, too. We're having beer and pizza. You like beer and pizza?"

"I like pizza."

"Okay. Coffee and pizza, then. What d'ya say?"

"Lenny, I can't."

"Sure, you can. Bring those damn reports with, if you want.

C'mon, Lieutenant. You gotta eat, don't you?"

"Better call your girlfriend first. See if it's all right with her."

"It will be, Lieutenant. I guarantee it."

Wesley looked at the stack of reports. They'd still be there tomorrow, wouldn't they? He could take a stack with him, and maybe he and Lenny would find time to read a few and discuss them before the night was through.

"Why not?" Wesley said.

"Let's go, then," said Lenny, taking a handful of envelopes to carry to the car.

Wesley grabbed a stack, too, and followed his young friend out of the office and into the parking lot.

Ellen called Suzi on the telephone before leaving work.

"I'm nervous, Sis," Ellen said. "I've planned a big meal to impress Michael, but I haven't cooked for a man in ages. What if Michael doesn't like beef stroganoff?"

"You worry too much, Big Sister."

"I just want everything to be perfect."

"You like him, don't you, Sis? I can tell. And if he likes you half as much as you like him, he won't pay any attention to the meal. You could feed him peanut butter and crackers, and he wouldn't mind a bit."

Ellen laughed. "The way to a man's heart is through his stomach, Sis. You make it sound like it's the other way around."

"If you have his heart, Big Sister, his stomach isn't important."

"That's not true."

"Sure it is, hon. Just ask Danny. That kid'll eat anything, won't he? Doesn't matter what you feed him, as long as you feed him *something*."

"But he's just a kid."

"Look. I'm having Lenny over for microwave pizza tonight. Do you think he cares that I'm a lousy cook? No. All he cares about is being invited to my place so we can be together. I could feed him mud pies and he'd still be happy. I like it like that, Sis. I don't want a man who's after my cooking. I want a man who's after my bod."

"You're terrible!"

"I am, aren't I?" She giggled.

Ellen giggled, too.

"Besides," Suzi said, "if it doesn't work out between you and Michael, there's always Tom Wesley. He likes your spaghetti."

"I think he likes my spaghetti better than me, Sis."

"Look, I gotta run. Lenny'll be over in an hour and I need to fix my hair before he gets here. Have a good time tonight, Big Sister."

"You too, Baby Sister."

Ellen left work at five, picked Danny up at the daycare center, and stopped at the grocery store on the way home.

Danny, seeming unusually cantankerous this evening, tore through the house looking for his coloring book and crayons. When he couldn't find them, he became whiny and sullen.

"Play with something else," Ellen suggested. "Or go watch television. I haven't got time to look for your coloring book, Danny. Not tonight."

"Why not?"

"I already told you we're having company tonight, didn't I? I've got things to do before the company comes."

Danny turned on the TV while Ellen checked the day's mail. There was a letter, not a bill, from the telephone company. Ellen opened it.

Service technicians have determined that the problem you recently reported is an internal problem unrelated to Bell System wiring or equipment. Please check your telephone and connecting cable yourself. If you are unable to correct the problem yourself, help is available at the nearest authorized service center during normal business hours.

Ellen sighed. She'd have to take time off work to bring the telephone in for repair. But tonight she didn't have time to think about it. She put the letter in her purse and forgot about it.

She went to the kitchen, wrapped four large potatoes in aluminum foil, put them in the oven, and left them to bake while she browned beef tips in a skillet. Then she cut up several yellow onions and set them aside for later.

Danny came into the kitchen whining that something on TV had scared him. He said there was nothing but news on all the channels, and the news about some man who'd been "Slashered." He didn't like TV when news was on. He whined that he wanted to stay in the kitchen where Mommy could protect him.

"I'll protect you if you protect me," Ellen said. "Sound fair?"

But Danny didn't seem to be listening. He was opening cabinets, pulling out boxes of cereal, and stuffing handfuls of sugary-sweet breakfast food in his mouth.

"Don't eat that now," Ellen protested. "You'll spoil your appetite."

"I'm *hungry*," Danny wailed.

"I'm fixing a good dinner tonight, Danny. I won't have you spoiling your appetite with all that junk."

Ellen tried to wrestle a big box of cereal from Danny's hands, but the boy wouldn't let go. She pulled one way while he pulled the other. Finally, the box ripped open and cereal flew everywhere.

"Danneee!" Ellen shouted.

Danny ran.

Ellen threw up her hands in frustration. Michael would be here in two hours. She looked at the mess Danny had made of the kitchen and wanted to cry. Instead of crying, however, she went to a closet and found a broom and dustpan. She had the cereal cleaned up and was putting the broom and dustpan away when she heard a noise in the living room.

"What are you into now?" she demanded, rushing to the living room to see.

Danny had dumped his toy chest out on the living room carpet. Toys, crayons, and Little Golden Books were scattered from the couch to the TV set.

"I can't find my coloring book," Danny whined.

Exasperated, Ellen yelled at the boy. "Go to your, room!" she demanded. "If you're going to make a mess, make it there where no one can see it!"

"I want my coloring book!"

Ellen took a step toward the child and he instantly raced away from her.

"You go to your room!" Ellen screamed. "Go to your room, or so help me…"

Danny ran upstairs to his room.

That was the last straw, and tears streaked Ellen's eyes. As they began to flow in earnest, she sank to her knees and sobbed quietly. Then, finally, she started to pick up each of the spilled toys from the floor and slowly replace them in the cardboard toy chest.

Danny could be such a pain sometimes, she brooded to herself. He really did need a father to teach him to behave, didn't he? Danny couldn't get away with things like that if Michael were around. Michael wouldn't let him.

The same way Bob wouldn't let him?

No, no. Bob and Michael aren't the same. Michael'd never—

Are you sure?

Of course I'm sure. Michael isn't a monster. Michael'd never hit the boy.

Wouldn't he?

Ellen's mind raced back to the last time Bob had been in this house, the last time he'd been allowed to see his son. She and Bob were legally separated at the time, but the divorce hadn't yet been finalized. Bob had legal visitation rights, but rarely used them. Then, just after Danny had turned three, Bob had insisted on giving his son a present for his birthday.

Ellen should have refused to let the man in the house when he knocked on the door at eleven o'clock at night. She should have known Bob had been out drinking, but he held his liquor so well because of his height and weight that no one knew when he was drunk or sober. Since she hadn't seen the man in more than a year, she didn't recognize the telltale signs of inebriation in his flushed face.

He'd brought a baseball as a gift, he said. Now that Danny was over his fever and was going to be a normal boy, the kid needed a baseball.

Ellen had relented and let him in. Danny was asleep, but Ellen let Bob take the baseball up to Danny's room and wake the boy from a sound sleep to hand him the present.

Why? Why did you let him do that?

I didn't know Bob would harm the boy. Honest to God, I really didn't know.

He tried to harm you, didn't he? When you were pregnant?

That was different.

Was it?

Yes. Bob didn't come here to intentionally harm his son. It was just something that happened.

An accident?

No, not an accident. But it wasn't something that Bob had planned.

Can you be sure?

Ellen tried to remember the details that she'd worked so hard to block out of her memory. Some things were too terrible to think about, and Ellen didn't like to think about that night at all.

Danny didn't want to wake up, she remembered. He opened his eyes and they shut again automatically. It was well past his bedtime and he'd been in dreamland for hours. He didn't want to come back, but Bob made him.

Bob had grabbed the boy's frail arms and clamped his fists around them until Danny screamed.

Ellen had screamed, too—screamed at Bob to let go of the boy's arms, to get the hell out of the house, to leave them alone—and Bob had swung around and hit her across the face with his fist. Not once, not twice, but repeatedly, until blood flowed from her nose and mouth, until her head throbbed like the inside of a drum, until, until she passed out from the pain.

That's what he'd come for, wasn't it? Not to hurt his son, but to hurt you?

But he'd hurt Danny, too. Danny had bruises on his arms that wouldn't go away for weeks.

What about your bruises, Ellen? How long did it take for your bruises to go away?

Ellen didn't want to think about it any more. Once again she quite effectively blocked all memory of that grotesque night from her mind, because, unfortunately, some of her own bruises had *never* gone away.

CHAPTER TWENTY-ONE

Wesley waited in the car while Lenny went home to change. Lenny had asked the lieutenant to come in and wait on the couch, but Wesley preferred to stay in the car and study unsolved homicide reports.

After quickly changing out of his uniform and into a T-shirt and jeans, Johnson called Suzi and informed her he'd be bringing a guest to dinner.

"Call your sister, why don't you?" he suggested. "Let's make it a regular party."

"Ellen's got a date tonight."

"Oh. I hope you don't mind Wesley coming over."

"Not as long as he doesn't stay all night."

"He won't."

"Good. Because I'm looking forward to taking you to bed later. I wouldn't want the lieutenant to get embarrassed when I drag you into the bedroom and make you moan."

"Keep talking like that, and I'll forget I even invited the lieutenant. I'll leave him sitting in the car all night and come over by myself in a taxi."

"You wouldn't do that to the poor man. Would you?"

"Try me."

Suzi laughed. "We'll have plenty of time later, Love, when we can be alone. Bring your friend on over and I'll throw the first pizza in the microwave as soon as you get here. There's cold beer already in the fridge."

"Put on a pot of coffee, will you? Wesley doesn't drink beer."

"Pizza and *coffee*? Ugh!"

"Ever tried it?"

"No. And I don't want to."

"Me neither. Make yourself decent, Suz. We're on our way now."

"I'm always decent," Suzi said. "But if you want me to change out of this see-through negligee I put on just for you, I will."

"See-through negligee?"

"Uh huh. Nothing underneath, either. I'll show you what it looks like after the lieutenant leaves."

"You're really wearing nothing but a see-through negligee?"

"I bought it just for you, Love. Now that I have your complete attention, I plan on keeping it."

"Suz…"

"Later, Love. I've got to go change and you need to keep your mind on the road to drive over here safely. See you in ten minutes?"

"Yeah. Ten minutes."

Suzi had changed into jeans and a short-sleeved blouse by the time they arrived, and Lenny thought she looked terrific—but he couldn't help wondering what she'd look like in a see-through negligee. It turned him on just thinking about it—and that, he eventually came to realize, was the reason why Suzi had bought the negligee in the first place.

Wesley felt like a third wheel on a bicycle. The way Lenny and the girl kept exchanging glances at each other, he knew he was interrupting important plans with his presence.

Right after dinner, he intended to call a taxi and get the hell out of their way.

Would it have been any different if Ellen had been there? he wondered. Too bad she and Danny couldn't make it.

Wesley settled down on the couch and buried his nose in the reports. It was a long shot and he knew it, but maybe something would turn up in one of the reports that would link the Slasher to an unsolved homicide elsewhere. Maybe, just maybe, some other detective had put together a list of suspects that included the name of a current Willow Woods resident.

His tired eyes scanned forty-two reports before he found one that matched the Slasher's *modus operandi*. Wesley stared unbelievingly at the autopsy photos. Then he read the autopsy report again.

Same M.O., no question.

The police investigation had been thorough, but dead-ended without any solid leads. It was one of two unsolved murders in a small California suburban community six years ago, and both cases were still active.

Remembering how Michael Thompson had used zip codes to locate sales within a wide geographic area, Wesley tried the same technique on towns in California. He sorted the envelopes onto piles by zip code, separating out ones that began with a 9.

Bingo!—three more towns with unsolved homicides, all in California, all in the same year, and all with similar M.O.s. How did the state boys out in California miss seeing such obvious similarities?

Two of the women were teenaged prostitutes—homeless runaways. Probably nobody gave a shit about them. One of the girls had been a waitress in an all-night coffee shop. None were married. Each had been stabbed—once in the heart—and then mutilated with deep post-mortem slash wounds to the upper torso. The familiar pattern of X-marks to the breasts—deep cuts that literally sliced each breast wide open like a piece of raw meat—was exactly the same on the California girls as on the Willow Woods victims.

How many murders took place in any given year in California? Too many. Some were solved, some weren't.

Wesley scanned the lists of suspects and came up empty. No name on one list matched a name on any of the others. What did that prove? Maybe nothing. But maybe it proved that the killings were done by someone with no prior association with the victims. Maybe the killer had picked the victims at random, and moved on to kill again, someplace else—moved on from town to town the way a traveling salesman might.

Wesley felt he was right on the edge of an insightful discovery that would lead him straight to the killer, but before he could make that discovery, Susan Lester interrupted his thoughts by shoving a plateful of piping-hot pizza right under his grateful nose.

Today was Michael's lucky day, no doubt about it. He'd been afraid the police might find a clue in Blake's office, but they hadn't. And he'd worried needlessly that one or more of the investigators—perhaps the bumbling Lieutenant Wesley—would come to his office and question him relentlessly, but that hadn't happened, either.

Killing Blake last night had turned his luck around completely. Michael was back in control, and everything was proceeding according to plan.

Tonight's date with Ellen Lester would be a celebration, he decided. He'd pick up a bottle of champagne on the way to her house, and they'd have a toast to his continued good luck, before he turned her over to the other Michael—and let him kill her.

Michael knew that he'd never be rid of the jinx permanently, but he also knew he could keep it under control by giving it what it wanted, what it needed.

He looked at the whole thing rationally, the way a businessman looks at things. Killing in order to placate the jinx was no different from paying the premiums on a life insurance policy—only, instead of a life insurance policy, it was a luck insurance policy.

Danny was scared.

This was the second time in less than a week that his mother had yelled at him, and he was scared to death by subtle changes he detected in her attitudes.

She was planning to leave him, wasn't she? He could hear her preening in the bathroom, shaving her legs and underarms, curling her hair. She never did any of that unless she had a special reason— like going out and leaving him here, alone, locked in his room.

Danny looked around at the encroaching shadows and shivered. Something bad was about to happen. He could feel it in his bones. Mom had told him that a man named Michael would be coming to the house tonight, and she wanted Danny to meet him and be nice to him.

Danny knew what that meant. What could he do to upset her plans? There must be *something* a five-year-old could do, but he knew he had to think of it quick. Time was running out and soon it'd be too late. The sun had already set, and the dreaded shadows in his room were looking darker and more sinister than they'd ever looked before. Soon the monsters would come out from their hiding places, and then it'd be too late.

"I want you to look at these," Wesley said, handing Johnson the

California autopsy reports. "Tell me if you think our Slasher was involved."

"More pizza, Lieutenant?" Suzi interrupted. "There are two pieces left. Don't let them get cold."

"I couldn't eat another bite," Wesley said, gently patting his stomach.

"More coffee, then?"

"Please."

While Suzi went to the kitchen to refill Wesley's cup, Johnson scanned the reports. Wesley could see excitement building in Lenny's eyes as the connection became obvious.

"It's him, Lieutenant. Same M.O."

"Sure looks like it, doesn't it?"

"How many women has this guy killed? Did you find any others in that pile of reports?"

Suzi came back with the coffee, and returned to the kitchen to fetch fresh beers from the refrigerator.

"I haven't had time to go through the rest of the reports, Lenny. I was hoping you'd help me look."

"Not tonight," Suzi said as she returned with the beers. "Tomorrow he can look at what you want to show him, Lieutenant. But tonight I want him to look at what I have to show him."

"This is important, Suz," Lenny said.

"More important than my see-through negligee?" Lenny turned beet red. "Besides," Suzi added, "you told me the state police were in charge of the Slasher investigation now. Shouldn't you simply turn all this over to them? Why do you have to do it?"

"Suzi's right," Wesley said. "Look, I've intruded on your plans long enough. Let me call a cab and I'll leave you two alone."

"You can't turn something like this over to those jerks," Johnson objected. "I met some of them this morning and they're all assholes."

"It's not your responsibility anymore," Suzi insisted. "It's not your job!"

Lenny looked at her incredulously.

"She's right, Lenny," Wesley agreed. "It isn't your job. Forget I asked you to help."

"I can't forget, Lieutenant." Lenny's face wore a pained expression. He turned to Suzi and said, "Your negligee will wait for another night, won't it?"

She looked hurt.

Lenny took her in his arms and hugged her. "Please, Suz. Try to understand."

"I don't," she said, pouting, on the verge of tears.

"Last week I might have been able to forget," Lenny whispered, stroking her hair. "I might have said that finding the killer wasn't my responsibility and not worried about it. But I can't do that anymore, Suz. Do you want to know why?"

"Why?"

"Because I'm in love with you."

Suzi pressed herself against him. "I love you, too," she whispered.

"And that's why I have to help with this, Love," he said. "The lieutenant is real close to finding the killer, and I have to help. We've got to find the Slasher and stop him before he kills again."

"What does that have to do with loving me?" she asked, sniffling back tears.

"Everything," he said. "You see, whenever I think about all those women who've already died, I automatically think of you, Suz. They're all around the same age as you, good-looking, single. Do you understand now? Do you know now why I have to help?"

"No," she said. "What are you trying to tell me, Lenny?"

"Every time I think about those women," he said, "I wonder who the Slasher's next victim will be. And, God help me, Suzi, I can't help worry that the next victim might be *you*!"

CHAPTER TWENTY-TWO

Ellen finished dressing and went to check on dinner. The potatoes were almost done in the oven, and the meat, simmering in her special sour cream and onion sauce on top of the stove, smelled delicious.

She set the table for three, then thought better of it. She put one set of the china plates she had inherited from her mother back in the cupboard.

Danny didn't like exotic foods anyway, so why bother. He'd just sit at the table fidgeting and fussing, picking at the food with fork and fingers, and not eating a single bite.

Her stroganoff would be wasted on Danny, wouldn't it?

So she fixed him a peanut butter and jelly sandwich, poured a large glass of milk, and brought it up to his room on a tray.

Why risk spoiling a perfect meal by having her son sit at the table?

Danny could meet Michael some other time, couldn't he? Why ruin her chances of ever seeing Michael again by introducing him to her son?

But isn't Danny the reason you invited Michael here in the first place? Isn't it to find a father for your son that you're going to all this trouble?

Yes, of course. But shouldn't I get to know Michael better before I let him meet Danny? Danny depends on me to protect him. What if—?

What if Michael is just like Bob?

Don't be foolish. They're not at all alike.

But you're not sure, are you?

No, I'm not sure.

But maybe, Ellen reasoned to herself, she'd soon get to know

Michael well enough to put these fears to rest once and for all. Tonight seemed the perfect opportunity to learn what the man was like.

Before the night was over, Ellen expected to know everything about Michael Thompson, including—if she got lucky—how good the man was in bed.

Danny stopped whimpering when his mother opened the door. She'd heard him! She was coming to comfort him!

Danny wanted to run to his mother and throw his arms around her legs. He wanted to tell her he loved her and promise her that he'd be good from now on.

She switched on the lights.

"I brought your dinner," she said. "I thought you might like a peanut butter and jelly sandwich better than stroganoff."

"Can't I eat with you, Mommy?" he begged. "With you an' the comp'ny?"

"Not tonight, dear. It's almost your bedtime."

"Can't I stay up? I wanna stay up and see the comp'ny come."

"The next time Michael comes to visit, I promise you'll meet him."

"No! Now!" Danny demanded.

But she wasn't going to give in. Danny could already tell by the set of her jaw, the look in her eyes. He'd have to try something else.

"Not tonight," she said. "Now you be a good boy. Eat your sandwich and drink your milk. Then, when you're finished, I want you to go to bed and go right to sleep."

Danny took a bite of the sandwich. "I'm scared, Mommy," he said with a mouth full of food. "I want you to stay here with me."

"I'll be right downstairs, Danny. You don't need to be scared."

"Can't I be downstairs with you, Mommy?"

"No, Danny."

Danny took another bite of the sandwich and washed it down with milk. He watched his mother watching him eat the sandwich.

"You don't love me anymore," he said.

"What a terrible thing to say," she told him. "Of course I still love you. I'm your mother, aren't I? I'll always love you."

"You don't act like it," he said.

"Oh, Danny, how can you say that?" She kissed the top of his head and tried to hug him.

"Cause you'd rather be with that Michael-man than me," he said defiantly, avoiding her hug.

"That's nonsense!" she said.

But the look on her face left Danny with serious doubts. Was it possible? Did his mother like Michael better than Danny?

"You gotta stay with me, Mommy," Danny insisted, throwing his tiny arms around his mother's neck. He clung to her as tight as he could. He felt tears in his eyes.

"Why, Danny!" she said. "You're trembling."

"I'm scared, Mommy. I don't want you to leave."

"Danny, Danny," she cooed. "There's nothing to be scared of."

"Monsters," he said, his voice quaking. "I'm scared of monsters. Monsters are real, Mommy. They are! They are!"

"No, they're not, Danny. You've got to get over this fear of monsters. Monsters exist only in your imagination."

"They're real," he sobbed. "You gotta stay here and pertec' me, Mommy. Puh-leeease!"

"Pretty please with sugar on it?"

"Yes. Pretty please with sugar."

She hugged him and kissed him. Then she pried his arms loose from around her neck. "I want you to put your PJs on and get ready for bed," she told him. "Okay?"

"You're not going to pertec' me from the monsters?"

"I'll be right downstairs, Danny, and I can protect you just as well from there. I won't let anything happen to you. I promise I won't."

Danny knew that arguing was useless. Mom's voice had a tone that told him her mind was made up. He took off his clothes and wiggled into his pajamas without saying another word.

"If you're finished with your sandwich," Mom said, "drink the rest of your milk and go brush your teeth."

She even went into the bathroom with him while he brushed his teeth. Then she waited outside the door for him while he used the toilet.

"Now it's time for bed," she said when she heard him flush. "No arguments. Hurry up and get in bed."

"But, Mommy…"

"No buts, young man. Into bed with you."

He went. "But, Mommy…" he tried one last desperate time as she kissed him goodnight.

"Don't worry, Danny. Mommy will be right downstairs where she can protect you. Now go to sleep."

As she turned off the lights and closed the door, Danny tried a final time.

"But, Mommy," he wailed as he heard her latch the door and lock it. "Who will pertec' *you* from the monsters?"

"I want to help, too," Suzi said. "Show me what you're looking for, and let me go through some of those envelopes."

"Fair warning," Lenny told her, "a lot of this is pretty gory stuff."

"Can't be any worse than what's on TV news, can it? Besides, I have a degree in electrical engineering with a minor in molecular biology. Let me put my education to work. I can be very scientific when I want to be."

"Here," Wesley handed her an envelope. "Inside you'll find a case folder that contains an autopsy report, photos of the victim, and a case report from the investigating agency. Check the autopsy report first. Go down the protocol until you find the heading that's entitled 'Circumstances.' Beneath that should be a subheading titled 'Body Factors.' If the type of wound includes both stab wounds and slash wounds, bring it to our attention. Different jurisdictions use different terminology. But somewhere on the coroner's report or medical examiner's report you'll find that information, though not necessarily in those words."

"Both stab and slash wounds?"

"Our local boy kills his victims with a single stab wound to the heart. After the victim is dead, this nut carves her up just for the hell of it."

"It's the stab wound that kills the woman," Lenny clarified. "The slashings are done afterwards for no apparent reason. He slices both breasts wide open with cross-cuts."

"Cross-cuts?"

"Like a big X," said Lenny. "Zorro carved a big Z. This guy carves a big X across each breast."

"And that's what makes our Slasher's M.O. unique," Wesley added. "Kind of like a trademark."

"So anyone who's been stabbed once and then slashed was probably killed by the Mad Slasher of Willow Woods?" Suzi asked.

"If the M.O.s match closely, it's a good bet the same man did the killings. A criminal's *modus operandi* can be as distinctive and incriminating as a fingerprint."

"Wesley thinks that this guy traveled around a lot in the past," said Lenny. "He's a real nut case that can't stop killing on his own, and we have to stop him or he'll keep on killing. Nobody nailed him in the past because he kept moving from town to town. But now that he's settled in Willow Woods, we've got a good chance to put him away."

"I started to follow up on this hunch before," Wesley said. "But when the bodies began to pile up, I sort of got sidetracked."

"What if the killer moves on again?" Suzi asked.

"Even if he does, we can track him. Now that I can prove he's killed in other states, I can call the FBI in on the case; with the FBI involved, the state politicians have to play by the book. But I don't think this guy's planning to leave Willow Woods anytime soon. I think he's got a job that's keeping him here."

"A job?"

"Yeah. I bet this guy has a job with one of the new factories or office buildings out by the interstate. Maybe he worked at a branch office before, or maybe he was a salesman. His job kept him on the move. But now maybe the company is consolidating its staff at the home office and the guy had to come here or lose his job. It's a possibility worth considering, isn't it? Those companies have brought tens of thousands of jobs to the area by building in Willow Woods, and tens of thousands of people from all over the country have flocked here to fill those new jobs. I'm betting one of those people is the Mad Slasher."

"You don't think it's Bob Norman anymore?"

"Not unless Norman was in California six years ago."

"Six years ago he was married to my sister."

"He didn't take trips to California, did he?"

"No."

"Then Bob Norman isn't the Slasher. I was wrong about him,

and I'm man enough to admit it. I guess I've been wrong about a lot of things lately."

"I don't think you're wrong about this," Lenny said. "I just found a match in Florida. Same M.O."

"When?" Wesley asked. "When was the killer in Florida?"

"Last year," Lenny answered.

"Now all we have to do," Wesley said, "is find a man who was in California six years ago, Florida a year ago, and lives in Willow Woods today."

"And Kansas City three years ago," Suzi said. "I just found another one with the same M.O."

"I brought you a present," Michael said. He handed Ellen a gift-wrapped package with a yellow bow tied on top. "And I brought a bottle of champagne to sip while you're opening your present. Where do you keep your champagne glasses?"

"Oh, Michael. You shouldn't have!"

"I wanted to. Where are the glasses?"

"Sit down and I'll get glasses. I don't have champagne goblets. Will juice glasses work?"

"Have any brandy snifters?"

"No."

"Get the juice glasses then."

Ellen got two juice glasses from the cupboard. When she returned to the living room, Michael was prying the cork from the champagne bottle.

BOP! The cork bounced off the ceiling and fell to the floor. Champagne bubbled from the open bottle and Ellen rushed forward with the glasses just in time to avoid a mess.

"To luck," Michael said as he poured the wine. "Let's toast to luck."

Ellen held up her glass and Michael did the same. "To luck," she said as the glasses clinked together.

"Open your present," Michael suggested.

"It looks too lovely to open. Did you wrap it yourself?"

"My secretary," said Michael.

Ellen loosened the ribbon and gently peeled off pieces of tape that kept the package sealed. The wrapping paper was too pretty to tear, and she planned to save it as a memento of Michael's thoughtfulness.

Inside the gift wrapping she found a fancy box. And inside the box was a brand new Blake Blades Best Cutlery set.

"Oh, Michael! I've always wanted one of these! They're so expensive!"

"Didn't cost me a penny."

She kissed his cheek. "Thank you," she whispered.

He smiled at her. "You look beautiful," he said in that sexy voice of his. "I'm the luckiest man in the world tonight. Thanks for inviting me here."

"I hope you're hungry," she said. "And I hope you like stroganoff."

They brought their glasses to the kitchen. Michael carried the bottle of champagne while Ellen placed the cutlery set on the cupboard counter, right next to the kitchen sink.

Michael insisted they finish the bottle of champagne before it went flat. "It'd be such a shame to let this go to waste, wouldn't it? Drink up."

Ellen knew wine would go to her head if she drank on an empty stomach, but that didn't matter tonight. She was already lightheaded from being in Michael's presence, and she liked the way she felt—all warm and tingly inside.

Michael refilled her glass, then topped off his own. "To the most beautiful woman in the world," he said, making a toast.

"And the handsomest man in the world," she said in return.

"Not the handsomest," he corrected. "The *luckiest*."

Ellen was sure he meant "luckiest" because he was here with her. It meant he appreciated her, didn't it? Her heart fluttered at the thought. He wasn't like Bob at all, was he? The two men were as different as night and day. Here was a man who appreciated Ellen and wasn't afraid to show how he felt about her. Michael would never do anything to hurt her, would he? Of course not!

Any misgivings she'd had about the man were put to rest. She felt she could trust him completely.

By the time the bottle of champagne had been emptied and they'd started on dinner, Ellen knew she was falling in love with Michael Thompson—hopelessly, helplessly in love.

CHAPTER TWENTY-THREE

The dark closed in on him and took away his voice. He didn't dare cry out. There were monsters everywhere and they were coming to get him. Alone in the dark, Danny thought he could hear them moving about, or was that only the sound of water running in the pipes when his mother turned on the faucet downstairs in the kitchen?

Danny heard the doorbell. The loud chime rattled his nerves.

He was sure he heard his mother open the front door. Then he thought he heard voices: his mother's voice and a man's.

Danny couldn't tell what they were saying. His room was above the kitchen, and his mother and the man sounded like they were seated on the living room couch.

The living room was beneath his mother's room.

He heard his mother enter the kitchen. She opened a cupboard. Then she quickly closed the cupboard and returned to the living room.

Danny could hear them talking again. Their words sounded like whispers. Were they talking about him? Surely, they must be! Danny's fear compounded. They had to be talking about him, didn't they? What else would they have to talk about? The sheltered, self-centered five-year-old couldn't imagine anything else as important as himself.

He heard them walk to the kitchen. Now he could hear their voices clearer, though it sounded like they were still whispering. Or were those whispers coming from the monsters under his bed? No, that was definitely his mother's voice.

Now it sounded like they were eating dinner. He thought he heard the clink of glasses, the scrape of silverware on china.

He strained his ears to hear what they might be saying about him....

After complimenting Ellen on her culinary skills, Michael manipulated Ellen into talking about her job at Evans Supply.

Obviously the champagne was having its desired effect, and he wasn't surprised when Ellen answered his probing questions with an openness that bordered on intimacy.

"Is Lane Evans someone I should worry about?" was the way he asked without arousing suspicion about his motives. "Should I consider the man my main competition for your... affections?"

"Oh, no, Michael," she answered quickly. "Mr. Evans is married."

"Some men don't let marriage stand in their way. Has Evans tried to put moves on you? Does he put moves on any of the other women who work there?"

"Of course not."

"Good. I can't stand a man who cheats on his wife. Men in Evans' position often do, you know."

"Not Mr. Evans."

"Are you sure?"

"Positive."

"You'd know if he received phone calls from women at work, wouldn't you? Or does he have a private line for them to call in on?"

"He has a private line. But—"

"Does he go out of town on overnight trips?"

"Not very often."

"But sometimes he does, right? Does he take his wife with him on any of those trips?"

"No."

"If I were married, I'd want my wife to be with me on out-of-town trips. Don't you think it strange that Evans doesn't?"

"I never thought about it before."

"Forgive me," he said, taking Ellen's hand and squeezing it gently. "Good salesmen always analyze their competition. I don't want to suddenly lose you to Lane Evans."

"Oh, Michael. Mr. Evans isn't competition. I could never be interested in him."

"But he might be interested in you, my dear. So, just to put my mind at ease, I want you to tell me all about the man. What's he like? What are his hobbies? What's his wife like? Does he have children and how many? Let me know all about him and I'll decide if I need to be jealous."

To hear Ellen tell it, Lane Evans was a virtual saint. Like most owners of their own businesses, Evans often put in long hours at the office. But Evans seemed to be all work and no play.

Michael found that hard to believe and said so. "Oh, Michael," she said. "You have nothing to worry about. Mr. Evans is a perfect gentleman."

Disappointed, Michael decided to forget about Lane Evans. With Blake and Gillespe out of the way, the Evans account was no longer essential to his plans.

And neither, he mused as he turned his attention to the lovely young woman sitting next to him at the kitchen table, was Ellen Lester anymore.

Ellen was ecstatic. Imagine! Michael cared about her so much that he was actually jealous!

Well, he certainly didn't need to worry about Lane Evans. Compared to Michael, Evans didn't have a chance, even if Lane were interested, which he wasn't.

But Michael was *definitely* interested. She could tell by the way he looked at her.

Oh, Michael. You make me feel so alive!

Ellen just knew that Michael had to be Mister Right. She'd hoped and prayed for a chance like this—to find the perfect man. And now her prayers had been answered.

"Why don't we go into the living room where we can be more comfortable?" she suggested.

"That sounds like a good idea. But first, let me help you with the dishes."

"Oh, no, Michael. I'll do the dishes later."

"I insist," he said, rolling up his sleeves. "Do you have a pair of plastic gloves I can wear?"

"Yes; but really, Michael, just leave the dishes on the table. I'll do them myself."

"Nonsense. Where are those gloves?"

Ellen saw his determination. She went to the cupboard and found a pair of rubber gloves.

"These should fit," she said. "They're one-size-fits-all."

Michael tried on the gloves. "Perfect," he said.

Oh, yes, Ellen silently agreed. *You are perfect, Michael. The perfect man. Who else but you could be this thoughtful?*

Never once had Ellen ever met a man like this—a man who was kind enough and thoughtful enough to offer his help with household chores. It never occurred to Ellen that Michael might have ulterior motives.

"Wisconsin," Lenny announced. "Madison and Milwaukee both, summer before last."

"Any suspects?"

"A whole list, Lieutenant. Want to see?"

So far none of the names on any one of the lists had matched suspects named on another list, and Wesley was beginning to feel discouraged. He hadn't had more than a quick cat-nap in the past forty-eight hours, and exhaustion had set in, too. "Maybe we ought to call it a night," he said. "I can't see straight anymore."

"I'll check them," Suzi offered. "What should I look for?"

"Names that turn up on more than one list," Lenny said. "Here, let me show you."

Lenny laid the lists of names out on the coffee table in front of Suzi's sofa and sat down on the sofa close to her. "These," he said, "are suspects from Madison, Wisconsin. Compare these names to the suspects in California, Florida, and Kansas. Then do the same with the Milwaukee lists. If any name appears on two or more lists, let me know immediately."

"Wouldn't it be easier to key this into a computer?"

"Sure. Tomorrow we'll get someone to do that down at the station. Wesley has a couple hundred more envelopes in his office, and we'll go through all of them as we get time. But right now, this is the best we can do."

"No, it isn't. I've got a laptop on my desk in the bedroom. You've seen it before, remember? I have a spreadsheet program that makes number-crunching or name-crunching seem like a breeze. I even have an image scanner and OCR software so we don't need to key individual names. Give me ten minutes to input the lists, another ten or fifteen to reformat, and I'll give you and the lieutenant a printout with every name alphabetized."

"Take all the time you need," Lenny said, and kissed her cheek. "I'll stay here and go through the rest of the envelopes with the lieutenant."

"I don't think the lieutenant will be much help," Suzi said, pointing to Wesley. "The poor man can't even keep his eyes open anymore."

Wesley, slouched down in an easy chair with his feet resting on a hassock, opened his eyes and smiled. "I'm still awake," he mumbled.

And then both eyelids drooped, his head nodded forward, and his jaw dropped open.

And he began to snore so loudly that Lenny and Suzi couldn't escape the sound of the lieutenant's wood-sawing until they both went into the bedroom together and booted up the computer.

How could his mother carry on a conversation and not once mention his name? Even when Mom and Aunt Suzi stayed up all night talking about other things, Danny usually heard his name mentioned a third of the time, but so far tonight he hadn't heard his mother say his name even once.

Keeping one ear focused on the conversation in the kitchen, Danny's other ear probed the darkness for movement in the closet. The monsters were unusually quiet tonight, almost as if they were waiting for something else to happen before making a move.

Something bad was going to happen. Danny could definitely feel it in his bones.

Suddenly his five-and-a-half-year-old mind made a quantum leap. What made tonight different from all other nights was the presence of a stranger in the house—a man named Michael whom Danny had never met nor seen—and that single presence had somehow upset the normal routine of the whole house and everyone and every *thing* in it.

Everything had changed solely because of Michael. Nothing was the same as it had been before Michael had entered this house.

Nor, Danny feared, would anything be the same ever again.

Already his mother had forgotten all about him—locked him away in his room, and left him alone here in the dreaded dark and forgotten him. He knew she'd forgotten about him completely because he hadn't heard her mention his name even once during all the time he'd been listening.

She'd forgotten, too, her promise that she'd protect him from the monsters.

Now Danny could hear those horrible monsters begin to stir. They were moving around in the dark in the clothes closet, behind the curtains that shaded his windows, under his very own bed. They were getting ready to jump out from their secret hiding places and grab him again.

And the only reason they'd delayed until now, Danny realized, was simply because of that man—that stranger—downstairs.

Maybe Michael was in cahoots with the monsters! Suddenly Danny's worst fears materialized in his imagination.

Michael wasn't just in cahoots with the monsters, he had to be a monster himself—maybe even the leader of the monsters!

And, while the monsters in Danny's room came for the boy and grabbed him, the monster downstairs would grab Danny's mother and cut her into tiny pieces and eat her up. And when the leader had finished with his own feast, he'd come upstairs and cut Danny up, too—cut him up into a zillion pieces so all the monsters could have an equal share.

It made perfect sense to the boy that such things were not only possible, they were indeed quite probable. Every night for nearly three years he'd been waiting for something like this to happen and now, finally, it *was* happening.

When strange noises began downstairs—hissing and gurgling noises that sounded like they were coming from directly beneath his bed—Danny never considered that someone might simply have turned on a faucet in order to wash the left-over dinner dishes in the kitchen sink.

Danny knew what those noises *really* were.

They were the sounds monsters make when they're coming to get you!

CHAPTER TWENTY-FOUR

Michael paid special attention to washing the silverware, scrubbing each piece thoroughly before rinsing. Not a single fingerprint would remain on any of the dishes when he finished with them. They looked spotless when he handed them to Ellen to dry.

"You must have had lots of practice doing dishes," Ellen said. She held a dishtowel in her hands and waited patiently for Michael to pass her the plates. "I didn't think a man knew how."

"My mother made me wash dishes when I was a kid." He hadn't meant to say that. It just slipped out when he wasn't thinking.

He never talked about his mother. Never.

"Tell me about her," Ellen asked. "What's your mother like?"

"She's dead," Michael said.

"Oh, I'm sorry."

"She died a long time ago," Michael said.

"Did your father raise you after your mother passed away?"

"My father died before I was born."

"Oh, Michael. I'm so sorry. Were you raised by another relative?"

Michael didn't want to answer her questions, but he didn't want to arouse her suspicions, either. Besides, what did it matter?

"I was raised by Roger Horton," he said. "Horton was the neighborhood grocer and he sort of took me in."

"Do you have any brothers or sisters?"

"No. I was an only child."

"I have one sister," Ellen said. "You met her the other night."

"Susan. Right?"

"Uh hm. My mother died when I was a senior in high school," Ellen said. "But my father's still alive."

"In Arizona?"

"You remembered."

"I try to remember everything," he said. "By the way, where's your son? I was looking forward to meeting him."

"It's past his bedtime already. I don't want him up late on school nights. He'd stay up all night if he could, but I won't let him. Growing boys need their sleep."

"He's five?"

"Almost six."

"I really would like to see him, even if he's asleep. Is he upstairs?"

Michael couldn't read the expression that flashed across Ellen's face. It was only there for an instant and then disappeared. But he thought he knew what it was anyway. It was *fear*, wasn't it?

"Maybe you could see him some other time," she suggested quickly. A little too quickly, he thought. *Why is she afraid to let me near her son?* Did she suspect? Was that why? Did she know he intended to kill her and her son, too?

"Perhaps on Saturday, then?" he suggested. "I could come over on Saturday afternoon and take both of you to the zoo. All three of us, together. Does he like the zoo?"

"That would be nice," she said. "We've never been to the zoo before. I'm sure we'll love seeing all the animals."

But you don't want me looking in on him tonight, do you? Michael wondered why, and it worried him that the answer was so elusive. Michael had to tag them both—Ellen and her son—at the same time. Otherwise, the boy might someday tag Michael back. And, since this game was played for keeps, Michael had to tag them both, permanently. First the mother, then the boy.

He finished washing the dishes and handed the last plate to Ellen to dry.

Then the other Michael reached for the Blake Blades Best Cutlery set on the counter next to the sink, and, with the thumb and forefinger of a gloved hand that left no prints, extracted a twelve-inch butcher knife from the box of Blake Blades Best Cutlery.

"You weren't lying about the negligee," Lenny said. "It really is see-through."

While Suzi sat at the computer entering data into memory, Lenny had asked permission to rummage through her closet for the negligee.

"I told you I was brazen," Suzi said. "I can't wait to wear it."

"Then put it on."

"Later, Love."

"I meant what I said, Suz. I am head over heels in love with you. You know that, don't you?"

"Come here, big boy, and kiss me while the computer prints out your report."

Lenny did.

Suzi reluctantly broke the kiss when the printer kicked the last sheet into the tray. "Want to see the results?" she asked, picking up the stack of printed pages.

"I only have eyes for you," Lenny whispered. "The lieutenant's asleep. Why don't we lock the door and go to bed. We can read that report in the morning."

"Aren't you curious? Now that the names are in alphabetical order, it'll be easy to spot any name printed twice. This will only take a minute, Lenny. You said it's important, didn't you?"

"Not as important as you."

"You're sweet." She kissed him chastely on the cheek.

"Okay," he said. "Let's look at the report." Together they scanned the list of names. None of the names appeared to be duplicated.

"That's funny," Suzi said, pointing at the Ts.

"What is? I don't see anything funny."

"Odd funny, not ha-ha funny. Maybe it's just a coincidence. Do you remember I told you that Ellen has a date tonight?"

"So?"

"So the man she's dating has the same name as someone on your suspect list." She pointed at the name. "Michael Thompson. See?"

"Oh, dear God! Sweet Jesus!"

"What is it? What's wrong?"

"We gotta wake the lieutenant. C'mon."

Lenny ran to the other room and Suzi followed. "Go to the kitchen and get the coffee pot. Hurry!" When she came back with the pot, Lenny was shaking the lieutenant's shoulders and shouting in the man's ear.

"Pour him a fresh cup of coffee and hold it under his nose. I've seen that work to wake him before."

"At least he's stopped snoring."

She held the steaming cup an inch from Wesley's nostrils. "Wake up, Lieutenant," she said. "If you don't wake up, I'll have to try tickling you."

One eye opened.

"S'watischish?" he mumbled.

"Michael Thompson," Lenny said. "He's our killer, Lieutenant. And right now he's at Ellen Lester's house with Ellen and Danny. That's why Ellen couldn't come for dinner. She has a date with Thompson tonight."

Wesley's eyes—both eyes—snapped open. His hand fumbled for the cup of coffee.

"Call her," he said in a gravelly voice. "Call her and warn her. Suzi, you call. Do it *now!*" He took a gulp of coffee. "Lenny, give me the details. Why Thompson?"

"His name came up as a suspect in the Milwaukee killing."

"You sure it's the same Thompson?"

"Same age. Name and age is all we put into the computer. But it's him, Lieutenant. It's got to be him."

"It don't got to be nothing. Bring me the Milwaukee file. Let me see for myself."

Wesley lit a cigarette and gulped the rest of the coffee. His first impulse had been to rush over to Ellen's and arrest Thompson, nail the bastard and make sure Ellen was safe. But now that he was waking up, he knew he couldn't do that without proof. What would Ellen think if Wesley burst through the door and arrested an innocent man?

She'd think you were a jealous lover, Lieutenant. First Bob Norman and then Michael Thompson. Jesus Christ! You can't put a man in jail just because he's interested in your girlfriend!

Johnson handed him the file. Wesley thumbed through it quickly, then concentrated on the suspect reports. A man by the name of Michael Thomspon had been interviewed by Milwaukee police one year ago last August. Thompson, twenty-three, was then a meat and produce buyer for a supermarket chain. He'd been in Milwaukee less than a week when the homicide of a Marquette University coed occurred. Michael Thompson was questioned only because an eyewitness had reported Thompson's car in the vicinity around the time of the murder. But Thompson had an ironclad alibi: though his hotel was across town, Thompson had dinner reservations in a German restaurant near Marquette on the night of the murder. Both the maître d' and the wine steward verified Thompson was eating when police discovered the body. It wasn't logical that a man would murder and mutilate a woman before sitting down to a full meal in a restaurant.

No, Wesley agreed, it *wasn't* logical. But insane serial killers are never logical, are they? Certainly not the Mad Slasher of Willow Woods.

Wesley remembered thinking that Thompson had something to hide when they had talked on Saturday. The lieutenant wanted to kick himself for not following up on Thompson sooner. Thompson had motive, didn't he? Motive enough for killing Gillespe and Blake, anyway. With them gone, Thompson was sure to take over as CEO of the company at the tender age of twenty-four. Ambition and money often made excellent motives for murder, and Michael Thompson appeared to be both extremely ambitious and sufficiently money-hungry.

And he had opportunity. As a vice president of Blake Blades, Thompson knew the routines of the factory like the palm of his hand. He knew when Gillespe was alone in the garage. He knew when Blake was alone in the office. He could approach both men without arousing their suspicions.

And he definitely had means. Thompson didn't need to buy the expensive cutlery the Mad Slasher used as a murder weapon. He could simply help himself to any knife Blake Blades manufactured, and nobody would ever question him about it.

But, more importantly, Thompson had been a meat and produce buyer for a supermarket chain. It was a safe bet that Thompson had traveled frequently in California to purchase fresh produce, to Florida for citrus, and the Kansas City stockyards to buy beef. Why was he in Wisconsin? For cheese, most likely. Or maybe bacon and sausage from Wisconsin meat packers. It all tied in.

Frank Monroe had once speculated that the Slasher might be a trained butcher or meat packer. Thompson was a salesman. *But he was a salesman who had previously associated with butchers and meat packers in the course of his normal employment.*

Wesley thought he knew now how that fairytale Prince must have felt, after searching his kingdom for a princess, he finally tried the glass slipper on Cinderella's foot and found that it fit so *perfectly*.

"Lieutenant, there's no answer at Ellen's." Suzi sounded worried, and Wesley couldn't blame her. "Maybe her phone's still out of order. She had problems with it over the weekend."

"It rings?"

"Yes."

"She doesn't have a cell phone?"

"No. She can't afford the extra expense."

"Then try the phone company. Ask them to check the line."

"Let me do it," Lenny suggested. He took the phone and dialed an operator, giving the operator Ellen's number. "This is a police emergency," he said. "I'm Officer Johnson of the Willow Woods Police Department."

A moment later Johnson gave Wesley the bad news. "It appears that Ellen's phone is unplugged. The operator can ring the line, but there's no impedance on the other end. Nothing's connected to the line."

"Let's go," Wesley said. "We have probable cause to bring Thompson in for questioning. We'd better get over there as fast as we can before—"

"I'm going with you," Suzi said, reaching for her purse. "She's my sister."

"No!" Lenny grabbed her arms. "You can help your sister more by staying here. I don't have a radio in my car and we might need backup. Please, Suz, listen to me. I want you to stay here and call the station. Give them all the information they ask for, but make sure they know the correct address. Can you do that? It might save your sister's life. Maybe mine, too."

"You need backup?"

"That's right. This is a possible hostage situation involving a woman and small child. Tell the dispatcher that Wesley and Johnson are on their way without radios. Got all that? It's important, Suz."

"I think so," she said.

"Good." He kissed her quickly, and dashed for the door while Suzi ran to the phone.

CHAPTER TWENTY-FIVE

Danny didn't want his mother to die. But, trapped in his room with a zillion monsters closing in on him, Danny knew of no way to save her.

But he had to save her.

Danny really and truly loved his mother, despite all the times he'd told her differently. In a very concrete way, Danny thought the world of his mother because she was his whole world, and he didn't want his world to end.

What would Superman do in similar circumstances? Batman? The Transformers? One thing was sure: They wouldn't sit here shaking like a leaf.

But Danny knew he wasn't a superhero. Sometimes he thought maybe he secretly was—so secretly that even he didn't realize his own capabilities. But, deep in his heart, he knew that was just a daydream and he was really only a scared little boy—a scared, ordinary little boy who had no superpowers at all, and who was special only to his own mother.

What could he do to save her from the monsters? Maybe he could make a deal with them—offer the monsters something of value in exchange. People made deals all the time, didn't they? Maybe monsters made deals, too. But what would a monster want?

"I'll give you all my comic books," Danny whispered at the darkness. "And my Little Golden Books and my coloring book and all my crayons. I'll give you everything I own if you'll let me get out of this room so I can save my mom. Okay?"

The monsters didn't answer. He could still hear them moving about in the closet and under his bed. If he could hear them, he knew they must have heard him.

Didn't they want his comic books? His Little Golden Books? His coloring book and crayons? Obviously, they didn't.

What else did he have to offer? His clothes—but monsters didn't wear clothes. His tricycle—did monsters ride tricycles?

He couldn't think of a single thing that might appeal to a monster.

"Puh-leeeease," he begged in a whispery whine. "Pretty please with sugar on it! Let me go so I can help my mom, and I'll give you anything you want!"

No sooner had he said that than he realized what he possessed that the monsters really wanted.

"No, I can't," he whispered. "I can't."

Surely there had to be another way. Anything but *that*. But he knew there wasn't.

If he wanted to save his mother, there was only one way he'd be able to get past the monsters and reach the door. He didn't know how he'd manage the locked door—maybe he'd have to kick it down the way he'd seen people kick down doors on TV—but he'd tackle that hurdle when he came to it. First, he had to get the monsters to agree to let him go.

"Okay," he said. "I promise to come back and give you what you want. But you gotta let me out so I can save Mom. After I save Mom from the other monster, then I'll come back and I won't try to hide from you ever again."

Danny waited for their answer.

"If you want to eat me up when I get back," he added, "I'll let you."

And, as if in answer to his offer, the sounds of running water abruptly ceased when someone turned off a faucet in the kitchen sink. The gurgling and hissing of the monsters under his bed grew silent, and Danny knew his offer had been accepted.

Ellen didn't know what to think. After Michael had mentioned his mother, Ellen immediately sensed a frightening change in the man's personality. It was as though there were two Michaels occupying the same body: One was the Michael she loved, and the other was something too terrible to think about.

And then, when Michael asked to see Danny, Ellen had felt an overriding necessity to protect her son from that second Michael

Thompson at all costs.

Call it women's intuition, Ellen thought. Call it mother's paranoia. Whatever it was, it had set off dire warnings that Danny might be in terrible danger.

Or maybe it was just her emotions running wild. Maybe she was overreacting. Ellen didn't know what to think.

For the first time in years Ellen was alone with a man she cared about, and that seemed quite wonderful and exciting—but it was scary, too.

Ellen had made a serious mistake once before, and she was scared that she might somehow make the same mistake again. Falling in love was risky business for a divorcée, especially a divorcée with a five-year-old son.

Now that the dizzying effects of drinking champagne on an empty stomach had dissipated after a meal, Ellen's inhibitions quickly rematerialized. Did she dare take any chances when she had a young son to protect? It was the way Michael had reacted to the mention of his own mother that aroused Ellen's initial suspicions about the man. When Ellen tried to probe further, Michael deliberately shut Ellen out and redirected the conversation away from his own family.

Suddenly Ellen realized how often Michael had redirected their previous conversations too, and for some reason that realization scared her half out of her wits. Michael knew almost everything about Ellen, while she knew absolutely nothing about him.

She'd told him, honestly and openly, all about herself—bared her soul almost as if she'd removed her clothes and allowed him to see her naked—because she had expected him to reciprocate.

Instead, Michael Thompson remained a mystery to her and his past—his family, his boyhood—seemed suddenly shrouded with suspicion.

And when Michael had asked to see Danny, there was something sinister about the way he'd asked to see her son that set alarms claxoning in Ellen's subconscious. Sinister undertones in the man's voice made Ellen suspect Michael of ulterior motives.

I really would like to see him, even if he's asleep.

Ellen remembered that Bob had once said something similar, and cold shivers coursed up and down her spine as the memory of that night and the consequences of her acquiescence came back to haunt her. This time, Ellen swore, she would do a better job of protecting her son.

When Michael suggested the zoo on Saturday, Ellen saw nothing wrong in the suggestion itself, but the look in Michael's eyes told her the man had no intention of coming over on Saturday. He had said that only to divert her suspicions.

Come off it, Ellen, she told herself. You're getting all nervous over nothing.

No, I'm not. Don't ask me to explain it, but the man standing next to me isn't the same Michael I thought I was in love with. He looks the same, but he's changed inside. You know, the same way Bob used to change after a few drinks—

Oh, my God! He's reaching for a knife!

Run! You've got to get away! He's going to kill you!

As Michael's gloved hand swung a twelve-inch knife straight at Ellen's heart, Ellen threw both the plate and dish towel she held in her own hands at Michael's eyes. The china plate shattered against his forehead an instant before the wet towel slapped his face, but the impact was enough of a surprise to make Michael miss her with the knife.

Without thinking, Ellen ran for the telephone to call for help. And then, when it was too late to run for the door, she finally remembered that the telephone was out of order.

Maybe it was because of the gloves, Michael postulated. Maybe gloves somehow diluted the magic of a honed blade. Maybe he had to hold the knife handle in a bare hand. This was the first time he'd worn gloves. This was also the first time he'd missed his mark in eight years, and a correlation seemed rather obvious.

He removed the rubber glove from his right hand and tucked the glove into a pants' pocket.

Michael's forehead was bleeding where he'd been hit by the plate. A small trickle of blood ran down the side of his face. He wiped the blood away with his left hand.

Michael had counted on the magic of a honed blade to offset the power of his jinx, but this time it hadn't worked. It worried him that his luck was running out this soon after tagging Blake. The jinx wasn't supposed to come back this fast.

But the other Michael shoved Michael's worries aside. The real Michael was relegated to the role of observer while the other Michael took over total control of Michael Thompson's body and mind. Now Michael couldn't stop himself even if he wanted to.

Holding the knife in his bare hand, Michael walked confidently into the living room and made sure the front door was double-locked. He hadn't heard the door open and close, so he knew Ellen hadn't left the house.

He located the telephone on a table near the stairs. He tugged on the phone cord and discovered the cord was broken and wasn't connected to the wall jack. That explained why he hadn't heard Ellen attempt to telephone for help. The telephone was useless.

It occurred to him that Ellen might have a gun in the house, though Ellen didn't seem the type to keep a gun in her home where a five-year-old might find it and play with it. Even if she did have a gun, he doubted she'd have the guts to use it. Ellen was too mousy to pull the trigger on a loaded gun. So, where was she?

Instead of running for the door or calling for help, Ellen must have gone into hiding. He imagined her huddled in the back of a closet or cramped beneath a piece of furniture, scared to death and shaking in her shoes. Where could she be?

Systematically, he turned over every table. He moved the couch away from the wall and searched behind and beneath the sofa and chairs. He opened the hall closet and rummaged behind coats and overshoes. He couldn't find her anywhere.

At first this game of hide-and-seek had seemed like fun, but now it was frustrating him, like that time when Michael was eight and had managed to tag a girl for the first time and then she'd tagged him right back.

Michael didn't play this game just for fun, he played *for keeps.*

After that girl had tagged him back, Michael made sure to use the magic words himself. With each word, he made doubly sure they'd never be able to tag him back. It was a ritual he'd developed entirely on his own, but it seemed to work miracles. Nobody had ever tagged him back since he started using his special ritual, because nobody could.

A single thrust of the knife punctured heart and lungs

simultaneously. Michael had practiced on sides of beef until he had perfect control of the blade. Then he'd gone to the library and looked up books on human anatomy to know exactly where to aim.

Once he tagged someone, he wanted them to stay tagged—permanently.

Just to be certain, he used the honed edge of the blade to slice the body open from sternum to stomach. And with each slash and slice he'd repeat the magic words: *Jinx, Sphinx, Rinky Dinks.*

And, for a while, the jinx would pass into the body of the person he'd tagged.

The jinx always returned to him, of course, eventually. Michael's luck didn't last forever. Lately, it didn't seem to last long at all.

When he was sixteen and killed his first victim—a girl he'd stalked for days before he dared to tag her—he'd rid himself of the jinx for six whole months before it found him again. The second time lasted almost as long, but each time thereafter his luck faded away faster and faster until now it seemed like he needed to kill once a day to keep the jinx away.

Tonight he'd kill twice—just for luck: First the mother, then the boy.

"Come out, come out! Wherever you are," he shouted. "Come out, Ellen. You can't hide from me forever."

But Ellen didn't come out from hiding.

He hadn't really expected her to.

"Okay," he said. "If you want to play this the hard way, I'm game."

He started up the stairs to find the boy.

CHAPTER TWENTY-SIX

Danny heard the monster's footsteps on the stairs. His first impulse was to run and hide, but he realized there was no place to run—and no place to hide.

Monsters were everywhere tonight—in his closet, under his bed, behind his curtains: all the places he could think to hide himself.

He'd made a deal with the monsters in his room, hadn't he? They had let him out of bed and let him get across the room. They'd even let him reach the door. Maybe they'd let him hide, too. But that wasn't part of the deal, and he knew it.

Danny had ventured, one hesitant step at a time, from his bed to the door. He'd half-expected the monsters to renege on their agreement and grab him, but they hadn't. He'd made it all the way from his bed to the door in complete darkness, something he'd never dared try before.

The door, as anticipated, was firmly locked from the outside. Danny, standing on tiptoe, could turn the doorknob easily enough. But the lock was a simple latch Mom had screwed to the outside of the door and it slid into a metal catch nailed to the doorjamb. Jiggling the doorknob didn't affect the lock one iota, plus the door opened into his room rather than out, thus making it impossible to kick open.

Danny had been pondering his problem of emergency egress when he'd heard a male voice shout, "Come out, come out! Wherever you are, come out!"

Then footsteps had started up the stairs—heavy footsteps, not the light pitter-patter sound of his mother's tiny feet.

Earlier, Danny had heard a plate shatter. Then he'd heard a brief commotion like someone running around downstairs.

Where was his mother, Danny wondered. Did the monster already eat her all up? Was it too late now to save her?

Danny found his fear of monsters had suddenly disappeared, only to be replaced by a hatred unlike anything he'd ever known before in his entire life.

Ellen remained hidden behind the living room drapes. Michael had no way of knowing those drapes covered a big bay window where Ellen kept an indoor greenhouse. Ellen had climbed up on the windowsill and hid amid her potted plants out on the ledge. He hadn't thought to check behind the drapes because there were no feet visible beneath the hemmed bottom.

Once, when Danny had been angry at her for not getting his way, Ellen had scoured the house for half an hour before finding the boy's hiding place. Danny had simply taken his crayons and coloring book, climbed up on the ledge, and played quietly in the afternoon sunshine. Ellen, however, had been near panic the whole time.

She was near panic now. If she came out of hiding, Michael would surely kill her; but if she didn't, Michael would surely kill her son.

Ellen had little doubt that Michael would kill the boy either way, but she couldn't just stay here knowing her only child was about to be butchered by a madman.

Peering around the edge of the drapes she saw Michael reach the top of the stairs. Surely there must be some way to stop him.

"Michael!" she yelled from her hiding place. "I'm down here!"

"Where? I can't see you."

"I'm right next to the front door," she lied.

"Show yourself," Michael demanded.

"No. You come down here and look for me."

"This is my game and we'll play by my rules. Your son is in this room, isn't he? If you don't come out, Ellen, I'll go in there and cut his throat."

"If you open that door, Michael, I'll open this one. I'll open the front door and yell my head off for help. I'll run next door and call the police."

That stopped him, just as he was about to unlock the latch to

Danny's door. It was an idle threat, but Michael couldn't know that Annie Galbraith, Ellen's next-door neighbor, was an eighty-year-old widow who barely heard you if you yelled directly in her ear.

Nor could he be certain that Ellen would never, under any circumstances, abandon her baby.

"Why, Michael?" she asked. "Why do you want to hurt my son?"

"I don't," he answered.

"What do you want, then?"

"I want you to come out where I can see you, Ellen."

"Why, Michael? So you can rape me?"

"I don't want to rape you," he snickered. "Whatever gave you that idea?"

"I don't understand why you're doing this. What do you expect to gain by hurting us?"

"Luck," he said.

"Luck?"

"I don't want to have to hurt your son, Ellen. You're the one I want. I promise to leave the boy alone if you come out and let me tag you."

"Tag me?"

"With the blade."

"You mean kill me?"

"Yes."

Ellen would have sacrificed herself willingly to save her son, but she could tell that Michael had no intention of ever allowing the boy to go free. Her sacrifice would surely be in vain.

"I've never hurt a child before," said Michael, as if reading her thoughts.

"How can I know for certain? How can I trust you?"

"Have you read in the newspapers or heard on TV that the 'Mad Slasher' has even once hurt a child? Of course you haven't."

"Oh, my God, Michael! *You* are the Mad Slasher?"

"That's right."

"You killed all those women?"

"All except one."

"Why, Michael? *Why!*"

"Because otherwise I'd be a jinx, Ellen. I know you probably don't believe that, but it's true. I never *wanted* to hurt anyone, but I must. It's the only way I can rid myself of the jinx."

"That sounds crazy!"

"No, Ellen. It's the truth. In the game of life there are winners and losers, victors and victims. In order to have winners, there must be losers, right? To have victors, there must be victims. By making you the victim, I become the victor. Nothing personal, you understand—it's just the way the world works."

"That's insane, Michael. *You're* insane!"

"I'm tired of talking, Ellen. Are you coming out where I can see you, or should I bring your son out here where you can see what you're making me do to him?"

Michael's hand slid the latch free of its catch.

"Wait!" Ellen screamed as Michael turned the doorknob and opened the door to Danny's room.

"Too late," he said, stepping into the room and disappearing in the darkness.

"Can't you go any faster?" Wesley demanded.

"Not without lights and a siren," Johnson said. "I'm risking an accident at every intersection we come to."

"Take the shortcut through the park, why don't you?"

"What shortcut through the park?"

"The walkway."

"The sidewalk?"

"Yeah. The brick walkway that goes straight through the park. Jump the curb at this end and follow the yellow-brick road. We'll wind up a block away from Ellen's house."

"You got to be kidding!"

"Uh uh. It'll cut our time in half. We'll get there in five minutes instead of ten."

"What about pedestrians?"

"Shouldn't be any. Park closed at sunset. After two murders, the city made the park off-limits after dark."

"I think I'd better take the long way."

"Then get out and let me drive."

"You serious?"

"Yeah. Deadly serious. Thompson's a killer and he's got Ellen and Danny."

"You made your point, Lieutenant. We'll go through the park to save time."

"Thanks, Lenny."

"Don't mention it, Lieutenant. Just hold onto your seat and pray."

Michael stopped just inside the door and waited. He had heard her leap from the window and run toward him as fast as her legs could move. She was coming up the stairs now, and Michael was ready for her.

He was to the right of the half-opened door, hidden by shadow. He gripped the knife in his bare, sweaty hand and waited for her to rush through the door so he could tag her—permanently.

Again Michael had played the carrot and stick game on Ellen, this time dangling her son in front of her nose as the carrot. Then he'd told her who he was—the "Mad Slasher"—so she'd have no doubts that he was capable of killing the boy. That was the stick— desire and fear.

Ellen desired to save her son. She feared what Michael would do to the boy.

Michael regretted what he was about to do to Ellen—and to the boy—but he'd meant what he'd said about victors and victims. Roger Horton had taught him that, and Roger Horton was right.

Michael had trusted Horton as a kind of father figure, a substitute for the real father Michael never knew. Dropping out of school at sixteen, Michael learned everything he needed to know about the ways of the world by apprenticing himself to Roger Horton.

Horton had exploited the boy mercilessly, promising Michael a partnership in his business if Michael would work harder, making the young Michael Thompson a willing slave. Michael worked seventeen hours a day, seven days a week, for a salary that was the bare equivalent of forty hours of minimum wage.

Then Horton sold out his grocery stores to a large supermarket chain, proving to the chain that his ghetto stores were making enormous profits. The chain gave Horton several million dollars which Roger Horton immediately invested in grain futures.

"Let this be a lesson to you, son," Horton told the boy. "Never trust anyone."

Horton was right, of course. Eventually, his lessons proved more valuable than money.

Horton's betrayal also proved that Michael would always be a victim—a loser—unless he found a way to rid himself of his jinx.

That's when he stalked his first victim, and became a victor.

His luck changed almost immediately. The supermarket chain made Michael an assistant manager, paid him a decent salary and, after Michael tagged his second victim, gave him a promotion and a raise.

Michael's victims were usually women—frail, fragile, lone, unsuspecting women. Sometimes, however, when he was sure a man wouldn't try to tag him back, Michael would tag a man.

Imagine Ellen thinking Michael wanted to rape her! Sex was unimportant to Michael. It was a mere tool he'd sometimes use to manipulate a woman, nothing more. If Michael needed sex, he'd go to a prostitute and pay for what he wanted. Sex, to Michael, was a simple business transaction—an exchange of money for something of value. That way he never felt obligated—the way his mother had made him feel obligated.

Don't think about her, cautioned the other Michael. *You know how upset you get when you think about Mother.*

Michael couldn't help but think of his mother tonight. How unalike she and Ellen were, yet they had one thing in common: motherhood.

As Ellen raced up the stairs to save her child, Michael was saddened by what he was about to do. He knew in his heart his own mother would never have risked her miserable life to save Michael. Lisa Ellers Thompson would have let her son die, and would have deemed it good riddance.

"You're a lucky bastard," Michael whispered to the boy he thought must be hiding under the bed. "But your luck is about to change."

Michael tightened his grip on the knife.

CHAPTER TWENTY-SEVEN

She was alive! Danny heard his mother's voice, and tears streaked down his face in a torrent of happiness. *She was still alive!*

But the bad man—the monster—was right outside his door. Danny cringed as he heard the bad man's words echo up and down the stairwell.

Your son is in this room, isn't he? If you don't come out, Ellen, I'll go in there and cut his throat.

Danny remembered the recurring nightmare that had haunted him seemingly forever. Were those the same words he'd heard in his nightmare?

Danny put his ear to the door and listened carefully to the conversation on the other side: First the man's voice, then his mother's.

Danny didn't know some of the words they used: rape, slasher, jinx, victors and victims. Other words were recognizable, but their meanings were vague: insane was one of those vague words. Hurt, kill, tag, winners and losers were familiar words to the five-year-old's limited vocabulary. He knew exactly what the man meant when he used them.

Danny heard the latch click open. The doorknob made a quieter click when it started to turn.

Trapped behind the door, Danny held his breath. If the monster shoved real hard, Danny knew the door could slam him back against the wall and crush him. But the door only opened halfway, and light from the fixture at the top of the stairs streamed into the room.

Danny heard the monster take two steps, then stop.

Screaming frantically as she ran, Ellen started up the stairs.

Danny heard her tiny feet take the stairs two at a time. This was Danny's worst nightmare come true. He'd seen what was about to come next a thousand times before in his dreams: First the monster would cut up Danny's mother, then the monster would come after him.

Only it isn't exactly the same as in my dreams, Danny realized. *The monster is already inside my room.*

Suddenly Danny knew how to save his mother. Utilizing every ounce of strength in his five-and-a-half-year-old body, Danny pushed the door.

Though he knew he'd be trapped in this room alone with a killer once the door swung shut, at least his mother would be able to get away.

At exactly the same instant that Michael's arm snaked out of the darkness with the Blake Blades Best butcher knife aimed at Ellen's heart, the door slammed into Michael's forearm. The twelve-inch knife flew from his sweaty fingers as pain radiated up his arm from the impact.

"Run, Mommy!" the boy screamed, trying to close the door the rest of the way. "Run!"

Michael reached for the boy in the semi-darkness and caught the kid's pajama top. Suddenly, a new pain shot up his arm as the kid's teeth sunk into Michael's wrist.

And then, before Michael could stop her, Ellen came through the partially open door and gouged at his eyes with her long and pointy, painted fingernails. More pain, this time from the gouges on his face where her nails raked away the skin. Letting loose of the boy, Michael spun around and lashed out with a fist, and missed.

What is this? his observer-half demanded to know. *First you miss when she distracts you with a plate and dishtowel. Then you miss when the kid slams the door on your arm. Can't you do anything right tonight?*

"I'm jinxed," Michael cried aloud. "I've run out of luck."

Then do something about it, you fool. Find the knife and get rid of the jinx—give it to them instead.

Ellen didn't allow him a chance. She plowed into him and forced him to the floor, going for his face again with her fingernails.

She continued to pelt and pound him, scratch and gouge. He

tried to push her away, to twist out from under her. But, no matter how hard he tried, nothing worked to rid him of the infuriated she-cat that had him cornered like a rat.

Play dead, his other self suggested. Let her think you're unconscious. If you're no longer a threat, she'll ease up. Then you can grab her.

Michael let his body go slack. Despite the blows that continued to rain down upon his face and neck, he didn't react. Eventually the storm passed, the rain became a light drizzle, and then...

He grabbed her.

"Gotcha!" he said, pinning her arms and flipping her body over.

"Gotcha good," he said as he slammed a fist into her face.

Fireworks went off in her head. Brilliant blues mixed with bright whites and blazing reds. Then the pain hit. All her energy was used up now. She had nothing left to fight with.

When she'd thought Michael incapacitated—at least unconscious, or maybe even dead—the last of her adrenalin dissipated.

Emotionally and physically drained, Ellen had stopped hitting him. Her hands were bloody and bruised, her fingernails ruined, and it didn't seem important to punish him anymore.

She'd turned her head for only an instant to look for Danny and that's when it happened.

Michael was going to kill her. He was going to beat her to death the way Bob had tried to beat her. He was the victor and she was the victim,

Ellen wondered if Danny had escaped. She hadn't seen him when she looked, but it was dark in the room and she didn't have time to look long.

Maybe he got away, she thought hopefully. *Maybe he's safe.* She didn't think she'd get the chance to know one way or the other.

Danny thought about running away to get help, but he didn't want to leave his mother alone with the monster.

Throughout the fight, he'd stayed out of the way. Ellen was winning, after all, and he didn't want to interfere.

But when Michael turned the tables on Danny's mother and began hitting her, Danny looked around for something, anything, to hit back with.

Then he remembered the plunger in the bathroom. He might be able to use the plunger like a baseball bat and hit Michael over the head with it.

Sure. That'd work.

Maybe if he crawled on his hands and knees out the door, he could sneak to the bathroom and back without the monster knowing.

Danny was halfway out the door when he looked back. The monster had stopped hitting Mom and was feeling around on the floor with one hand like he was trying to find something. Danny watched with dread as the monster turned his head, first one direction and then the other.

He's looking for me. Danny thought. *If he looks this way, he'll see me.*

Danny knew he had to move fast. He started to get up and make a run for it.

And that's when he found the knife.

Ellen faded in and out of consciousness. She tried to clear her head, but it still felt like the Fourth of July—skyrockets, starbursts, pinwheels, and roman candles continued to explode, complete with sound effects—in her battered brain. Then the pyrotechnics ended.

I'm dead, she thought.

But would she hurt like this if she were dead?

She remembered the beatings Bob had inflicted on her, and she knew she wasn't yet dead. If she were dead, she wouldn't feel this pain. Human beings are tremendously resilient, their bodies and minds adaptive to trauma as one type of growth process. Ellen had been through beatings like this before. This time it wasn't such a shock to her system, and it didn't take as long as the last time to recover some of her senses.

She realized Michael had stopped hitting her when the next blow—the one that would probably kill her—failed to materialize. She tried to open her eyes just a little, but both eyelids were swollen shut. The ringing in her ears made it difficult to hear.

She could feel Michael's body on top of hers, his buttocks resting on her stomach. He was sitting up and straddling her, his legs pinning each of her arms.

What's he wailing for? Why doesn't he just kill me and get it over with?

Ellen knew Michael intended to kill her. He couldn't let her live with the knowledge of who he was and what he'd done.

Is he going to rape me before finishing me off?

Michael had told her he wasn't interested in rape, and Ellen had believed him at the time. Rape was the farthest thing from the madman's mind.

Slowly it dawned on Ellen what Michael wanted to do—what he had planned to do to her all along. *He's going to use that knife on me. But he dropped the knife. Now he's looking for it.*

Ellen seldom listened to news reports on radio or TV. She paid scant attention to the front sections of the daily newspaper. She knew very little about this man the media called "The Mad Slasher of Willow Woods." But she knew enough to realize that this was the same madman that cut up his victims after killing them, used a butcher knife on human flesh the way Ellen used a butcher knife to slice a beef roast. Why? she wondered. *Why was the knife so important?*

Obviously, it must matter to Michael. He'd stopped hitting her in order to look around for the knife.

Maybe he'll get off me. Maybe he'll leave me to fetch the knife. Maybe I'll have a chance to escape when he goes for the knife.

Ellen felt weak and dizzy. She doubted she possessed the energy to make a run for it. Michael would catch her in a minute, but she had to try. Ellen wasn't the kind of person who simply rolled over and died without a fight.

If there was an ounce of energy remaining anywhere in her tortured body, she'd die fighting. When the doctors had told her that Danny would die of fever, Ellen had fought that fever and won. Was this any different?

Ellen forced one of her eyes to open only a crack. In the half-light, Ellen could see that Michael's head was turned toward the door.

His attention was riveted on what he saw there. He wasn't aware she'd opened her eyes.

"Give it to me, boy," the man said menacingly. "Bring it here and give it to me, or I'll come over there and take it away from you."

"No," Danny said, his tiny voice quaking.

"I mean it, boy. You know what'll happen if you make me mad, don't you? I'll beat your bottom until it bleeds."

"No," Danny said again.

Ellen could see her son clearly now. The cobwebs had cleared from her mind and her vision was nearly normal. Danny stood silhouetted in the doorway, his hair mussed and unruly.

Thank God! Her son was alive!

"Now, boy," Michael demanded. "Bring it here."

"No," Danny said, and he took a step backward. Michael started to get up. Ellen could feel the weight on her stomach lessening.

His knees pressed into her wrists as he prepared to dismount. Then, like a cowboy getting off a horse, Michael swung one leg off. That's when Ellen, her hand freed, made a lightning-like last-ditch effort.

Michael screamed as Ellen's ragged fingernails dug deep into the underside of his scrotum. Jagged and broken, her nails were still quite deadly. Deadlier than those nails, though, was the vise-like grip she had on his testicles. She clamped down and squeezed as hard as she could with thumb and forefinger, raising the sound of his scream another octave or more.

"Run, Danny!" she yelled. "Run!"

Danny ran, but not the way Ellen intended.

Instead of running downstairs and going for help, Danny ran toward his mother, into the room rather than away.

Everything was happening so fast that Ellen couldn't see what Danny held in his hand.

"Run!" she screamed at her son. "Get away!"

But Danny wouldn't listen. Once, twice, three times he swung both hands at Michael's back.

"Like David battling Goliath," thought Ellen proudly. "He's a brave little boy, isn't he?"

And then Michael's high-pitched screams died in his throat as his body jerked and twisted, spasmed and heaved.

Ellen lost her grip on Michael's manhood. One of her fingernails cracked all the way to the cuticle and blood gushed out and stained the front of Michael's trousers. Suddenly Ellen saw blood everywhere. Her hands had turned red, her dress was covered with it. That's when she saw the blood-covered knife in Danny's hands— and the gaping gash in Michael's neck that spurted blood like a fountain.

CHAPTER TWENTY-EIGHT

Michael felt the blade slice into his own neck. The agony and ecstasy of it seemed purely exquisite compared to the grotesque pain piercing his groin.

He tried to say the magic words that would make him immune, but he couldn't stop screaming.

Then the blade cut into him again, and he knew he'd been tagged good this time.

Michael Thompson, the man who'd been jinxed all his life, knew he'd now have to stay jinxed for the rest of what precious little remained of his unfortunate life.

The blade cut into his neck a third time, and both Michaels lost control of their one body. There was no more pain now, no more agony. Only the ecstasy remained.

As the blood intended to supply his brain with needed oxygen pumped copiously from his slashed carotid instead, the world grew dark. For an instant he thought the fading light in the stairwell was being extinguished with a dimmer switch.

There was barely enough light left in the room for him to see the boy, though he wasn't able to discern an expression on the miniature face.

"Here, Mommy," said the boy, handing the knife to his mother. His voice sounded distant, far away. Ellen said nothing as she took the knife from her son.

There was nothing she needed to say.

And there was nothing Michael Thompson could say or do to prevent Ellen from raising that Blake Blades Best twelve-inch butcher knife over Michael's still-beating heart.

He couldn't even scream when she brought the blade down— and the blade punctured his clothes, his skin—and tagged him "It" permanently.

Wesley had already unfastened his seatbelt and he jumped out of the car even before Johnson could bring the car to a screeching halt in front of Ellen's two-story frame house. He could hear the wail of police sirens several blocks away, but he didn't dare wait for backup. If Thompson were indeed inside the house, a minute or two delay might mean the difference between life and death for Danny and Ellen both.

During the ride over from Suzi's apartment, Wesley thought about how to enter without jeopardizing any lives. A surprise two-frontal attack wouldn't divide the Slasher's attention for long, but it was all Wesley could think of that might work. He'd rush in through the back door while Johnson went in the front. They might be able to sandwich the Slasher between them.

Circling around to the back of the house, Wesley tried the back door. Just as he'd suspected, the door was locked.

A second later, Johnson rang the front doorbell. At the same time, Wesley smashed a window in the back door, reached inside, and unlocked the door. If he were wrong about Thompson being inside, Wesley would be guilty of breaking and entering. He prayed he was wrong. He'd gladly go up on charges if only the kid were okay. Tom had already lost his own two children. He couldn't bear the thought of seeing another child die.

Johnson continued to ring the doorbell.

Wesley went quickly and quietly through the kitchen, then through the living room with its upturned furniture. Then Wesley unlocked the front door and let Johnson in.

"Upstairs," he whispered.

Wesley went first with Johnson close behind. He took the stairs two at a time until he reached the last step, then braced against the stairwell and listened. He heard someone sobbing in the boy's bedroom.

"Police!" Wesley announced in a loud voice. "Come out with your hands behind your head."

Danny came to the door. The boy was covered in blood. Before Wesley could stop him, the boy threw himself at Wesley's waist, and hugged the cop as if his life depended on it.

"She'll be okay," Frank Monroe told Wesley after Ellen had been sedated and removed to a hospital via police ambulance. "She's in shock right now, but she'll come out of it."

"What about the boy?"

"He'll be fine, too."

"You sure, Doc?"

"You recovered from shock after your wife died, didn't you? It may take a while, but they'll both get over it. They're alive, and that's the most important thing. They'll eventually heal."

Wesley breathed an audible sigh. "Thank God," he said.

"So this is the Slasher, eh?" the coroner asked as he viewed Michael Thompson's corpse. "Looks like he got exactly what he had coming to him, doesn't it?"

"Looks to me like Ellen saved the taxpayers some money," Wesley said. "And that's all it looks like."

"So she did. Won't need a trial now, will we? We still need to hold an inquest, though. She'll have to testify at the inquest."

"Isn't there some way around it?"

"You know better, Tom."

"She had to kill him, Doc."

"Yup."

Wesley looked away while the coroner completed his preliminary examination.

"You kinda like her, don't you, Tom?"

"Who?"

"Ellen Lester."

"Whatever gave you that idea, Doc?"

"Lots of things. Like the way you're worried about her, for example."

"It shows, huh?"

"Yup."

"I don't even know her, Doc. I mean, I played checkers with her son once. But we've never gone out or anything."

"You'd like to go out with her though, wouldn't you? Wanted to ask her out before, I bet, but the Slasher took up all your spare time."

"Something like that, Doc."

"She's going to need help, Tom. The boy, too. Think you can help both of them?"

"All I can do is try."

"You're a good man, Tom. But don't take too much responsibility on yourself again and wind up in a mental hospital. The time to see a shrink is before you need one, not after. Like this fellow, for example. Maybe a shrink could have helped him once upon a time. Or maybe not. But after Humpty Dumpty falls off the wall, it's harder'n hell to put him back together again."

"You saying I need to see a shrink?"

"Ellen does. That's a fact, Tom. Wouldn't hurt you to see one, either. Maybe you can find a good group therapy session and go together. It helps to talk things out."

"Level with me, Doc," Wesley asked. "How bad did this affect her?"

"Can't say for certain, Tom. Nobody can. Only time will tell, won't it?"

"I guess you're right, Doc."

The doctor took one last look at Thompson's body before covering it with a sheet. "One thing's for certain anyway," he said, "this man's dead. With multiple stab wounds to the head and neck, torso, limbs and genitals, the Mad Slasher will never kill again."

"How many times did she stab him, Doc? Got a rough guesstimate?"

"More than a dozen, I'd say. We'll never know for sure exactly what happened, but the autopsy will tell us more. Any idea why she didn't stop with stabbing him just once or twice?"

"Yeah, Doc," Wesley said, as he accompanied the doctor out of the house. "She said she wanted to make sure he wasn't faking this time."

Danny felt better when Officer Johnson brought Aunt Suzi to stay with him in the hospital.

The doctors had given him shots with a needle, and he didn't like needles.

He wanted his Mommy, but they wouldn't let him see his Mommy. She needed rest real bad, they said. He needed rest, too. Maybe tomorrow they'd let him see his Mom, but they wouldn't make any promises.

So, when they brought Aunt Suzi to stay with him, he was real glad. And then he got real sleepy and didn't remember anything else until the next morning.

Sometime after lunch, Lieuten't Wesley came to see him. Danny told the lieuten't about everything, and then the lieuten't asked Danny to tell him the same story all over again. Danny didn't want to, at first. But when Lieuten't Wesley said that Danny and his mother were very brave and deserved a medal for what they did, Danny decided it was a good story and didn't mind telling it over again.

Danny and the lieuten't played checkers after that, but a nurse came in and made Danny take a pill that made him sleepy. Danny must have slept for a while. When he woke up, Lieuten't Wesley was asleep sitting up in the visitor's chair in the corner.

Danny felt safe with the lieuten't there. He played quietly with his crayons and let the lieuten't sleep.

That night Aunt Suzi came back to stay with him, and Officer Johnson stayed too. Aunt Suzi wanted Danny to call Officer Johnson "Uncle Lenny," but Danny didn't think he should.

The next afternoon Danny went home with Aunt Suzi and "Uncle Lenny" to Suzi's apartment. Danny stayed with his aunt until his mother was well enough to come home from the hospital. Lieuten't Wesley visited Danny every day at Aunt Suzi's, and Danny beat the lieuten't in checkers twice in all that time his mother was away. Danny didn't mind losing to the lieuten't, and when he won, it was something very special.

The day came, finally, when they all went to the hospital in Uncle Lenny's car and Danny and his mother were reunited.

It was a special 'cassion. Kinda like a birthday. Or maybe like beating the lieuten't at checkers.

They didn't bring Mom home with them that day, but the very next day they did.

Aunt Suzi and Uncle Lenny had cleaned up the house. Danny's room had new carpeting, a fresh coat of paint, and brand-new curtains with a matching new bedspread. Pictures of Batman, The Caped Crusader, were printed on the curtains and bedspread. Danny felt safe with Batman to protect him.

Mom was still on med'cation. She sounded funny when she talked—like her mouth was full of mush or something—but she hugged Danny and kissed him a lot, and Danny was glad to be home with her again.

Aunt Suzi moved in with them for a while, helping with the housework and taking care of Danny while Mom was "resting." Mom was tired all the time 'cause of her med'cation, Aunt Suzi explained. The only time Mom seemed really awake anymore was when Lieuten't Wesley came over. He'd ask her to go for long walks and she'd always say yes. Sometimes Danny went with on their walks too, but most of the time Mom and the lieuten't went alone.

One day, Lieuten't Wesley asked Danny to call him "Tom," but Danny didn't want to. Aunt Suzi suggested "Uncle Tom," but Danny thought that sounded worse than "Uncle Lenny." Danny kept calling Tom Wesley "Lieuten't," and Lieutenant Wesley didn't seem to mind at all.

Every day that passed, now, Mom seemed more and more like her old self. Soon, Danny knew, Mom would be well enough to go back to work, and then Danny would have to go back to kindergarten and day care.

Actually, he didn't think he'd mind anymore going to kindergarten. Somehow, thinking about that big bully Johnny Radcliffe didn't seem to scare him half as much as it used to.

CHAPTER TWENTY-NINE

Johnson drove Ellen and Wesley downtown to the courthouse on the day of the coroner's inquest. Suzi stayed home to take care of Danny.

Though the coroner's inquest was supposed to be an informal, closed-door session, the state's attorney and the elected coroner tried to turn it into a media event. Reporters and camera crews seemed to be everywhere.

"Is it true that Thompson admitted to being The Mad Slasher?" one reporter asked as he confronted Ellen on the courthouse steps as she entered.

"Is it true that you castrated the Slasher, Ms. Lester?" asked another reporter.

"Did he try to rape you?"

"How long had you known Thompson before you killed him?"

"How well did you know him?"

"Is it true you were lovers?"

"Wasn't he younger than you?"

Wesley and Johnson shielded Ellen as best as they could, but Ellen was in tears by the time they got inside the building.

Camera crews greeted them in the hallway, and another throng of nosy reporters pressed in on them in an elevator. By the time they reached the courtroom where the hearing was held, Ellen was a nervous wreck.

The coroner opened the inquest right on time. Interested parties, from governor's representative Arthur Godwin to medical-legal investigators to actual witnesses such as Ellen Lester, were called to testify. The purpose of a coroner's inquest, the coroner explained during his opening remarks, is to shed light on all the circumstances surrounding a "suspicious death." If it can be determined that a "wrongful death" has occurred, the coroner is required by law to turn the case over to the state's attorney for prosecution.

Deputy Coroner Frank Monroe testified that Michael Thompson was the victim of widespread, multiple stab wounds over large portions of his body. The instrument of death was a Blake Blades Best twelve-inch butcher knife, part of a Blake Blades Best Cutlery set. He talked about "traumatic injury patterns" and entered into evidence photographs of the victim taken at the crime scene and during autopsy. The apparent severity of the stab wounds, in his opinion, seemed deliberate and excessive. The only hesitation marks appeared to be three incisions on the victim's neck, two of which were only minor injuries that could not, in and of themselves, have caused death.

"In my opinion," Doctor Monroe said, "the cause of death was not from those neck wounds but from deliberate and repeated stab wounds to the thorax and abdominal regions. The manner of death should be considered homicide, and it is the duty of this inquest to determine if such a homicide is justified by extenuating circumstances involved at the time of death. What happened to the victim afterwards is an independent occurrence and not related to the death itself."

Lieutenant Thomas Wesley testified to finding the victim in Ellen's house with Ellen kneeling next to the body. She still held the murder weapon in her hand and sobbed hysterically as she plunged the knife repeatedly into the deceased's already-mutilated torso. Wesley had to physically subdue Ellen Lester to get her to stop.

Then Ellen took the stand. As the only living adult witness to the homicide of Michael Thompson, Ellen Lester's testimony was crucial.

She related that she had invited Thompson to dinner at her house on the evening of the murder, that Thompson tried to stab her with a knife in the kitchen of her house shortly thereafter, that she'd avoided being killed only by throwing a plate at him, that she'd hidden in fear until Thompson threatened her son with the knife instead, that she had attacked Thompson only to protect her son from a madman who had readily admitted to being the Mad Slasher of Willow Woods, that Thompson had pretended to be subdued and then counterattacked when Ellen least suspected it, that Thompson had held her on the floor and had hit her in the face until she lost consciousness, that it was only because Danny—her five-year-old son—had saved her from certain death, that she was able to acquire the knife and, she claimed, she had stabbed Thompson only in self-defense. She said she feared for her own life and that of her son. She couldn't remember how many times she stabbed Thompson, she said, because everything after that was hazy and blurred in her memory.

"But why did you stab him so many times?" the coroner demanded. "Once he was dead, why did you continue to stab him?"

"I had to make sure he was dead," Ellen answered. "I couldn't take the chance that he might be faking."

An emergency room physician testified to Ellen's condition when she appeared at the hospital on the night of the murder. She'd been severely traumatized from repeated blows to the head, he claimed. Her face was bruised and swollen, she suffered from severe concussion, and she was in obvious mental and physical shock.

Then Arthur Godwin was called to the stand. Godwin, the head of the governor's task force investigating the Slasher murders, testified that Michael Thompson was a serial killer who had previously killed more than one hundred victims in eleven different states over an eight-year period. Despite his outwardly normal appearance, evidence had recently come to light—from forensic psychiatric analysis—that Thompson suffered a personality disorder and may have been violently insane.

The last witness to testify was Lisa Ellers Thompson, Michael's mother.

"He was a jinx," Mrs. Thompson, an obese woman in her mid-forties, said of her son. "I knew he was no good before he was born. I knew I should have had an abortion, but I couldn't afford one. Michael was no son of mine, I tell you. He was a jinx like his father."

After all testimony was taken into due consideration, the coroner, in consultation with the state's attorney, ruled Michael Thompson's death a "Justifiable Homicide."

Ellen broke down in Wesley's arms, sobbing with relief.

Wesley had tears in his eyes, too.

"It's over," he told her, holding her tight. "It's finally over."

The dead had been accounted for. Now it was time for the living to get on with their own lives.

Wesley took a week's vacation. He stayed home for two days and caught up on missed sleep. Then he went for a haircut, shopped for new clothes and shoes, and bought an automobile.

Then he asked Ellen out on a date.

Driving a car was a lot like riding a bicycle, he immediately dicovered. Once you learned how, you never forgot.

Falling in love worked much the same way. Wesley and Ellen had both been in love before, only not with each other. It was a familiar, but breathtakingly new, experience for both of them. They discovered many things they had in common and a few things they didn't. They even learned to respect their differences because neither would let anything disrupt the beautiful friendship developing between them.

They cared about each other. Nothing else seemed quite as important, except Danny—and Danny was no problem. Lieutenant Wesley liked Danny, and Danny liked having the "lieuten't" around to play checkers with when Danny's mother was too busy cooking or cleaning to play.

The following week Ellen returned to work, Danny went back to school, and Wesley's wonderful vacation ended.

"Doc wants to see you," Johnson said when Wesley walked into the station on Monday. "Doc didn't want to interrupt your vacation, but he said he had to see you as soon as you got back."

"He say why?"

"He's been thinking about the Slasher case. Something doesn't seem to fit, and he needs your opinion."

"Let's go see him, then. We'll take my car so I can show it off."

"Doc know you're driving again?"

"Not yet."

Johnson chuckled. "You're gonna surprise the hell out of him, Lieutenant."

Wesley's new car was a solidly-built Ford Bronco that seemed more like an army tank than a passenger car. "Any sonofabitch that hits this," Wesley said, "won't be able to damage it much."

"What made you want to drive again?"

"You did," Wesley said. "When I realized I had to depend on someone else to get me someplace in a hurry, I decided I wanted to be behind the wheel. If Ellen and Danny need me in the future, they won't have to wait for a slowpoke like you to get me there in time."

They found Monroe in his office. When Wesley attempted to coax the doctor out to the parking lot to see the car, Monroe declined.

"I have something more important on my mind," said the deputy coroner. "Do you remember Joan Norman?"

"What about her?"

"Godwin had data from those unsolved homicide reports fed into a mainframe computer. Every one of the Slasher's known victims—with the exception of Mrs. Norman—had four long slash wounds on her upper torso: two slashes across one way and two down the other way, like the killer tried to carve two large Xs into the breasts. That was the Slasher's trademark, you remember, and we never gave the particulars to the press."

"Sure, I remember. We deliberately withheld that information in order to validate a confession."

"Or eliminate copycat killings, if there were any. Well, I think we may have one in Mrs. Norman."

"A copycat killing?"

"Mrs. Norman had multiple slash marks across her torso, but they differed markedly from all the others. Since the Slasher changed his M.O. on Gillespe, I didn't follow up on it at the time. But now that I know that Thompson simply wanted Gillespe out of the way, the only deviation from his set pattern is the Norman killing."

"You trying to tell me Thompson didn't kill Joan Norman?"

"Take a look." The doctor produced a computer printout from the state crime lab. "Notice any discrepancies in the Norman case?"

"Contusions," Johnson said. "She had contusions, didn't she?"

"Antemortem bruises that didn't blanch when I tested lividity," clarified the doctor. "I incised the contusions and flushed the surrounding tissues to be sure. Contusions are often overlooked in livid areas, and I think Mrs. Norman's killer tried to cover up her contusions with slash marks. Only they were the wrong kind of slash marks, weren't they?"

"Nineteen separate slashes on Mrs. Norman," Wesley noted

from the report. "Only four on each of the others."

"Plus the stab wound," Monroe added. "Thompson used an upthrust to penetrate both heart and lungs with a single motion. Joan Norman's stab wound didn't have the same direction to it."

"What do you mean, Doc?"

"The other victims were standing up when they died. Mrs. Norman was prone. Here, let me demonstrate."

The doctor took a ballpoint pen and laid it in the palm of his hand.

"Assume the point on this pen is the point of a butcher knife. Thompson gripped his knife like a sword, knifepoint in the same direction as his thumb. In this manner he had maximum control of the blade as well as the point." The doctor turned the pen around. "Whoever killed Mrs. Norman used his knife like a dagger. He had excellent downward thrust, but had to reverse the knife to manipulate his blade. Ergo, Thompson was an expert with a knife who wanted to control both stabs and cuts without wasted motion. Joan Norman was killed by an amateur who first stabbed her, then took the time to reverse the knife, and finally used the blade to make his incisions."

The doctor handed his pen to Wesley. "Try it yourself, Tom. Hold it like a dagger and try to stab me. Doesn't work when I'm standing up, does it? You'll have to twist your hand to get an upperthrust, and then you'll leave a horizontal, not a vertical, wound in your victim."

Wesley turned the pen in his hand. "I see your point, Doc," he said, wincing at his unintended pun. "If I hold it this way—with the point facing the same way as my thumb—I can bring it up to stab, down to slash."

"Simple mechanics," said the doctor, sounding pleased with himself. "The wrist and elbow joints dictate limitations of efficient manipulation."

"Mrs. Norman was prone?" Johnson asked. "You mean flat on her back?"

"Exactly. She'd been badly beaten by her assailant. She was probably unconscious at the time of her death."

"I was right about Robert Norman then, wasn't I?" Wesley said. "Norman killed his wife and made it look like the Slasher."

"Can you prove it, Tom? We know Thompson didn't kill Joan Norman. But can you prove that Robert Norman did? When you flew off the handle at Norman before, you prejudiced this case in his favor. You'll need ironclad proof to get the DA to issue an arrest warrant."

"Norman's probably disposed of the knife by now," Johnson said.

"But what if he hasn't?" Wesley wondered. "It'll be all the proof we need to nail Norman to the wall. Let's go see the judge and get a search warrant. This time, I think he'll agree we have probable cause to poke our noses around in Norman's apartment."

CHAPTER THIRTY

"Where's Lieuten't Wesley, Mommy?" Danny asked his mother as she tucked him into bed.

"He has to work tonight, dear."

"He promised he'd pertec' us," Danny said, accusingly. "He can't pertec' us when he's not here!"

"He'll drive by during his break, Hon. And we'll keep in touch by telephone. We can call him, and he can call us."

"Can we call him now?"

"No, dear. Now you have to go right to sleep so you can be all bright-eyed and bushy-tailed tomorrow at school."

"I don't wanna be bright-eyed and bushy-tailed! And I don't wanna go to sleep! I want Lieuten't Wesley to be here!"

Ellen sighed. "I wish he could be here, too, dear. But he can't be here every night, can he?"

"Why not?"

Again Ellen sighed. "Be a good boy and go to sleep, Danny. Please?"

"I can't. The monsters will get me."

"I thought you weren't afraid of monsters anymore."

"I'm not when Lieuten't Wesley's here. But he's not here."

"I'm here, Danny. I'll protect you."

"You won't leave? Promise me you won't leave!"

"I'll be right next door, Danny. And I won't close the door."

"You won't turn out the lights?"

"No. You can sleep with the lights on, if you want."

"Stay with me, Mommy! Pertec' me!"

"I'll stay with you for a little while longer. Okay? But then we both need to get some rest."

"Thanks, Mommy," Danny said, throwing both arms around his mother's neck.

"Now tell me, Danny, why are you suddenly so afraid of monsters again? A brave boy like you doesn't need to be afraid, does he?"

"Yes, I do. I do."

"But why, Danny? You were so brave when you saved me from... from that *other* monster. I didn't think you were scared of anything anymore."

Danny began crying, sobbing softly on Ellen's shoulder.

"Oh, Danny," Ellen said, cuddling her son close. "I know. I know. But everything's all right now. Hush, dear. Everything's all right."

"No, it isn't," he whispered.

"Of course, it is. Nothing will ever hurt us again, Danny. I promise."

"I made a promise, too," he whispered. His voice was so low she could hardly hear.

"What kind of promise?" she wondered aloud.

"I made... a promise... I... I promised the monsters..."

"What did you promise the monsters, dear?"

"I promised... if they let me... save you... that I'd let them... eat me up!"

"Oh, Danny," she laughed. "Don't you know that promises to monsters don't count?"

"They don't?"

"No, of course not."

"Are you sure, Mommy?"

"Yes, Danny. Mommy's sure."

Danny thought about that for a moment.

Then he kissed his mother goodnight, laid down on the bed, and asked his mother to tuck him in one more time.

Ellen worried about her son. Wesley had warned her that this might happen, and she'd been expecting a delayed reaction to trauma to hit Danny and her at about the same time.

Because this was the first night that she and Danny had been alone in the house since she'd come home from the hospital, it seemed natural that tonight was when that reaction would hit, and it had—both Danny and her—at the same time.

But Ellen thought she'd hid her nervousness from her son quite well. But now, alone in her room, she couldn't help but worry.

She got up out of bed, went into the bathroom, and took a sleeping pill. Then she peeked in at Danny just to make sure he was asleep—and safe.

She'd just gone back to bed when she heard the phone ring in the living room.

She didn't want to run downstairs to answer the telephone, but that incessant ringing would eventually wake up Danny if she didn't. Besides, it might be important—it might be Tom Wesley.

She threw aside the light blanket and hurried downstairs.

"Hello?"

"Ellen?"

It wasn't Wesley. The gruff voice seemed vaguely recognizable, but she couldn't place it precisely. Her memory was still hazy with medication, and the recent sleeping pill only made it worse.

"Yes. This is Ellen. Who are you?"

"Ellen, this is Bob. Bob Norman, your ex-husband."

Ellen gasped. It had been two—almost three—years since she'd last heard Bob's voice. It sounded *different* than she'd remembered.

She was too shocked to hang up. The phone felt glued to her ear.

"I'm sorry if I woke you," he said "I'm a night person myself and sometimes I forget that other people go to bed before midnight. The reason I'm calling, Ellen, is this: I have lots of money now, and my lawyer says I can save a bundle on taxes by setting up an irrevocable trust for my son's education."

"A trust?"

"Yeah. Money Danny can use for college."

"College?" Danny was only five. Ellen didn't want to think about him going away to college yet. It seemed like such a long way off.

"If we do some long-range planning now, the lawyer says, Danny'll have enough money for any college he wants to attend— even Harvard or Yale. We'll funnel a hundred grand a year into an education trust—"

"A hundred grand? One hundred thousand dollars?"

"Yeah. It'll save me twice as much in taxes."

Ellen's mind reeled. One hundred thousand dollars invested each year, compounding over ten or fifteen years, would amount to a fortune.

"I figure I owe it to you, Ellen. And to my son."

"Bob, I can't believe you're doing this." Ellen couldn't believe she was still talking to the bastard either, but she was.

"It wasn't my idea. The lawyer suggested it. I mean, what good is it having a kid unless you can save a bundle on taxes?"

Now Bob sounded like the man Ellen knew and despised. Bob wasn't interested in Danny at all, was he? Bob saw a way to cheat the taxman and couldn't pass it by.

But Ellen saw it as a way to pay for her son's education, the way Mom's life insurance had paid for Suzi's. When Danny was old enough to go to college, tuition would cost a fortune. This might be her son's one chance to afford college, and Ellen knew it.

"Listen," Bob said, "I've got to get some papers signed before tomorrow so the lawyer can start the ball rolling on Danny's investments. I've already signed the papers, but you have legal custody so you have to sign them too. I'll bring them over and—"

"No!" *Oh, God! No!*

Alarms went off in Ellen's head. Even with the tranquilizing effect of her medication and sleeping pills she could hear alarms blaring in the background of her muddled mind.

"I won't come in, Ellen. I'll just bring them to the door and you can sign them. It'll only take ten minutes."

"No!"

"You want to piss away Danny's college education? All you gotta do is sign some papers, for chrissakes!"

"Why tonight? Why can't I sign them at the lawyer's office tomorrow?"

"Because I might change my mind. Tonight I'm feeling generous. Tomorrow my mood might change and I'll find some other way to fuck the IRS. You be a bitch about this, and I'll just fuck you too."

"How do I know you won't change your mind anyway? Even if I sign those papers, you could tear them up and throw them away."

"Stupid broad, you get to keep a copy of all the papers. It's an irrevocable trust. Once you have a copy with both our signatures, you'll have me over a barrel and it won't matter if I change my mind."

Don't trust him. He's a liar and a cheat.

But what if he means it? What would it hurt to look at the papers?

Can I afford to take a chance with Danny's future? I don't have to let Bob inside the house.

"Make up your mind, Ellen," Bob said. "I haven't had a drink all day and I'm starting to get thirsty. I can run these papers by your house on my way to the country club."

Ellen hesitated.

"Or," he said, "I can tear 'em up and throw them away."

"You're sober?" she asked.

"Absolutely. Scout's honor."

"You weren't a Boy Scout, Bob."

"Don't I sound sober, Ellen?"

"I can't tell."

"Last chance, Ellen. What'll it be? Are you going to sign or do I tear these up and pour myself a drink?"

"I won't let you in, Bob. But you can pass the papers through the mail slot in the front door if you want."

She heard him laugh. "That's mighty big of you," he said. Ellen slammed down the phone. Her hands were shaking.

You don't have to see him, she told herself. *You can make him wait on the porch until you sign the papers.*

Ellen debated going back to bed and simply blotting Bob from her mind. She could forget about Bob and the money for Danny's education through the miracle of modern medicine, couldn't she? Another sleeping pill and she wouldn't hear a thing when Bob rang the doorbell.

But Danny might. Danny might hear the bell and come downstairs and open the door. He might let his father into the house while Ellen was asleep. Danny didn't know any better. She decided she didn't dare go back to sleep.

Maybe she should telephone Tom. Wesley had told her to call him at the station if she needed him, and now she knew she needed him.

Ellen had deliberately and foolishly avoided talking to Tom about her ex-husband, and Tom had been a perfect gentleman and never pried into her personal past. But now Tom needed to know the kind of man she had mistakenly married. If she wanted to be open and honest with Tom Wesley, she had to tell him about Bob.

Ellen picked up the phone and dialed the station's non-emergency number. A detective named Ellis said that Wesley and Johnson were out of the office, but he'd ask the dispatcher to give them a message. She left her name and number and told Ellis it was important that Wesley call her as soon as possible. Ellis promised to turn it over to dispatch right away, but if Wesley didn't have a radio she was out of luck. He might not get the message until he came back to the office or telephoned in.

Why was Tom out of the office? Ellen wondered. Where the hell was Tom Wesley when she needed him?

Wesley had been trying to locate the judge since five o'clock that afternoon, tracking His Honor from the courthouse to his home, then to a bar association banquet at the country club. The judge adamantly refused to issue a search warrant for Norman's condo, and nothing Wesley said would change His Honor's mind. Bob Norman was a respected member of the community and a member of the same country club, and the judge couldn't believe Norman was a cold-blooded killer.

That's when, surprisingly, Arthur Godwin, stepped in. Godwin, seated at the judge's table, had listened to Wesley's arguments with obvious amusement. But just as Wesley was about to give up and leave, Godwin suggested the judge might want to reconsider his decision.

"After all, Bud," Godwin told the judge, "it was my task force that determined Thompson couldn't possibly have killed Joan Norman. I think the lieutenant has probable cause for a search of Norman's premises. If you won't issue a search warrant, I'll help the lieutenant find someone more reasonable—like Judge Hamilton over at the next table."

Wesley got a signed search warrant from Bud. "Thanks," he told Godwin.

"Glad I could help," said Arthur Godwin. "You're a good cop, Lieutenant, but a piss-poor politician. Don't ever run for office. You're too damned stubborn to know how to compromise and ask a friend for a favor."

Norman didn't answer the door when Wesley rang the bell at Norman's condo.

"I don't think he's home," Johnson said. "What do we do now?"

"Now we break the door down," said Wesley. "I've got an axe in the back of the Bronco. Run down and get it for me, will you? I'll wait here."

"That door's solid, Lieutenant. It'll take forever to chop through."

"Then hurry up and get that axe. The sooner we get started, the sooner we'll finish."

CHAPTER THIRTY-ONE

"The mail slot isn't big enough. They won't fit. You'll have to open the door."

"No," Ellen said.

"Look. I'm leaving all the papers on the porch and backing away. Just open the door and pick them up. I'm not going to try anything."

Ellen didn't believe him.

"Look out the window," he said. "I'm off the porch now. You can open the door."

Ellen looked through the bay window. Bob was backing away from the porch.

Did she dare open the door?

"Sign those papers and Danny'll be set for life," Bob said. "C'mon, Ellen. Don't be stupid."

Ellen went to the kitchen and rummaged through a drawer.

Then she returned to the door with an eleven-inch butcher knife in her hand.

Maybe it wasn't a Blake Blades Best—the police had confiscated Michael's gift and Ellen never asked for it back—but the blade she held in her hand would protect her almost as well.

It was the same knife she'd used to threaten her husband six years ago.

Ellen checked the window again. Bob was ten feet away from the porch. She unlocked the door. Opening it just a crack, she peeked outside. The papers were there on the porch.

Bob hadn't moved. He stood ten feet away, watching her. She started to shake all over.

"Go ahead," he urged. "Pick them up."

Holding the knife in her trembling right hand, she reached for the papers with her left.

"Read them," Bob said. "You'll see I didn't lie to you. All I want is the tax deduction."

Ellen snatched the papers from the porch and slammed the door. Still shaking, she sat down on the couch. The sheaf of papers were exactly what Bob had described on the phone: legal documents in quadruplicate that defined parties involved in a binding agreement. The party of the first part, one Robert Daniel Norman, agreed to deposit funds in an irrevocable trust to ensure the education of the party of the second part, one Robert Daniel Norman, Junior. The party of the first part agreed to deposit monies in excess of one hundred thousand dollars annually in the trust, allowing those monies to compound and accumulate until such time as the party of the second part entered college, or reached age twenty-one, whichever came first. Neither party could touch those funds until maturity, at which time all monies theretofore accumulated in the trust would belong solely and separately to Robert Daniel Norman, Junior.

Along with legal papers were IRS forms granting a non-custodial parent the right to claim Robert Daniel Norman, Junior, as a dependent for income tax purposes.

Though Ellen didn't understand the wording in places and the documents were too long to peruse completely, she read enough to know that Bob hadn't lied. For once in his life, Robert Daniel Norman, Senior, was doing something nice for someone else—though his reasons were purely selfish.

"You done yet?" Bob asked impatiently.

Ellen searched for a pen. She found one in the bottom of her purse, but it was out of ink. She turned her purse upside down and scattered the contents, looking for another pen. She found lots of bobby pins and safety pins, a compact and lipstick, wallet, checkbook, address book, fingernail file—no pen. She had dozens of pens in her desk at work, but none that she could find at home. Pencils, yes. Coloring crayons in every shade and hue. But no pen.

"Hurry up, will ya?"

"I'm looking for a pen."

"You need a pen? I've got a pen."

"I'll find one. Give me a moment."

Ellen went upstairs and looked through her other purse. She found a penny in the bottom of the purse, but no pen.

She entered Danny's room and began to search through the mess in his closet.

"Mommy?" the boy asked, rubbing his sleep-filled eyes.

"Yes, dear. Mommy's here. Go back to sleep."

This time Danny did as he was told. Once the boy was asleep, he wouldn't wake up completely for anything. He always went right back to sleep and slept like a log. Getting him to go to sleep in the first place was the difficult thing.

Ellen, too, was sleepy. Suddenly, her eyelids felt like rocks. The sleeping pills had taken effect and she didn't know how much longer she could fight off her drowsiness. She decided to borrow Bob's pen and simply get this over with as quickly as possible.

"Put it on the porch and back away," she told him through the door.

She watched from the window as he laid a pen on the porch. Once again, he backed away and waited.

"How is he?" Bob asked when she opened the door and reached for the pen. "I read in the newspapers about what happened. Is Danny okay?"

Ellen was surprised by the concern in Bob's voice.

"He's my only kid," Bob said. "First the Slasher kills my new wife, then he goes after my kid. Danny didn't get cut, did he?"

"No," Ellen answered. She was startled to hear that Joan Norman had been one of Michael's victims. Ellen deliberately avoided news reports about the Slasher and didn't know the names of any of the victims.

"Why did Thompson do it? I heard on TV that the Slasher told you everything. Did he say why he picked on me? Why he wanted to kill my wife? My kid?"

"He... he was crazy."

"He must have said more than that, didn't he?" Ellen didn't want to talk about it. She picked up the pen and shut the door, but Bob wouldn't let it go. "What did he tell you, Ellen? I need to know what he said."

Ellen ignored him. She found where Bob had already signed each of the papers or forms, and added her own name and signature in the appropriate places. Then she kept out one copy to put in a safe deposit box at the bank and took the other copies to the door.

"Why won't you tell me, Ellen?" Bob demanded. "Answer me, dammit!"

"Back away from the door, Bob," she answered. "I don't want to argue."

"I saw you on TV, Ellen. You and that police lieutenant. The two of you looked real chummy coming out of the courthouse after the inquest."

Ellen said nothing. She was too tired to argue. But Bob, obviously, wanted an argument.

"I don't want you talking to that cop, Ellen. Stay away from him."

Still Ellen said nothing.

"You hear me?" Bob said, his voice threatening. "You stay away from that cop!"

Was Bob jealous? It sounded like he was. If Ellen wasn't so tired, it might even have pleased her that he was jealous of Tom Wesley.

"I'm not married to you anymore," Ellen told her ex-husband. "I can see anyone I want."

"I'm warning you, Ellen."

"Go away. Just go away and leave me alone."

"Give me the papers," he said. "Then I'll leave."

Anxious to get rid of him, Ellen unlocked the door and shoved the papers outside. If she hadn't been quite so sleepy, maybe she would have realized sooner that, this time, Bob Norman was waiting on the porch for the door to open.

Wesley had turned the kitchen upside down looking for a Blake Blades Best Cutlery set. So far he hadn't had any luck.

Johnson, meanwhile, had explored the bedroom. "In here, Lieutenant. I think I've got something."

"What'd you find?"

"If you look closely, you'll notice there's blood on the carpet. It's hard to see bloodstains on a purple-colored rug, but there are four or five spots that weren't cleaned up."

"Where?"

"On the floor by the bed."

Wesley got down on his hands and knees and examined the carpet. Blood had soaked into the weave, making the wool carpet stiff in several places near the bed. "Use Norman's phone and call in," he told his partner. "We need a forensics team to tell us if this dried stuff matches Joan Norman's blood type."

"Right."

Wesley pulled the covers off the mattress. The mattress pad was brand new, spotless. But the mattress itself was heavily stained where blood had soaked through the previous mattress pad.

"Bingo!" Wesley said, elated.

"They're on their way," Johnson said, hanging up the phone. "And Ellen called for you an hour ago."

"She leave a message?"

"She talked to Ellis. Wants you to call her as soon as possible, but didn't say why."

"Couldn't be too important if she dialed Ellis instead of nine-one-one. Let's find that knife. I'll call Ellen later."

Three smaller bedrooms and two baths adjoined the master bedroom, and Wesley and Johnson systematically tossed each of them before moving on to examine the huge living room. Two evidence technicians arrived from the county forensics team and joined in the search, but the knife was nowhere to be found—until Johnson opened a liquor cabinet behind the built-in bar.

"Hey, guys," he shouted. "Guess what Norman hid behind a bottle of Jack Daniel's!"

"You gotta be kidding," Wesley said.

"Nope. It's right here. A complete Blake Blades Best Cutlery set. There are," he counted, "six big butcher knives in a wooden cutlery block. Bunch of newspapers in here, too."

"Newspapers?"

"Yeah. A whole stack of newspapers."

Wesley turned to one of the techs. "Bag the knives, run them through the entire series. I want prints, DNA, blood analysis, the works. Let me know what you find out on the mattress and carpet, too. If I'm out of the office, leave a message with Ellis or Peters."

"It'll take a few days on the DNA, Lieutenant."

Wesley shrugged. "Try to rush it, okay? Call me as soon as you come up with something definite."

"Will do, Lieutenant."

Wesley turned to Johnson and smiled. "Well, kid," he said, "I guess that wraps it up. I'll call Ellis and put out an APB on Norman. Then I'll call Ellen."

"Better look at this first, Lieutenant." Johnson removed a handful of newspaper clippings from the cabinet.

"Whatcha got?"

"A complete file on the Mad Slasher. From the first killing here in town to some of the follow-up stories that appeared after the inquest. Norman made his own notes on a few of these. I think you better read them."

Wesley took the clippings and glanced at each in turn. Norman's earlier notes were mere pencil underlinings. The most recent clippings, however, were highlighted with yellow marker and had marginal notes scribbled in red ink.

The latest news story featured a photo of Ellen and Wesley walking down the courthouse steps after the inquest.

Highlighted in the newspaper copy was a quote attributed to Ellen Lester. "Miss Lester testified at the inquest that Michael Thompson admitted to being the Mad Slasher and told her about killing all but one of the victims."

Penned in the margin were the words: She knows!

"My God!" Wesley said.

And then he ran for the elevator with Johnson following hot on his heels.

Bob bolted through the door before Ellen knew what was happening.

One slap across the face, and Ellen dropped the knife.

"What were you planning to do with this?" he laughed, picking the knife up from the floor. "Kill me the way you killed Thompson?"

He slapped her again.

Ellen, dazed, tried to back away. She backed up into a wall.

"We're going to have a little chat, you and I," he said, brandishing the knife at her face. "What did the Slasher tell you about Joan?"

"N—N—Nothing," Ellen managed to say.

Bob poked the knife into Ellen's left breast, hard enough to draw a trickle of blood. "Oh, come on. He must have said *something*."

"Owww! You're hurting me."

"I'll hurt you worse, unless you start telling the truth."

"What do you want me to say?"

"The truth, dammit! You know what I'm talking about. Don't you?"

"No. I'll say anything you want, Bob. Just don't hurt me."

"That's better, Ellen. We've always had an understanding, you and I. I tell you what to do, and you do it."

"Y—yes."

"Sometimes you surprise me though. Like the time you threatened to cut off my nuts with this knife. Remember that, Ellen?"

"Y—yes." Tears were streaming down her face.

"Maybe I ought to cut off your tits. Give you a taste of your own medicine." He moved the knife point over her breast. "But I won't."

Instead, he used the knife to slit her nightgown down the front.

"You always were a good looking woman, Ellen. Even when you were pregnant, you were better looking than Joan ever was."

"Then why did you marry her?" Ellen sobbed. "Why did you leave Danny and me to marry her?"

"You know why. Your money ran out, honey. And Joan had bundles to burn."

"You didn't love her?"

Bob laughed. "I loved her money. She gave me everything I wanted because she thought I adored her. But she had to come home early from a damn party that got cancelled, and caught me with another woman. She said she was going to kick me out but I wouldn't let her. I tried to pound sense into her. I was drunk at the time, and I must have hit her too hard. I don't know my own strength when I'm drunk."

Ellen said nothing. Bob's revelations shocked her into silence.

But thanks to the medication and the sleeping pill, Ellen's mind was able to cope. This seemed like a bad dream—a nightmare—to her inner self. She was sure she'd wake up any moment now and discover none of this had happened.

"You're not surprised," Bob said. "I knew you wouldn't be. When I read that the Slasher had told you everything, I worried you'd tell that cop what you know about me. But you haven't told him about me yet, have you?"

"No," Ellen said. She hadn't told Wesley about Bob yet.

"But you're going to tell him, aren't you? I can't let you do that, Ellen. That cop's out to get me. He asks too many questions. Sooner or later he'll ask you the wrong questions, and you'll tell him all about me—how I used to beat you up, how I almost killed you that last time you saw me. Then you'd remember that Thompson admitted to killing all but one of those women, and you'd know which one the Slasher didn't kill. I came here tonight to find out if you'd told the cop yet and to warn you—scare you—from telling. But I can't trust you, Ellen. I knew I couldn't trust you the moment I saw this knife in your hand. Now I'll have to kill you, won't I? The way I killed Joan."

"You killed Joan?"

"I had to. Even after I'd tried to knock some sense into her, she wouldn't listen. She said she'd divorce me and make sure I'd never see a penny of her money. I couldn't let all that beautiful money just slip through my fingers, could I?"

"The police will know. They'll know it was you." Her muddled mind still thought this was a bad dream. She tried to reason with the dream.

"Not if you don't tell them, Ellen. The police might suspect me, but they won't be able to prove it. They'll think there's a copycat killer—a nut case—who heard on TV that you murdered his hero."

Ellen still couldn't believe this was really happening. As if watching a dream unfurl, she saw Bob Norman raise the knife and plunge it downwards at her chest.

It wasn't until she heard her own scream and felt the incredible pain in her breast that she realized this wasn't a dream.

CHAPTER THIRTY-TWO

Danny didn't want to come back from dreamland yet.
He fought the pull that drew him back. Loud noises like the telephone or doorbell sometimes brought him back before he was ready, and the loud scream he'd just heard tugged at his unconscious in a similar fashion. He'd heard screams aplenty in nightmares before, but those were always his own screams and they never stopped ringing in his ears until Danny opened his eyes and consciously made them stop.

This scream, however, died in the air before Danny came fully awake, and that fact frightened him enough to give up his fight to remain in dreamland. He felt himself being bodily dragged through the murky borderlands of nightmare—the place where the most horrible monster of all fed on his imagination. Then dreamland disappeared, his eyes snapped open, and he found himself in his own bed, in his own room.

"Mommy?" he cried out.

Since the lights were on and the door to his room open, Danny rolled out of bed and ran immediately to his mother's room.

"Mommy?" he asked again.

That's when he heard the noise—a loud *thump*—downstairs in the living room.

Thinking he'd simply heard his mother knock over a piece of furniture, Danny didn't hesitate to run downstairs. All he wanted was his mother to tuck him back into bed—the way she always did when he awoke in the middle of the night—and hear her say, "Go back to sleep, dear. Everything's all right."

But as Danny reached the bottom of the stairs and entered the living room, he saw a hulking beast bending over a familiar-looking shadow on the floor.

The monster turned around to face him, and Danny knew his nightmares weren't ever going to end.

Wesley whipped the Bronco into four-wheel drive and cut straight through the park. Unfortunately, he couldn't follow the yellow-brick road straight from Norman's Tower residence to Ellen's two-story home, but he could still save time by tearing up park turf.

Please, God, he prayed. *Let it be enough to save Ellen's life. And Danny's.*

Wesley hadn't talked to God since that day of the accident. Any God who snuffed out innocent women and children on their way to worship Him, Wesley felt, wasn't worth wasting prayers on. But now he didn't know what else to do.

It was always possible, of course, that Norman's clippings were idle doodles and didn't mean what Wesley thought.

It was possible, too, that Norman was merely at the country club, or some such other favorite watering hole, enjoying cocktails with rich friends.

Then why did Wesley have this incredible certainty gnawing at his gut that Robert Norman was, at this very moment, threatening to murder his ex-wife?

Because you're a cop, he told himself. *You have a cop's instincts.*

The evidence was overwhelming that Robert Norman had murdered his second wife, Joan Gould Norman, and tried to pin Joan's murder on The Mad Slasher of Willow Woods. And now the same evidence indicated that Norman wanted to kill his ex-wife, Ellen, because Ellen had killed The Mad Slasher.

Ellen's testimony that Michael Thompson had admitted to all but one of the murders, evidently, was what convinced Norman that Ellen was a potential danger that had to be eliminated. How many innocent bystanders had Wesley seen killed simply because they were potential witnesses? Too many. Nearly one-third of all homicide victims were potential witnesses to a crime. They just happened to be in the wrong place at the wrong time and were eliminated along with the main target, or hunted down afterwards so they couldn't talk. Wesley felt in his gut that Norman couldn't afford to take a chance that Ellen might talk to the police, especially since Norman had seen a picture of Ellen and Wesley together.

Ellen hadn't wanted to talk to Wesley about Norman because she'd still been in shock. And Wesley hadn't previously pressed her for information because he cared more for her as the woman he loved than as a witness. Besides, Wesley had thought they'd have plenty of time for talk after Ellen got well. Now, he feared, there was no time left at all.

He swung the steering wheel hard to the left to avoid a row of bushes planted directly in his path, and the Bronco's back end skidded sideways across the dew-dampened grass, tearing up chunks of sod with its rear tires. For an instant Wesley thought the vehicle would overturn.

Instead of hitting the brake, Wesley gave it the gas. His foot stomped the accelerator all the way to the floor.

And the four-wheel-drive Bronco shot forward like a bullet, righting itself in the process.

"If we get out of this alive," Johnson said, "remind me never to ride with you again."

"If we get out of this alive," Wesley told his partner, "I'm going to retire from the force and become a racecar driver."

This was the *real* monster, the one Danny had seen in his dreams every night for nearly three years. It had always seemed like only a dream .before, but now Danny knew it hadn't always been only a dream. Danny had just turned three when this monster came into his room and hurt him. He'd been fast asleep—far off in dream-land—and this monster had grabbed him and hurt him badly, pulling him back to reality and nearly breaking both his arms.

And when Mom had tried to stop this terrible monster from hurting Danny more, the beast had turned on her instead—hitting her and calling her names and making her bleed.

This was no imaginary monster that hid under the bed or in the closet and never came out when the lights were on. Oh, no. This was a real monster.

And that's exactly what Danny had tried to convince his mother all these years—that monsters didn't exist only in nightmares, *monsters were real!*

But his mother never believed him. It was almost as if she hadn't wanted to listen to the truth.

Now Danny saw his mother and instantly realized that it was already too late to try to pertec' his mother from the monster. Ellen's body lay on the floor in a widening pool of blood. This monster had already killed her.

Because Danny had seen something similar before—both in his dreams and that night when the monster called Michael Thompson had died in Danny's bedroom—he wasn't shocked into immobility. Instead of freezing his feet to the floor, fear made his feet move without need of conscious direction. He fled up the stairs and ran straight to his room, slamming the door behind him, before the man could catch him.

"Danny," the man called to him. "I'm your father. Don't you recognize me?"

Danny did recognize him. And now Danny also recognized that the monster he'd feared all his life was his own father—the father he'd never really known.

When other kids had talked about their fathers at school, Danny had wanted a father too. He'd pieced together an imaginary "Pop" to meet his needs. But this man wasn't his father. This man was a *monster.*

"I've got a present for you, Danny. Don't you want to see what it is?"

Danny had already seen the blood-covered blade of the butcher knife in his father's hand. He'd seen the "present" Mom had received.

"Daddy's coming upstairs to tuck you into bed, Danny," the monster called up from the foot of the staircase. "You like to be tucked in, don't you?"

Danny ran to his bed. He had no intention of being tucked under the covers by his father, nor had he any intention of hiding. He stood on the bed and tried to reach the latch on a window with the tip of a finger. If he could open the window, perhaps he could yell for help—or, if he absolutely had to, jump.

Danny pushed on the latch, but it wouldn't move. The footsteps outside his door reached the top of the stairs.

The doorknob turned.

Danny shoved at the window latch with all his might. It moved. "Get away from that window, kid!" the monster yelled as he entered Danny's bedroom.

Danny desperately tugged at the bottom of the window. He didn't have strength enough to pry the frame loose from the painted windowsill.

Then the paint cracked. The window began to budge.

"Get away from there!"

The man hurried across the floor towards the bed. And Danny raised the window half an inch—an inch—two inches—and then he *screamed*!

Want we should do it the same as last time?" Johnson asked.

"Yeah," Wesley agreed. "You take the front and I'll take the back."

"You sure Norman's in there?"

"I'm not sure of anything."

They could see Ellen's house in the distance now, lit up like a Christmas tree. It was nearly midnight, and the house should have been dark.

As they got closer, they saw that the front door was half-open.

Wesley's heart sank. "We're too late," he said, choking back tears.

"You don't have to see this, Lieutenant," Johnson said, fearing the worst. "Stay outside and back me up."

"We go in as planned," Wesley said. "If that bastard's still inside, I want him."

Unbuckling their shoulder harnesses so they were ready to leap out as soon as the car came to a halt, Johnson reached for his weapon with one hand and opened the door with his other.

Wesley rode up over the curb and parked on the lawn.

"Go," he said.

Johnson hit the porch and braced at the door while Wesley quickly ran around the side of the house, just in time to hear Danny's ear-splitting scream come from above his head.

His .357 Magnum filling his hand, Wesley looked up. There, in the second-floor window, was the face of Danny Lester, and right behind him, a knife raised over Danny's head like a dagger, was Robert Norman.

Wesley reacted instinctively. His hand brought the .357 Magnum level with his eye, his thumb moved the hammer back to full-cock, his finger was already squeezing against the hair trigger.

This has to be perfect the first try, he told himself. *If I'm off by an inch, I'll hit the kid.*

Off by an inch the other way, he knew, and the round would miss its mark. Norman could still bring the knife down and…

An enormous flash lit up the night right in front of his eyes, and he heard the familiar "BOOOOOMMM!" that always reminded him so much of the resounding cannonfire at the thrilling climax of Tchaikovski's 1812 Overture.

The glass in the window shattered into a million pieces and the wall behind the window splattered with flesh and blood and bits of broken bone. Wesley discovered that his hand was badly shaking, and suddenly Lieutenant Thomas Wesley of the Willow Woods Police Department felt sick to his stomach and knew he was going to throw up.

Ambulances came and went, Doc arrived and made a preliminary examination, TV crews set up cameras across the street, but Wesley hadn't moved. His stomach was empty and even the dry heaves had finally passed, but he didn't dare go into that house. There was nothing he could do now anyway.

He'd fired his best shot, and *missed*. He'd aimed for Norman's shoulder, a clean shot that would have shattered the man's clavicle and immobilized him, but Norman must have moved just as Wesley had pulled the trigger and the hollowpoint had hit the man in the forehead and made the head explode like a pumpkin thrown at the wall behind him, *like a jack-o'-lantern with a lit firecracker inside instead of a candle.*

Wesley sat on the wet grass behind the house and chain-smoked half a pack of cigarettes. Johnson had been too busy to bother him, and no one else knew he was here.

He needed the time to think. Wesley had always known that someday he'd have to kill a man in the performance of his duty. He'd accepted that as a fact of life for a police officer—an occupational hazard, so to speak. But he'd never known that someday he might want to kill a man the way he'd wanted to kill Robert Norman. Did any man deserve to die the way Norman had?

All his life Tom Wesley had believed that human life was

precious—a God-given gift. No man or woman had the right to take another's life. That was what had made Wesley want to become a homicide cop in the first place.

Cops were supposed to protect human life, not take it. It was a conflict Wesley knew he had to resolve if he were to remain a police officer.

Finally, he made a decision. Wesley got up from the grass, walked around to the front of the house, and entered.

He had a job to do.

EPILOGUE

Danny had a brand new Dad.

He thought "Dad" sounded much better than "Tom," and better even than "Lieuten't."

Dad wasn't a lieutenant anymore anyway.

Mom was crying when she and Dad walked down the aisle in the church after the wedding ceremony, but she was smiling, too. Danny knew her tears were tears of joy.

Aunt Suzi and Uncle Lenny had taken care of Danny while Mom was in the hospital, and now they would take care of him while Mom and Dad went away on a "honeymoon."

Danny didn't mind.

After the honeymoon was over, Mom and Dad would come back. He knew they would always love him and protect him. They could go away as often as they wanted, but he knew they would always come back.

Mom and Dad had bought a new house—a three-bedroom ranch-style house with all of the bedrooms on the same floor with the living room and the kitchen—and Danny couldn't wait to move. He'd start first grade in a new school. Danny didn't mind one bit leaving that big bully Johnny Radcliff behind when Danny and his family moved from Willow Woods to the state capital.

Dad had asked a man he knew in gover'ment for a favor, and the man gave Dad a job as an administrator at state Police headquarters. Tom Wesley was now Captain Tom Wesley of the state police.

That meant Dad could work regular hours and be home in time to eat supper and play checkers and help Mom tuck Danny into bed every single night.

Aunt Suzi and Uncle Lenny planned to move to the capital too, as soon as Aunt Suzi graduated from graduate school—and she and Lenny got married.

Someday Danny would go to graduate school, too, thanks to some papers his birth father had signed. Danny was Robert Norman's "Legal Air," whatever that meant.

After that terrible night when Dad had saved Danny from his real father, a few people had claimed that Wesley deliberately killed Robert Norman just to get the man out of his way. They said that Dad had never intended to wound the monster, pointing out at the inquest that Wesley was "out to get" Danny's father in order to marry Danny's mother. By killing Norman instead of wounding him, Wesley gained access to Norman's ex-wife and the millions of dollars Danny would someday inherit after the Norman-Gould estate was finally settled.

Danny knew that was just a lie made up by the news media. Wesley was too good a cop to ever do something like that.

Dad had no way of knowing beforehand about the clause in those legal papers that named Danny as "Legal Air" should the senior Norman die. Danny was absolutely certain that Tom Wesley had no other motive for killing Robert Norman than simply to protect Danny's life.

The coroner's jury and Internal Affairs at the Willow Woods Police Department eventually agreed.

Because Dad had no way of knowing, either, that Mom was still alive. How could he have planned to marry a woman that he believed Norman had killed?

Fortunately, Mom didn't die. The knife had entered her body at the wrong angle to penetrate her heart. Ellen spent months in the hospital having operations and undergoing therapy, but she recovered completely.

Danny, too, had recovered completely. He'd suffered minor injuries from flying glass, and he'd been scared half to death. But now he was fine.

Even his bad dreams had gone away.

Soon Mommy and Daddy would be home from their honeymoon, and then Danny would challenge his new Dad to a game of checkers. Danny loved to play games because every game had winners and losers, and Danny now knew he would never ever be a loser again but always be a winner.

ABOUT THE AUTHOR

Paul Dale Anderson loves to read and write horror, dark fantasy, thrillers, and science fiction. He's an active member of SFWA, HWA, and ITW, and was previously represented by Barbara Puechner of the Peekner Literary Agency. When Barbara died with his breakthrough novel still half-finished, he switched to writing non-fiction. Paul went back to college and earned an MS Ed. and most of a doctorate in Educational Psychology and earned an MA in Library and Information Studies from the University of Wisconsin. He taught creative writing for Writers Digest School (both Novel and Short Story) and for the University of Illinois at Chicago.

He returned to fiction writing with a vengeance in 2012, completing his breakthrough novel and seventeen other novels, and began writing fresh fiction that crossed genres.

Two of his published novels, *Claw Hammer and Daddy's Home* sold very well, and several of his anthologized short stories have reappeared from major publishers. One of those short stories adapted to graphic novel format was recently re-released in hardcover and paper in J. N. Williamson's Illustrated Masques.

He is also a Certified Hypnotist and National Guild of Hypnotists Certified Instructor.

BOOK LIST

Supernatural Horror:
Abandoned
Axes to Grind
Darkness
Inevitabilities
Light
The Devil Made Me Do It
Time
Written on the Wind
Winds

Psychological Horror:
Boxcutter
Claw Hammer
Crowbar
Daddy's Home
Ice Pick
Meat Cleaver
Pickaxe
Sledgehammer
Woodchipper
Jackhammer
Pinking Shears
Spilled Milk
The Girl Who Lived Megan's Story

Suspense Thrillers:
Delusions
Deviants
Figments
Incongruities
Options
Running Out of Time

Curious about other Crossroad Press books?
Stop by our site:
http://store.crossroadpress.com
We offer quality writing
in digital, audio, and print formats.

Enter the code FIRSTBOOK
to get 20% off your first order from our store!
Stop by today!

Made in the USA
Lexington, KY
22 March 2017